A NIGHT AT THE INN

The inn was the foulest abode that Miss Ellen Marling had ever entered, but the raging storm outside had made further travel impossible. The Marquess of Trent declared this to be so, and Ellen was forced to agree—and forced to agree as well to share a room with Trent, since only one was free.

Now with the gravest misgivings she found herself alone with the notorious marquess. Her misgivings only deepened when she saw him lock the door, then prop a chair under the knob. And it was small comfort to have him explain that it was to prevent them being robbed and murdered.

As Ellen, horror-stricken, watched the marquess calmly draw his shirt over his head, she was sure of only one thing: she was inexorably caught between death and dishonor. . . .

Scandal Bound

Anita Mills

A SIGNET BOOK

NEW AMERICAN LIBRARY

SIGNET TRADEMARK REG. U.S. PAT. OFF. AND FOREIGN COUNTRIES
REGISTERED TRADEMARK—MARCA REGISTRADA
HECHO EN CHICAGO, U.S.A.

SIGNET, SIGNET CLASSIC, MENTOR, ONYX, PLUME, MERIDIAN
and NAL BOOKS are published by NAL PENGUIN INC.,
1633 Broadway, New York, New York 10019

First Printing, June, 1986

1 2 3 4 5 6 7 8 9

PRINTED IN THE UNITED STATES OF AMERICA

For Larry

1

"You make such a charming bride, my dear," her father whispered from his position in the receiving line.

Her smile was frozen into place as she accepted the good wishes and probably the sympathy of those members of the *haut ton* in attendance. To her left, her new husband beamed and wiped the perspiration from his florid face. Occasionally, he stopped nodding long enough to manage a proprietary pat against her shoulder, letting his hand drop to her waist and lower—a grim reminder to the young woman that she belonged to him from that day forward. Revulsion flooded over her every time he touched her.

"Buck up, my sweet—soon enough we shall be alone," her corpulent lord murmured next to her ear.

Ellen Marling Brockhaven steeled herself against a public display of distaste as she determined to fix her attention on the guests at her wedding dance. Her proud papa had achieved his goal of selling his eldest daughter to the wealthy but aging Lord Brockhaven for the not inconsiderable sum of twenty thousand pounds in settlements—a figure that Marling, a greedy man with no fewer than three daughters and one son to provide for, could not resist, despite the girl's spirited battle. Only his threat that if Ellen did not accept his lordship's very generous offer, her seventeen-year-old sister Amy would be obliged to take her place had forced Ellen to bow to the inevitable. The courtship had been brief, despite her every effort to discourage Sir Basil—a singular impossibility, given the baron's overweeningly high opinion of his own charm. She had once commented to her brother, Julian,

7

that Brockhaven's sense of self-importance matched his size.

Ellen reflected bitterly that she had never had a chance on the marriage mart. Her clutch-fisted father regarded the expense of a Season an unnecessary frivolity until it became apparent that his eldest daughter was all but on the shelf. Now her only consolation was that she would see that Amy was presented properly with more than a few undistinguished dances at the Bath assemblies. Unfortunately, she would be forced to present the girl under the aegis of Lord and Lady Brockhaven, and Amy had conceived an active dislike of the baron.

Ellen's role as a sacrifice to her father's greed had not been an easy one—one look at the red-faced, pudgy Lord Basil and his small, beady black eyes was enough to put any female's stomach into revolt—and she now faced the prospect of living with such a husband with dread. To make matters worse, her unwanted lord was taking every opportunity to paw, squeeze, and fondle her.

A quiet, pleasant girl whose best claims to looks were a pair of large, expressive blue-violet eyes and thick, lustrous dark hair, Ellen could only curse whatever charm had caught Brockhaven's attention. Though six years the elder, she lost in any comparison to Amy, a young beauty of diminutive stature, riotous dark curls, and flawless features. It was generally conceded, even by those who loved her, that Ellen's nose was a trifle too long, her hair too straight, and her stature too tall for real beauty. And despite her quiet demeanor, she often dismayed her parents with her dubious habit of being too candid for a female. While other ladies took every opportunity to fan themselves flirtatiously, the eldest Miss Marling met a man's gaze squarely, disconcerting him with her unwillingness to succumb to any fantastic flights of praise or extravagant compliments.

As the last of the guests filed through the reception line, Lord Brockhaven took his bride's gloved hand and raised it to his rather full lips. "I believe, my dear, that we must lead the first set out. But," he lowered his voice conspiratorially, "there is nothing to say that we must tarry here all night. We shall slip away as soon as may be polite, and have a more intimate party of our own upstairs."

Visibly repressing a shudder, the new Lady Brockhaven shook her head as she followed her husband onto the dance floor. She managed to give him a tight smile and respond, "I hope, sir, that I am not such a bad hostess as that. Besides, I am quite determined to dance until dawn."

"Ah, but I have other plans, my dear," Sir Basil told her. "However," he conceded, "I am not adverse to your indulging yourself for, ah, shall we say another hour."

In desperation, Ellen threw herself into the dance with the appearance of enthusiasm while she mentally reviewed avenues of escape. When the dance was over, her heavily perspiring lord insisted on procuring a glass of champagne for her. She shocked him by throwing it down in a single gulp and reaching for another.

"Ellen," he protested, "I should not like to see you disguised on our wedding night!"

"I doubt even an entire bottle would render me senseless, my lord," she managed through clenched teeth.

"Nonetheless, my dear, you must remember now to conduct yourself with the circumspection of behavior required by your elevated station. As my baroness, I shall expect you to set the style for all that is proper."

She tried to blot out the punctilious coxcomb at her side by closing her eyes momentarily and then opening them to roam over the crowd. Sipping her second glass of champagne defiantly, she had to own that she knew almost no one there and could turn to none for help. Her father had preferred the less expensive life of a country squire and ridiculed those who wasted their substance on a London establishment. And on those few occasions when it was necessary to lease a town house, he had not been inclined to entertain even a small circle of acquaintances. There was no doubt about it: had she not chanced to stand up with Brockhaven at one of those insipid Bath assemblies, she would never have had the misfortune of meeting the baron at all. It was with an imminent sense of defeat that she raised her glass again.

"Your pardon," an immaculately clad buck of the first order apologized as he bumped into Ellen and spilled the rest of her champagne on her silver-spangled silk dress.

"Devilish sorry, of course, but this place is a damnable squeeze."

Brockhaven bristled indignantly before the fellow turned around to face him. "You clumsy oaf, look what you have done! You have ruined three hundred pounds in that dress." And then he paled visibly, his eyes seeming to start from his head as he stared at the offender. "Trent! Egad!" His plump fingers crept involuntarily up to pull at his cravat while he moved back a step. "Beg your pardon, my lord. I am sure she did not see you."

A gleam of amusement lit the otherwise cold eyes as they took in the baron's discomfiture, but there was nothing but boredom in the voice that responded, "The fault was mine, Brockhaven, and you find me happy to pay for the gown, though I own I had not expected it to be worn above once."

Ellen's eyes widened as she stared at the exceedingly handsome, obviously arrogant man before her. Even from her limited experience, she knew she faced a true buck of the *ton*. His well-proportioned body loomed above her dumpy husband's by three-quarters of a foot; his face was sculpted like one of Lord Elgin's famous marbles with high cheekbones, straight nose, and very cold blue eyes; and his hair was cropped in the current mode à la Brutus, but its disarray seemed less the result of the careful contrivance of a Byron and more from its own natural curl. His clothing, while extremely plain in contrast to Brockhaven's rather flashy style, was absolutely correct and perfectly tailored. His eyes flicked over Ellen without the least hint of interest before he bowed politely and turned back to his friends.

"Basil," Ellen rounded on her husband indignantly, "why did you feel it incumbent to apologize when 'twas he who jostled me?" But the baron was still too visibly shaken to answer. "Basil, who *is* he?"

"Trent," he finally muttered succinctly. He slowly let out his breath in relief as the gentleman in question moved away from them. "Strange that he should be here, for I've no recollection of inviting him," he mused aloud, adding, "and you can be sure that this is not the sort of entertainment he favors."

"You look pale as death."

"Aye." Brockhaven's black eyes turned back to her and he noted, " 'Tis never healthy to raise one's voice to the Marquess of Trent, Ellen. I shudder to name those who have."

"A duelist?" She raised a skeptical eyebrow and took another look at the retreating figure. "Really, my lord, but he does not look so very dangerous to me—cold, perhaps, but not dangerous."

"Much a green girl like you would know of the likes of him," Sir Basil scoffed. "I can assure you that he has never frequented the Bath assemblies, my dear, and is rarely seen at Almack's, though I cannot for the life of me imagine how he could be admitted at all," he disgressed. "No. He favors the muslin company, and the latest *on-dits* among the *ton* are about which mistress he means to mount next."

"What a pity for his wife."

"Ain't got one," Brockhaven snorted derisively, "for there's not a female alive as can bring him up to scratch. Havey-cavey bunch, the Deveraux. His father set the *ton* on its heels when he made off with Lady Caroline. Shocking thing it was," he remembered, then collected himself to add repressively, "but I would not speak of such things, my dear."

"Why not? If I am to live in London, I will hear the gossip anyway."

Before Brockhaven could answer, an exquisite in a watered-silk waist coat bowed over her hand to request the next waltz. Sir Basil stepped forward possessively, prompting her to dazzle her would-be partner with a smile and reply, "I should be pleased, sir."

She danced almost incessantly, feigning a gaiety that she did not feel, until her hour was gone. Basil Brockhaven stood along the wall watching her when at last the Earl of Rossington led her off the floor, then he moved forward purposefully to take her arm.

"Come, Ellen, it grows late and I would retire."

"Ah, pray let me go up first, my lord, that my maid may assist me," she ventured hastily. "You may come up in half an hour."

"I'm afraid I've already dismissed the girl, my dear,

but you will find me quite adequate to your needs. I am not without experience, after all."

Panic seized her as his fingers pressed into her arm. "Champagne, sir," she tried desperately. "I believe I should like another glass first."

"Ah, my lovely, but there is already a bottle in our bedchamber."

Unable to cast about for a further delay, Ellen reluctantly allowed herself to be led up the staircase. Basil Brockhaven opened the door to a chamber that would have been impressive under other circumstances. Branches of candles lit up the room, casting a warm glow on the polished mahogany furniture and the satin-striped wallpaper. An elegantly draped four-poster bed was positioned at the far corner to allow the rest of the chamber to be used as a combination sitting and reading room. An alcove off to the left served as a dressing room and contained a *poudre* table laden with various pots of pomades, powders, and scents, testimony to the artifices Brockhaven employed in his quest for youth. Ellen's glance traveled around the room, taking in any detail that might provide an avenue of escape. The doors to the right of a large wardrobe appeared to open only into closets, while double French windows gave the only access to the outside—and they were some fifteen feet above the ground.

"Do not look so glum, my dear." Brockhaven smiled as he poured two glasses of champagne and advanced toward her. "After all, 'tis your wedding night, and by the morrow, you shall truly be Lady Brockhaven."

"Sir Basil," she tried desperately, "I cannot go through with this." She reached for her glass and drained it before he could even begin to sip. "As I have tried to tell you these last weeks, sir, we should not suit."

"Nonsense, my dear. 'Tis but maidenly reserve, I assure you." He set his goblet down and possessively drew her into his arms, his blunt fingers working the fabric of her gown against her flesh, his wet lips smacking kisses from her throat to her mouth.

Nausea rose in her as he began kissing her in earnest. She let her glass fall and shatter, the shards flying upward. Sir Basil stepped back momentarily.

"I am terribly sorry, my lord," she murmured, "but you startled me. Perhaps if I had another glass . . ." her voice trailed off dubiously. "You see, I, uh, well, I never, um . . ."

"If you think another glass will help, you may have mine."

"Uh, no. What I meant to say, Basil, is that perhaps if I were alone to undress . . ."

"All right," he capitulated gracelessly. "I will get you another glass, and while I am gone, you may remove your gown and petticoat."

She waited until he was safely out of the room before taking the only opportunity available. Throwing open the window, she stepped gingerly to the sill and peered below to where the faint illumination of the ballroom showed a thick shrubbery. Hoping it would break her fall, she closed her eyes and jumped.

"What the devil . . ."

Strong arms grabbed her and wrestled her to the ground while a masculine voice murmured softly, "What have we here—a housebreaker?" He pinned her to the ground for a second before discovering, "Dammit, you are a female!" He stood up unsteadily and pulled her after him. "Ought to march you back in and find out what's going on here."

"No! Oh, please do not," she hissed desperately. "And pray keep your voice down. I am running away."

He tried to focus on her in the darkness. "One of the housemaids, eh? Well, he'll not bother you now that he has a young wife."

Realizing her captor was quite disguised with drink, she decided to brazen through an improbable explanation. "You do not understand. I *have* to get to my aunt's in Yorkshire, sir, and Lord Brockhaven will not let me leave. I am not a housemaid!"

"Yorkshire! Egad, 'tis the length of England, girl."

"But if you would but release me and direct me to the nearest posting house, I would not trouble you further." She could sense his hesitation and pressed her chance. " 'Tis nothing to you, after all, whether I stay or go."

"Very true, and I've little enough liking for the fat

robin myself. All right," he made up his mind abruptly, "I'll take you to a posting house."

"Would you?" she breathed in relief, almost unable to believe her good fortune. If he could but get her off Brockhaven's grounds, she might make her escape. "Oh, sir, I'd be ever so grateful!"

"Yes, well, let's get a look at you in the light before we determine just how grateful you ought to be." He clasped her hand and led her to his waiting carriage, where he tossed her up under the disapproving stare of his driver and then followed her into the dark coach. Settling back against the thickly padded squabs, he stared broodingly at her. Even as her own eyes adjusted somewhat to the darkness, she still could not see him, but she could literally feel his eyes on her.

"Don't suppose you thought to pack a bag?" he asked abruptly as the coach lurched into motion.

"I am afraid I had not the time," she admitted ruefully.

A sigh of obvious disgust escaped him. "Aye, I thought not. Females never seem to plan things out, do they? I ask you, how can you expect to get to York without so much as a change of clothes?"

"I told you—I had not the time to pack, sir, and the problem is mine."

"And I suppose you do not even have the price of your passage to York, do you?"

She sat stock-still in her seat for a moment and then shook her head. "No, but I have my jewelry. Surely that will gain me admittance to at least a mail coach."

"It'll get you robbed, more like," he responded dryly. "What is it?"

"A wedding ring."

"No," he was positive, "that won't do. Well, if I am to be an unlikely Galahad, I suppose that 'tis up to me." He rapped the ceiling and yelled up at his driver. "Madame Cécile's, Timms! And be quick about it! Miss, er—?"

'Smith," she supplied quickly.

"Aye. Miss Smith must have some clothing to take to Yorkshire with her."

"But, yer lor'ship," the driver protested, " 'tis two in the mornin'!"

"How long have you been with me, Timms?"

"Two weeks, sir."

"And who pays your wages?"

"Yer do."

"Then stifle it and do as I ask."

"Aye, sir." Above them, the driver put his whip to the team of big blacks and muttered audibly, "Quality! They think th' worl' lives fer 'em!"

"Mesself, I wouldn't quarrel with 'im none," one of the coachies advised, "fer a wilder lord ye'll niver see. 'Tis best ter jest do 'is biddin' and take yer money. Right gen'rus he is, ain't he?"

Inside, the man across from Ellen shifted his hat over his eyes and leaned back. She strained to make out his features in the darkness. There was something slightly familiar about that voice, but she could not quite decide what. She felt a sense of unease and had to reassure herself with the thought that he could not possibly be worse than Basil Brockhaven.

The carriage halted so suddenly that she found herself thrown across the seats and into the stranger. He caught her easily and pulled her onto his lap. "Egad, girl," he murmured above her as she struggled to right herself, "you are as light as a bag of feathers. How old are you?"

She stiffened and pushed forcefully against his chest until he let her go and she fell to the carriage floor. Grabbing for a pull strap, she lifted herself up into the seat. "I am three-and-twenty, sir," she answered haughtily, "and I am unused to being mauled by strangers."

"If you call that mauling, my dear, you have much to learn on the subject." He leaned past her to open the door, swung his body across, and jumped down into the street below with an agility that belied his state of inebriation. "However, I believe we have arrived at Cécile's, so instruction on the subject will have to wait. Timms," he yelled at the reluctant driver, "be quick and rouse the house. We have not all night."

Responding with alacrity, one of the coachmen slid down from the box and nodded to his master, "Timms is new, sir. I'll take keer o' it fer ye."

"Very well, Dobbs, but get on with it."

After about five minutes of the coachy's relentless pounding, they were rewarded with a glimmer of light and a spate of French words unknown to the usually conversant Ellen Marling. Finally, the bolt was drawn and the door opened to reveal a hastily dressing servant.

"Milor'!" the fellow protested. " 'Tis after two!"

"Aye," Ellen's benefactor acknowledged dryly, "and now that we all know what time it is, you will be pleased to advise Madame that I am come to collect the clothes she has made for Signora Mantini."

Ellen leaned curiously to catch a glimpse of her rescuer, but was thwarted when he stepped in front of the carriage to talk to the Frenchman. She was having second thoughts about him, particularly after his comment about instruction in mauling. It came home to her that she had not the least idea who he was and it was just possible that his attentions were not honorable in the least.

"But Madame is asleep, *monsieur!*" she could hear the servant protest.

"Then get her up. I am not used to waiting, fellow."

"But, milor'—"

"Very well. You may inform Cécile when she wakes that I have taken my custom elsewhere."

"I will see if I can rouse her, milor'," the servant capitulated.

"Frenchies!" the coachy spat out in disgust. "And after all yer's bought 'ere."

Madame Cécile herself suddenly appeared in the doorway in her satin wrapper and surveyed her night visitor. "Trent! I might have known 'twas you, milord. No matter." She shrugged with Gallic indifference. "We can box most of what you have purchased in minutes. If you will but come inside to wait, 'twill be done with dispatch."

Ellen sank back against the squabs in shock, unable to believe that of all the people she could have encountered in her mad enterprise, she'd fallen into the hands of a hot-tempered rakehell. For a moment, she considered yet another escape, but then realized that she knew nothing of the vast city of London except it was dangerous at night. Well, she would thank his lordship sincerely, take the mailcoach to York, and that would be that.

True to her word, the modiste reappeared to direct the tying on of no fewer than six boxes. While Ellen watched, Trent came out and said something she could not hear.

The little French dressmaker's laughter floated up to where she sat. Then the door opened and the marquess swung up his tall frame while ordering Timms to get moving again.

"The English!" Madame Cécile's man fumed from the steps. "Their nobility have no manners."

"Not all of them," Cécile reminded him. "And you cannot judge any by the Marquess of Trent, Paul, for he quite lives by his own rules. La, what a man! If I were but twenty years younger . . ." Her voice trailed off dreamily and then she caught herself with a sigh, "But I am not. Come, let us get to bed if we are to be able to greet the customers later."

In the carriage, Ellen shook her head in disbelief. "I cannot credit that you did that, sir."

"Why?"

"Well, won't the Mantini be angry that you have taken her clothes?"

"Probably." He shrugged. "But I paid for them. Besides, I care not a jot what she thinks. She has no cause for complaint with my generosity."

Ellen leaned forward to tell him, "Pray do not think me ungrateful, my lord, but I cannot accept them. For one thing, I have not the money to pay, and for the other, 'tis unseemly."

"Why not? I can assure you that, with the exception perhaps of a slight fullness in the bodice, they will fit."

"But I could not. If you would be so kind as to set me down at the posting house, my lord, I would trouble you no longer."

"No. You cannot go racketing about in a common coach without so much as a maid or abigail with you. Besides, I have decided to accompany you."

"Oh, no! That is, I could not presume. Pray do not— 'tis *most* unnecessary, my lord. Really, if you will but set me down—"

"Can't. We are already on our way, my dear, and I am decided. Who knows? A little rustication might be just the ticket. London's become a deuced bore these days."

"*What?* Oh, but you cannot! I mean, we are not even acquainted, sir."

With a hint of amusement in his voice, he swept off his

hat and leaned forward. "Alas, my lamentable manners, my dear. Allow me to present myself. I am Alexander Deveraux, frequently called Trent by many, although my intimates call me Alex."

"I still cannot presume on your kindness, sir," she repeated firmly. "Besides, I cannot arrive at my aunt's in your company—or any gentleman's, for that matter. 'Tis not certain that I shall even be welcome by myself."

"That being the case, Miss, er, Smith, I should consider it incumbent on me to support you when you beard the old lady."

She sank back in dismay, unable to even consider her aunt's reaction to her arriving in the company of a man like Trent. The street lanterns were passing more quickly as the coach picked up speed, and she had absolutely no means of getting out of it. With a sinking feeling, she realized that her companion, although appearing moderately sober, was too far gone for reasoning.

As if reading her thoughts, he repeated, "We are already on our way, my dear. And who knows? By light of day, I might find you attractive enough to keep you for a while."

"And despite the strange circumstances of our meeting," she replied stiffly, "I must ask you to believe that I am not that sort of female."

"No? We shall see, Miss Smith. But, as for now, I am more than a little foxed and need to sleep off Brockhaven's champagne."

2

ELLEN NAPPED OFF and on as the carriage sped through the night and well into the morning. The sun came up finally and afforded her a better opportunity to observe her carriage mate, so she studied the sleeping man opposite. He did not look so very dangerous, after all. In fact, the relaxation of sleep gave him the appearance of being younger and almost vulnerable. The cold blue eyes that had given him such a forbidding aspect at her wedding dance were closed, leaving only the dark smudges of thick black lashes against rather fair skin. The planes of his face were not so rigid or pronounced either, and he seemed more youthful. The night before, she had judged him to be somewhere in his thirties, but now he appeared several years younger. Yet, awake or asleep, she had to admit he was a strikingly handsome man. He stirred slightly and pillowed his head more comfortably against the corner of his seat. His thick black hair was ruffled in charming disarray.

Almost as if by intuition, he became aware of her scrutiny, opening one eye slightly and wincing at the sight of her. He closed it and blinked several times, as if unwilling to credit what he'd seen. Finally, he straightened up in his seat and ran his fingers through his rumpled hair. He eyed her irritably now.

"Your pardon, madam, but were you not last night's bride?" His eyes traveled over her wrinkled wedding dress with its grass and champagne stains, and he sighed heavily. "I am afraid I must have been even more foxed than I thought, so you will have to enlighten me with the whole, if you please." He shook his head as though to

19

clear it, and stared briefly at the rolling countryside through the coach window. "And pray do not leave out where we are."

"Well, I am not precisely certain as to where we are, my lord, except that it is somewhere on the road to Yorkshire. And in spite of my protestations, you would insist on coming with me when all I asked was escort to the nearest coach house. I am running away, you see."

"No, I don't see," he snapped irritably. "The whole, if you please, and spare me any enactment of a Cheltenham tragedy, for my head aches like the very devil." Clearly his gallantry of the night before was forgotten and replaced with ill humor. He leaned forward, fixed her with those cold blue eyes, and waited.

She briefly sketched the improbable events of her escape and his assistance, remembering to include their stop at Madame Cécile's. "So, you see, sir, that is quite the entire tale," she told him. "I did not ask you to come—'twas you who insisted."

He sank back with a groan. "And now what the devil am I to do with you? I have done some incredibly stupid things in my life," he admitted, "but this is surely the worst. And you are not even a beauty, so I have not that excuse."

She bristled at his rudeness and was on the point of retorting hotly that her appearance had nothing to do with her very real need to escape a loathsome husband, but he raised a hand to silence her before she could speak.

"It is the plain truth, ma'am. If you did not have those unusual eyes, you would not attract a second glance. You are too slight of form to intrigue a man," he pointed out bluntly.

"Listen, you, you insufferable oaf," she choked out when she found her voice. "As though I care about such things! I find the lot of you disgusting, boorish, and self-centered. And you are wrong, anyway. I attracted Brockhaven despite all my attempts to discourage the man."

"A fat, aging roué," Trent scoffed.

"Listen, my lord," she managed to reason in a calmer voice, "if you will but set me down at the next posting house with enough money for my passage, as I asked you to do from the very beginning, I shall not trouble your lordship further. You may even have my wedding ring for surety that you will be repaid."

"Set you down without a maid or abigail?" He raised a disapproving eyebrow. "My dear, every manjack on the stage would be sure to think the worst of you."

"As you were prepared to do yourself?"

"Acquit me! I admit to many liaisons with your sex, ma'am, but I have never resorted to rapine. I am not totally lost to propriety, no matter what you may have heard. But you have landed us both in the basket with your rash actions. I ought to—"

Before he could finish the thought, she leaned forward in alarm. "You would not try to return me to Brockhaven! You could not!"

"Lud, no! I should look the veriest fool bringing you back in the morning, shouldn't I? While a man may be forgiven any number of little affairs with soiled doves, widows, and even other men's wives, it is outside the bounds of decency to run away with another man's virgin bride. Even I should draw the line at that," he told her in disgust. "But now that you are here, what the devil *am* I to do with you?"

"My lord, if I have to repeat one more time that it was you who insisted on bringing me this far, I shall scream in vexation." She drew herself up disdainfully and added with an affronted sniff, "It was not your affair, after all. And even an unfeeling cad could not have wished my fate on anyone. I could not go through with it. The husband chosen for me is old, fat, and disgusting. I could not bear the sight of him."

"Then why did you agree to marry him?"

"You do not know how it is. You think we all have a Season to parade around London, attending balls, musicales, and whatever, until some lord declares himself smitten with our charms and offers marriage, don't you? Well, in my case, I had not even one Season. My father considered it a waste of his money, if you must know. And then, when I was past twenty-two, it occurred to him that I was on the shelf. Then he whisked me off to

Bath for the Short Season, pushed me at Brockhaven, and considered his paternal duty done."

"And you took Brockhaven because no one else came up to scratch, eh?"

"No, it was not that way at all, my lord. The very first assembly I attended, Sir Basil attached himself to me, and my father was overwhelmed at his good fortune," she remembered bitterly, "for it meant he would not have to buy me any more finery. And when Brockhaven offered twenty thousand in settlements, my father said I should be happy to accept without so much as consulting me. When I refused, my father offered him my seventeen-year-old sister. You cannot understand, but Amy is sweet and kind and so beautiful, I could not let them do that to her."

"I see. You were sacrificed for twenty thousand pounds."

"Yes. My father called me ungrateful, my lord, and starved me for three weeks before he came upon the idea of giving Sir Basil Amy instead. I guess I was weak and thought I was being noble. But when it came to—to living with Brockhaven, I could not."

"Well, it would have been better for both of us had you just blown out the candles and pretended he were someone else."

"Quite easy for you to say, sir, for you have not the dubious distinction of being Lady Brockhaven. I, on the other hand, would have had to look at the disgusting popinjay for the rest of his life. And with my current fortune, he would live to ninety just to plague me."

"I doubt he could make it another ten years, given his fat," Trent hazarded. "But what is done is done, I suppose. We can only hope that this aunt of yours will support you in this."

"My aunt is Lady Sandbridge." She had the satisfaction of seeing his eyebrows shoot up in surprise. "Until now, I have been quite her favorite relation, and I can only hope that she can prevail on Papa to seek a separation between Brockhaven and me." She looked up and met his eyes soberly. "Though it will be difficult to explain this if I arrive in your company, my lord."

"Aye." He nodded in resignation. "She will think you

have eloped with me. The tale gets worse the more I hear of it."

"You hold too fine an opinion of yourself!" she snapped in exasperation. "I should not have gone as far as the nearest corner with you had not my situation been desperate. I am no opera dancer—or any other kind of trollop!"

"We were not speaking of your good name, ma'am, but rather of mine. But the more I look at you, the more I am certain I shall be acquitted of any such intent."

"You, sir, are insulting."

"But truthful."

"And stop calling me 'ma'am'—I abhor it!"

"Since I have not met you, I have not the least notion of what to call you."

"I am Ellen Marling—or I was until yesterday—and I prefer to be called Miss Marling."

"Well, Miss Marling, then. We shall not have a shred of reputation left if this gets out." Without warning, he began to chuckle a warm, throaty chuckle. "But I must say, my dear, that you are vastly calm about it. Most gently bred females would be treating me to fainting spells or vapors or tantrums. You, on the other hand, seem positively proud of yourself."

"I am." She smiled ruefully. "I have come to realize that I should rather have no reputation at all than be Lady Brockhaven."

He sobered suddenly. "There will be a terrible scandal, you know, and Brockhaven may even divorce you." He paused as another thought struck him. "And do not be thinking I can be brought up to scratch with some farradiddle that I compromised you. I warn you right now that I am not a marrying man and I cannot be made into one. Any effort to lead me into parson's mousetrap would be wasted, Miss Marling. And now that 'tis settled who you are and where we are going, I have a devil of a headache to sleep off."

"I would not have you if you begged me, my lord, so we are quite safe with each other, are we not?" she retorted acidly. "I should prefer a worthy gentleman."

"A foolish dream, girl. If this gets out, no respectable man would have you."

"Go on to sleep, my lord, and leave my future to me."

He covered his eyes with his hat and settled back. In a matter of minutes, he was breathing evenly, and his features softened with sleep. She watched him enviously as she shifted her cramped body into various positions, vainly seeking comfort in the confines of the carriage. After an hour or so, the coach rolled to a halt in an innyard and one of the coachmen jumped down to bang on the door.

"Yer pardon, yer lor'ship, but 'tis the Hawk we've come on."

The marquess straightened up and surveyed his surroundings sleepily. As his eyes again took in Ellen's crumpled appearance, he shuddered and remembered his absurd situation.

"Best bespeak a private parlor, Dobbs, and get a room where Miss Smith may refresh herself."

His man disappeared into the inn for a few minutes and then returned with word that his lordship's requirements could be met. Without waiting for the order, the coachey began untying one of the boxes on top of the carriage.

"You go on, ma'am, and follow Dobbs," Trent directed her. "Hopefully, he has chosen a box with something you will dare to wear publicly"—he grinned—"for I've a notion that much of what was ordered for the Mantini was of a more intimate nature." He opened the door again and jumped down to assist her out. Reaching up to her, he caught her at her waist and set her down as easily as if she had been weightless. "You are the merest dab of a girl for one so tall," he observed.

"Thank you." She smiled sweetly. "And you are a veritable lummox."

"You are certainly the first to say so."

She gathered up her skirt hem disdainfully and followed the coachman into the inn, where she was directed to a room by the innkeeper's wife. Once alone, she rummaged through the box of the Mantini's clothes and was dismayed to find that Trent had been right. She finally found a relatively plain lavender muslin day dress and some underwear. Peeling out of her despised wedding gown and petticoats, she reached for the fine, flesh-colored silk pantaloons and the zona. As she fitted the latter around her, she was disgusted to find that it provided very little support for her bosom at all. With a sigh as to the injustices of nature, she pulled on the lavender dress and found that the *signora*'s tastes ran to the revealing even for daytime wear. She sat down before a mirror and began repairing the damage to her coiffure while pondering what to do about the dress. An impatient knock sounded sharply at the chamber door and the marquess's voice carried through it.

"I do not like to be kept waiting—five minutes and I begin to eat."

"Wait. Do you have a handerkerchief?" she asked hopefully.

"Of course." He pushed open the door and stepped in, his gaze traveling from her flaming face to the deep décolletage of the gown. "Ingenious, my dear," he murmured as he proffered the fine Venetian lace-edged square. "I doubt I have ever supplied one for that purpose before."

She grabbed for the handkerchief and turned away to tuck it into her bodice. "I cannot believe that the Mantini would wear this in company," she muttered half to herself.

" 'Tis one of her more discreet gowns." He grinned. "Come on, we waste time and I am hungry."

The repast prepared for them was nothing short of fantastic. Ellen settled into her chair opposite the marquess and tucked a napkin over her lap. She had never seen so much food set out for two people, for she was used to traveling in the company of her father, who insisted on breaking their fast with tea and a few biscuits with jam. It was not because they were poor, but rather because he resented spending his money.

Lord Trent cut off a slice of ham and laid it across her plate. "Do not be saying you could not eat a morsel, Miss Marling, because I cannot abide a die-away miss. Pray keep in mind that we shall not be stopping again until late."

"I should not dream of it, sir," she assured him while she helped herself to an egg, a couple of muffins, and some sausages. Daintily cutting up the meat, she proceeded to eat. Trent finished first and then began watching in fascination as she ate everything she had taken on her plate. Finally, when she popped the last bit of muffin in her mouth, he felt compelled to push a plate of rolls toward her.

"You might as well try these, too. Really, Miss Marling, but you must have had a nurse that thought it a sin to waste food."

"Even a crumb." She nodded. "But how did you know?"

"I had one like that—Button, we called her."

"I had not supposed that the Marquess of Trent ever had a nurse."

"All English children of our class have nurses, my dear."

"Well, I cannot imagine you to ever have been a proper English child," she managed with a smile.

"Oh, I was a scapegrace," he admitted cheerfully, "but not because Button did not try." He took out his watch and frowned. " 'Tis late, and we'd best be getting back on the road. I am afraid you will have to give Timms a more precise direction than just York, in case there is a shorter route. I've no wish to play nursemaid any longer than necessary, for I have enough problems with pursuing females."

"If that is supposed to mean that I shall be soon casting out lures to you, my lord, you are way wide of the mark," she answered sweetly as she rose from the table. "I do not find ill-tempered men attractive in the least."

While she made her way back to the carriage, he paid the shot and then huddled with Timms and the coacheys. When he came back, he found her standing outside the coach admiring the elegant equippage by light of day. Frowning, he moved to open the door and hand her up. "You should not be standing unattended in a common innyard," he chided as he swung up beside her and settled in the seat across. "It would not do for you to be recognized."

"My circle of acquaintance is quite small, my lord—'tis not I who would be recognized." She spread her skirts out on the seat and resigned herself to more long hours cooped up in the carriage.

Once the coach started rolling, they made good time.

She attempted a few desultory comments for conversation, but he appeared preoccupied with other things, and she finally abandoned the effort. Both napped off and on until at last they stopped again. This time, Dobbs procured some bread, meat, and apples, and a bottle of wine from another inn along the way, and they ate inside the coach while it lurched into motion again. She viewed the small nuncheon with disfavor as she divided it.

"I have heard of those who travel light, my lord, but this is ridiculous. Never say that you mean to rely on so little to sustain yourself."

"And I was about to say the opposite for you, Miss Marling— you have an uncommonly healthy appetite for a thin female." He pushed another apple her direction and added wryly, "I do not suppose you thought to lift Brockhaven's purse before you jumped from his window, did you?" He watched her color guiltily. "Of course you did not. And I had not the least intention of traveling the length of England when I left my house, either."

"You mean we do not have any money?"

"I have enough, ma'am!" he snapped back. "But if you expect me to keep a roof over your head, you will practice a little economy. It was not until I paid the shot at the Hawk that I realized just how light my purse is."

Mortified, she ate in silence and kept her eyes on the food in front of her.

Goaded by her embarrassment, he leaned across and corrected the impression he'd given her. "I am not so light in the pocket as I made it sound, my dear, but we will have to watch the expenses."

"But you are a marquess."

"And you imagined I carried my blunt with me? What a strange notion of marquesses you must have, Miss Marling."

Stung, she bit back another acid remark and twisted the ring from her finger. "Here, my lord. Perhaps this can be sold the next place we stop."

"Do not be absurd. I may not be the Bank of England, my dear, but I would cut up pretty warm if it came to that. I just do not happen to carry my gold with me."

"Take it."

"I could not take your wedding ring."

"I assure you, my lord, that it has not the least sentimental value to me. If it will buy even one meal, it's yours." When he would not take it, she let it fall on the floor of the carriage. Finally, he bent to retrieve it and slipped it on the little finger of his left hand. He leaned back and shaded his eyes again with the hat. It was inconceivable to her that he meant to sleep again, but he did. She had to content herself with curling up on her side and covertly studying the strange man across from her. He was not so bad, she decided. In fact, he reminded her of her brother, Julian, at times. Perhaps it was that all young men of wealth were given to excesses, with the very rich reaching a level of boredom that required increasingly dissolute behavior to interest them at all. Lulled by the constant swaying of the coach, she abandoned the attempt to figure him out and drifted off to sleep herself.

"Ma'am."

It seemed like she could not have been asleep above a few minutes when he was shaking her awake. "Where are we?" she yawned sleepily.

"We are at the Blue Boar, and by the looks of it, 'tis crowded. We could push on, I suppose, but I think we ought to plan on supper and beds here. At least I have heard this place keeps clean linen."

She had never before entered an inn for lodging on the arm of a strange man, and she was acutely conscious of the appearance they must give without so much as a maid or valet between them. Trent grasped her elbow and led the way.

"And how might we serve you, sir?" the inkeeper asked while he looked them up and down. Behind him, his wife hovered curiously.

"I am needful of a chamber for my wife and myself," Trent stated baldly.

At almost the same time, Ellen spoke up, "We are needing chambers for my brother and me."

"So, that's how it is, eh?" The innkeeper's wife pushed herself forward and stood with her arms on her hips. "I knew it was havey-cavey business the minute I saw 'em. Well, sir," she addressed Trent, "you can take your doxy elsewheres. We run a respectable establishment here."

"I am the Marquess of Trent," his lordship snapped at the landlord. "and I will have a chamber!"

"Aye, and I am the Prince of Wales," the fellow snorted derisively as he took in Trent's travel-stained evening clothes and his full day's growth of dark beard. "Nay. Be off with you! We don't run no place like that."

As soon as they were back in the carriage, Trent rounded on her. "Wonderful! 'Tis amazing how you got us thrown out of the last inn for miles."

"You surely did not expect me to share your chamber, my lord," Ellen shot back, unrepentant.

"Acquit me! I have not the least design on your person, ma'am, but could you not see the crowd in the taproom? They just might have had one chamber, but 'twas certain they did not have two. The next time, I shall do all the talking and you will keep your mouth closed—that is, *if* we can even find another place."

"Then bespeak two rooms, my lord."

The sun set, making the road dark and ominous as they barreled down a lonely stretch of it. Trent stared glumly out the carriage window into the blackness. "I do not like being abroad at night in a strange area and riding in a carriage emblazoned with my arms. 'Tis almost an invitation to robbery. I should have abandoned you to your fate and taken whatever bed they had back there. I doubt they would have quibbled with that."

"Halt!"

He'd no more than voiced his fears than a warning shot rang out and horsemen approached from the side of the road. "And now, what do you think of what you've gotten us into, Miss Marling?" Trent demanded. He slid his hand into his cloak and drew out a silver-chased pistol that gleamed in the darkness. "Damn!"

The coach driver reined in as the men drew nearer. Dobbs leaned over and whispered to Timms, "Best duck, fer 'is lor'ship ain't about ter git robbed."

At almost that same instant, another shot rang out and one of the riders fell heavily from his horse. The others spurred their mounts and bolted away without a thought for their fallen comrade.

Dobbs took the reins from Timms' nerveless fingers and nodded knowingly. "Told yer he wouldn't stand fer it."

Inside the carriage, Ellen stared at the still-smoking pistol. "That was fine shooting, my lord. He must have been fifty paces away and in the dark."

"About sixty," he corrected coolly. He checked the barrel and slid the pistol back beneath his cloak. "I'll reload later. Let's go, Timms," he yelled up to his driver.

"But, I mean, aren't you going to see if that man needs a doctor? You cannot just go off and leave him," Ellen protested.

Trent laughed cynically. "He's past redeeming, my dear—shot clean through the heart, I assure you."

"But you cannot know that."

"I never miss. Deveraux are noted marksmen."

It was obvious that he considered the subject done, but Ellen could not help persisting, "You cannot just leave him there!" She reached across the seat and caught at his coat sleeve, imploring, "You cannot! Even dead, he should have the dignity of identification and burial, my lord. If you will not see if he requires assistance, at least seek out the local constable and report his whereabouts."

"You know, you are deuced softhearted over a damned highwayman," he complained, and then relented with a sigh. "All right. Dobbs, get down and see to the fool. Miss Smith is concerned that he may be bleeding to death."

"A highwayman, sir?" Reluctantly the coachman unhooked the lantern from the box and stepped down gingerly to examine the fallen robber. "Gor," he breathed in awe. "Yer lor'ship got 'im clean in the 'eart. He niver e'en felt it."

"Satisfied, my dear?" Trent leaned back. She could sense his mocking look as he added softly, "A Deveraux never shoots except to kill his man."

"A remarkable family, the Deveraux," she snapped with asperity. "A pity they have never exerted themselves to be civil. No doubt they could have excelled at that also, my lord, if they were so inclined."

"A flush hit, Miss Marling," he acknowledged, "but I doubt even my esteemed relatives have been called on to assist a runaway bride who does not know when to hold her tongue."

Unable to think of a suitable reply, she allowed the

conversation to drop again with an expressive sigh. Closing her eyes, she leaned back and feigned sleep. The coach lurched forward, jostling its occupants again as it regained speed and eventually returning to its constant swaying motion. Trent stretched his arms and shoulders several times and crossed and uncrossed his legs for exercise. Setting his hat on the seat beside him, he brushed back his unruly locks with the palm of his hand, and then having nothing else to do, he set to contemplating his companion. Sparking a flint to light the inner coachlamps, he waited until they glowed softly and then trimmed the wicks down until they provided enough illumination that he could see her.

In fairness, he had to own that she was not an ill-looking girl, despite the gibes he had cast at her. He fell to wondering what she could look like decently gowned, with a maid to style that thick dark hair. In other circumstances—certainly a wedding to Brockhaven could not put any female in looks—but in other circumstances, he wondered if she might not be passably pretty. From what she'd said, he gathered she was about twenty-three—still too young for the aging baron. Indeed, the thought of Sir Basil's bedding any young female revolted even Alex Deveraux. It was unfortunate that Ellen Marling could not have rejected Brockhaven out of hand, he mused, for she was certainly in for a very unpleasant scandal now. One thing he had to give her, though: there was no female of his acquaintance, respectable or not, who would have dared to do what she'd done. To defy everyone, to risk both limb and reputation, to literally jump out of a window to escape the attentions of a repulsive husband, was an act of either great folly or great courage. He drew back from his meandering thoughts with a jolt. He must be getting soft in his thirtieth year, he decided, for pity was something he seldom felt.

"Yer lor'ship!" Dobbs leaned over the side of the box and called down, "There's an inn ahead. D'ye want ter stop?"

"Aye," Trent yelled back.

Ellen opened her eyes finally as the coach came to a halt in a deserted innyard. A cat scurried out of the way as Dobbs dropped to the ground and began banging of the door until a slatternly woman stepped into the coachman's lantern light. The orange glow gave her an unpleasant scowl.

Ellen looked out and shuddered involuntarily. "This looks like a place to be murdered in, my lord," she muttered low.

"How very gothic you are, my dear," he murmured back. "I cannot speak for you, of course, but I am ready to seek a bed." He opened the door, ducked his head, and stepped down into the courtyard before turning back to assist her. While she pulled at the badly wrinkled skirt of the lavender gown, he moved to speak with the woman at the inn's entrance.

"We require lodging for the night—or what is left of it. So, if you would make up beds for me, these men"—he gestured toward Timms and the coachman—"And—"

"How do you do?" Ellen stepped forward to possess herself of Trent's arm and held on tightly. "I am Mrs. Smith. Smith and I are wishful of either an adjoining chamber or a single large one. The adjoining one would be best, of course, because he snores terribly, but—" She felt like a fool and her face flamed in embarrassment, but she did not like something about the place.

"Ellen," Trent hissed, "I am perfectly capable of making the arrangements. Well, you heard my wife, madam." He put an arm around Ellen and squeezed her shoulder.

"Ain't no such thing here. 'Tis rooms at either end of the hall or one at the top of the stairs."

"Well, then, it seems like one will have to do—right, my dear?" He gave Ellen's shoulder another squeeze and propelled her through the door of the inn. "I daresay you can stuff your ears with something, can't you?"

Ellen surveyed the grim little room they'd entered and noted the dearth of other guests. A rat, or else a very large mouse, scurried around a corner, causing her to jump against the marquess. "One will be fine," she agreed readily.

The innkeeper appeared from the lower stairwell, his dirty shirt and trousers attesting to the general unkempt condition of everything there. He wiped his hands on an apron that Ellen decided looked bloodstained. With a jolt, she realized that his interested gaze had moved to rest on the low neckline of the Mantini's dress. Her face coloring with embarassment, she twined her arm through Trent's and shrank behind him.

For his part, the marquess appeared not to notice anything amiss as he nodded in the innkeeper's direction. "My wife and I have not eaten, and neither have my men. Perhaps it would be possible to order a cold supper?" he asked hopefully.

"As to that"—the fellow bobbed his head affirmatively— "I am sure that Mrs. Grumm has some beef left. We slaughtered today."

As soon as they were alone in the dingy taproom, Ellen rounded on Trent. "How you could eat a morsel in this place is beyond me, sir. And he did not say what he slaughtered, did he? I do not wish to stay here, my lord."

"And I would go no farther tonight, ma'am." A wicked gleam crept into the blue eyes. "Especially not in light of the newest development in this strange journey. I can scarce wait to see you in one of the Mantini's sleeping dresses."

"You insufferable—" Her retort was cut off by the appearance of Mrs. Grumm with a plate of cold meat and bread. Setting two mugs of ale on the table, the woman spilled them onto the soiled cloth. With a shrug, she wiped the rims with her finger.

"Anything else, Mr. Smith?"

"No—nothing save clean sheets."

"Ugh!" Ellen vented her feelings as soon as the woman was out of hearing. "Really, sir, I wonder at you. I would doubt there's a clean sheet to be had in this whole place." She looked around her disdainfully and added, "I see no signs of other custom, but then no doubt the service discourages return visits."

"Be still and eat, girl," Trent recommended. "If you insist on insulting the old hag, there's no telling what she will serve you." He cut a slab of cold roast and slid it onto her plate. "Here—it does not taste bad." Slicing off a thick hunk of bread, he transferred the meat to it and pushed it toward her. "It's been at least seven hours since last you ate, and I would not be kept awake with your stomach growling at me."

Gamely she picked it up and took a bite. Trent watched

while she tried to chew the dry food and slid her mug across the table. "It's ale, and I doubt you have ever tasted it before, but it will wash that down."

Without thinking, she removed the handkerchief from her bodice and carefully wiped the rim before she sipped. When she looked up, she caught Trent's wicked grin and followed his line of vision. "Oh." Her face flamed as she hastily retucked the damp cloth back into place.

When Mrs. Grumm finally reappeared, it was with candles to light them upstairs. Trent drained the last of his ale and wiped his mouth with a frayed napkin before standing and stretching his tall frame.

"Ready, Ellen?"

She eyed him dubiously now, uncertain as to what he must think of her and yet unwilling to give herself away to the waiting Mrs. Grumm. "I—I suppose so," she answered finally.

She trod the stairs with trepidation behind the marquess, afraid of what he might do. She sincerely hoped that she would be able to convince him that she was not fast and that she would not behave in an improper manner.

"Really, my dear, must you give it out that I snore?" he murmured as he shut the door behind them. "And if you are willing to share my chamber now, why the devil did you not do so at the other place?" He eyed the room with distaste. "At least there we should have been more comfortable." He turned his back and bent to remove his shoes while adding, "And at that place, 'twas because beds were scarce. You certainly have not that excuse here."

She stood rooted to the floor when he stood up and began unbuttoning his wrinkled coat. "You will find what you need in that box. Dobbs brought it up while we were at supper," he told her conversationally as he draped the coat over a chair and loosened his wilted cravat. Tugging at it until it hung limply at his throat, he then turned his attention to removing his waistcoat. Her face flamed when he looked up and stopped.

"What are you doing, my lord?" she choked.

"Getting ready to seek my bed, and I recommend you do the same, Ellen."

"I did not give you leave to use my name."

He raised a black eyebrow as he began undoing the studs at his wrists. "A little late for such formality, don't you think, my dear?"

"I am not your dear, either!" She wiped damp palms against the muslin skirt and faced him bravely. "My lord, you have the wrong impression if you think that I—that I . . ." Her voice trailed off as she realized she had his full attention.

"Do you not think I can tell a respectable female when I see one, Ellen?" he asked in amusement. "I have been funning with you, but my eyes tell me you are devilish straitlaced, my dear, and I certainly am not given to rapine."

"But you are undressing!"

"Only this far, I promise. You would not want me to get into bed in my shoes and coat, would you? Think how uncomfortable we should both be."

"I cannot share a bed with you, my lord!" she gasped, mortified.

"Well, since I see naught but this straight wooden chair, there doesn't appear to be a choice, does there? Ellen—Miss Marling—if it becomes known that you have been alone in my company for an hour even, the prattlers will have it that the worst has happened, anyway," he told her practically. "I advise you to take off your shoes and loosen your corset if you are wearing one, and crawl into bed. 'Tis late and we've a long way to go tomorrow." He walked over to stand in front of her. She stared in fascination where he'd unbuttoned the neck of his shirt and black hair curled there. "Look—you are safe enough with me, Ellen. As I told you before, you simply are not in my style." He picked up the chair where he'd draped his coat and carried it to the door.

"What are you doing?"

"Leaning this under the doorknob, my dear. I am not so obtuse that I do not know why you have insinuated yourself into my chamber, and I've no wish to be kept awake with your fears. You may sleep secure that any attempt to enter this room will waken me."

"You do not like this place, either!"

"No, I do not, but I do not intend to sit up all night." He picked up his cloak where Dobbs had laid it and drew out his pistol. "See, I have this right here beneath my pillow, all primed and ready. Now, take off your shoes and lie down so I can douse the light." He folded back the covers and waited. "Well?"

"I—I cannot."

"Ellen . . ." There was a hint of warning that his patience was coming to an end.

"I cannot sleep in the same bed with you."

"Do I have to throw you in? Have you never slept with a sister or another female?" He watched her think about it. "Well, pretend we are brothers, then."

"No!"

"Shall I take off your shoes and your corset for you? Is that what you want? Because I am not above doing it if it will get me a night's sleep."

"All right." She swallowed hard to hide her embarrassment and edged over to the bed to sit. When he started to turn his back, she blurted out, "You don't have to do that, my lord, for I never wear a corset." Then she slipped her flat kid shoes off and lay down along the edge of the bed as though she were on eggshells.

"That's better." He moved to the other side and blew out the candles before lying down. "Now, let us pull up the covers, if you please. I am not so hot-blooded that I do not need any, no matter what you may have heard." He sat up to rearrange the coverlet over them. "And do not be taking the whole—I cannot abide struggling for possession—and my brother was always wont to play tug-of-war over them at night." He lay back down and turned away from her. "Good night, Ellen. You need not fear I shall ever tell the story, my dear."

3

"EITHER YOU PRODUCE the girl, or I want my settlement back, Marling. You have no notion of how mortifying it is to be deserted on one's wedding night," Brockhaven grumbled. "And do not be saying you've no notion of her whereabouts, either, for she cannot have just disappeared."

"Really, my lord, I am unable to convey the extent of my disappointment to you. Naturally, as her parent, I am as concerned as you about the situation." Marling mopped his brow at the thought of losing twenty thousand pounds. "You have my word that I shall notify you the instant I hear from her. Thank heavens you had the presence of mind to give out that she has taken ill."

"Nevertheless," the baron sniffed, "my own servants know it for a lie. If I am to save any face at all, she will have to be returned to me within the week, do you hear? I expect you to find her." Angrily pushing his hat on his head, Brockhaven executed a stiff bow to Thomas Marling. "One week!"

"Aye, I understand," his host acknowledged. "But I cannot guarantee that I shall even get wind of her direction by then."

"One week," his lordship reiterated with awful finality as he slammed out the door.

"Dear me, Thomas, but what an ugly little person he is. I can quite sympathize with Ellen for running away, you know. But then I never did favor the match," Eleanor Marling reminded her husband.

"Twenty thousand pounds, Nora—twenty thousand pounds! What an ingrate you have reared!" Thomas Marling's sense of outrage bordered on apoplexy. "She was Lady Brockhaven! Do not be forgetting that, my dear. She was to be mistress to a great estate with a bloody fortune at her disposal."

"You speak as though she were dead, Thomas."

"Well, if I do not find her before she costs me the settlement, she might as well be, for all I shall care. Twenty thousand pounds! I shall not welcome her back in my house—not ever."

His wife's eyes widened at the vehemence in his voice. "But you cannot be such an unnatural parent as that!" she gasped.

"What a simpleton you are, my dear. Do you not realize how she has ruined the future of your other children? We have nurtured a viper in our midsts, Eleanor."

"Pooh. The scandal will blow away long before Amy is to be presented, I am sure, and I should think that half the *ton* cannot but sympathize with poor Ellie. As for Julian, he never favored the match in the first place, and I cannot think he will consider his future ruined because Ellie could not stomach Brockhaven." Eleanor Marling laid a placating hand on her husband's shoulder. "And since Lucinda is but ten," she reasoned, "she cannot be touched by the scandal at all."

"Amy will not be presented, madam!" he snapped. "I did my duty by Ellen and see what it got me. Very likely I shall not have a groat when Sir Basil is finished with me."

"Nonsense, Thomas," his wife sighed at his parsimony. "You know we are comfortably circumstanced. Besides, 'twas not duty but greed that prompted you to positively throw your eldest daughter at that old roué. I tell you now, Thomas, that I shall not sit idly by and let you sell Amy as you did Ellie."

"And I will not have you encouraging her to rebellion as you did your eldest. You'll not see me foot the bills for another Season for an ungrateful chit."

"You will not have to," Eleanor told him mildly, "for your notion of a Season is quite inadequate, anyway. With Amy's beauty, she will take in an instant, and I'll not deny her the chance. I intend to give her over to your sister Sandbridge—I am sure she will know how to go about it with some style."

"I forbid it."

"And I have already posted a note to her. Without doubt, she will come as soon as she is able—and I should not like to hear the rare peal she'll read over you. After all, Ellen is quite her favorite."

"Aye, a blistering for my ears, I'll be bound. 'Twas my hope to see it all settled before she found out." He sank into a chair and eyed his wife with disfavor. "Aye, and she'll make it cost me."

Marling had never been able to stand up to his only sister. Even when they were children, she had dominated him and bent him to her stronger will. Now she would descend on him like some avenging angel to take him to task for forcing Ellen into a distasteful marriage. Damn the chit! Why could the girl not have accepted her lot? Why did she have to behave like a goose and bolt? Any fool could've told her she'd outlive Brockhaven and be a rich widow someday. And where the devil could she have gone? He could not swallow that tale about her escaping through the window—the damned thing was a full fifteen feet off the ground. Besides, even if she had, where would she have gone? She was a green girl with no knowledge of London. There was something havey-cavey about the business, he'd be bound. He snapped his fingers in inspiration. Just let Brockhaven try to get his money back—he'd accuse his lordship of doing away with her. Aye, let him get out of that. Turning his attention back to his wife, he glared at her and declared, "Very well, madam, let Augusta come. I shall not be here."

"I did not think you would, Thomas, for I know you cannot stand her because she is usually right."

Seventeen-year-old Amy Marling ventured into the room and looked from one parent to the other. It was obvious from the flush on her father's face that they had been in a spirited argument. She ignored him to address her mother.

"I just saw Sir Basil. Was Ellie with him?" She paused at the warning in her mother's expression. "Is something amiss, Mama?"

"Aye, something's amiss!" Thomas Marling exploded.

"That depends of how you view the story," her mother interposed, "for Brockhaven was here to tell your father that Ellen has run away."

"Really! Then I hope she did it before he touched her. I know I could not have borne his fat fingers on me." She gave a defiant toss of her dark curls when her father scowled at her. "Well, 'tis true—I'd never have gone through with the wedding."

"This is not a fit subject for a young female. Go upstairs, miss."

"Fiddle, Thomas. 'Tis time she knew what Ellen did for her. 'Tis true, my dear, that your father would have just as soon married you to Sir Basil to get the settlements."

"And I should have," Marling muttered sourly.

"Then I would have bolted, too, Papa."

Faced with the censure of both wife and daughter, Thomas Marling launched into a tirade about the respect due the head of the household and then stalked off when he realized they were barely attending him.

As soon as he was out of hearing, Amy turned back to her mother. "But where can she have gone? And what will keep Lord Brockhaven from forcing her to return to him if she is found?"

"I do not know the answer to either question, my dear, but you must promise me that you will not give her away to your father if she contacts you."

"As if I would!" Amy retorted hotly. "Mama, I couldn't!"

Eleanor surveyed her middle daughter critically and liked what she saw. Once she had feared the lovely child would be too biddable in the hands of her scheming father, but no longer. And this time, Eleanor would not fail her. Amy would not have to take an aging and repulsive husband like Basil Brockhaven as long as there was breath in her mother's body. A pity she had not been as firm of spine for Ellen. Aloud, she just agreed. "See that you do not, child. When Augusta gets here, I expect her to straighten him out on that head whether he stays to hear it or not."

"Never say she knows about it."

"She will when she gets my letter."

"Oh, poor Papa!"

"Exactly."

They were interrupted by the intrusion of twenty-year-old Julian Marling, a tall, handsome young man who favored his younger sister in looks. He stopped by the doorway long enough to ask, "Brockhaven gone? I cannot stand that man—fat macaroni that he is."

"Oh, Julian! 'Tis famous. Ellie's bolted!" Amy bubbled.

"Bolted? Capital! Knew she would not go through with it."

"Yes, well, before you go too far, Julian, you'd best hear the whole of it," his mother cut in. "No one has seen Ellie since Brockhaven would have it that she jumped out of a second-story window. He came to demand her return or his money back."

"Papa ought to have thrown it in his face."

"You know him better than that. He's too pinchfarthing to do any such thing. If he finds her, he'll send her back to Sir Basil."

Julian flicked some lint from his navy-blue coat of best superfine before answering, "Not if I have anything to do with it, he won't. I should have rather seen her an ape leader than tied to the old rake."

"Much you did at the time," Amy reminded him. "You were just like everyone else: you danced at her wedding!"

"I did not!" he retorted, stung. "If you must know, I didn't stay for the dance because I couldn't bear seeing the fat baron leer at her."

"Children! There is enough blame to share, believe me. None of us did anything, and poor Ellie had to do the best she could. Oh, but I wish we knew where she was, whether she is safe, even. London is no place for a girl alone."

"Now, Mama," Julian soothed, "ten to one, she's rented lodgings and is but waiting for Papa's temper to cool. She'll come home, you'll see. Besides, if anything terrible had happened to her, we would have heard of it."

Unconvinced, Eleanor Marling could only stare out

the window into the London street. "Well, I cannot but hope you are right."

"Mama, she's all right. And when she does come back, Julian, Aunt Augusta will be here to see that she does not have to go back to Sir Basil. You know what Aunt Gussie can do to Papa."

4

ELLEN AWOKE TO find herself quite alone. Alarmed, she sat up and looked around the room for some sign of Lord Trent. His coat still hung on the chair back and his shoes were where he'd discarded them, but there was an eerie stillness about the place. She rose and went to the window to look down on the courtyard where his carriage had been the night before, and there was no sign of it. It was inconceivable that even a man like the marquess could have left her to face the nasty landlord alone, and yet she knew instinctively that he had gone. Then she noticed the partially exposed butt of his pistol under the pillow. No, she decided with relief, he would never have left that behind.

She hastily changed into another of the Mantini's day dresses, a sprigged muslin, and stuffed Trent's handkerchief into the softly gathered bodice before draping the Mantini's cloak over her arm to conceal his pistol. Tiptoeing to the door, she cracked it an inch and peered out. The silence was overwhelming. Slowly, she edged her way down the stairs, keeping close to the wall and stopping when the steps creaked to listen for some sound of life.

The entire lower floor was deserted: there was no sign of Trent, his servants, or the Grumms. Her heart pounded uncomfortably beneath her ribs as the stillness frightened her. Crossing the empty taproom, she let herself out into the courtyard and could see the still-fresh tracks of the big carriage. A chicken squawked and ran from her, but it was the only sign of life in the innyard. Noticing that the stable door was ajar, she clutched the pistol more tightly and went to investigate. Once inside, she found nothing except a pair of broken-down nags, a two-wheeled cart, and some tack badly in need of repair. It did not appear that the Grumms had prospered in the inn. She sat down dispiritedly on a mound of hay and took stock of the situation.

Just as she'd made up her mind to try saddling one of the nags, she heard the sound of hoofbeats coming down the deserted lane. She froze in indecision—it could be Grumm or it could be anyone. Determined not to give herself away, she moved to the back of the stable and waited while someone dismounted outside and approached. With thudding heart, she heard the door creak open. Sucking in her breath, she dropped the cloak and spun around with Trent's pistol aimed squarely at the door.

"And I was worried about you!" Trent smiled. He reached to take the weapon, disengaging it from her paralyzed fingers. Thinking her about to swoon, he put an arm around her and led her back to the hay pile.

"I was so frightened," she murmured in understatement as she gripped his hand tightly. "There was no one here, my lord—no one at all." She swallowed convulsively, unwilling to give vent to the tears of relief she felt welling up. "I thought you had deserted me."

"I gave you my word as a Deveraux that I'd see you to York, Miss Marling."

"Not knowing any other Deveraux, my lord, I had no way of knowing how binding such a promise was," she retorted. "Besides, what was I to think? You were gone, your carriage was gone, your servants were gone—even the Grumms could not be found. You might have wakened me, or left me a note, or something!"

"I expected you to still be abed." He sank down beside her and managed a wry smile. "You were more right about our esteemed innkeeper than I care to admit, my dear. Timms heard them rattling the door where I'd placed the chair, and he surprised them. By the time I got the door open in the dark, he and Dobbs had subdued Grumm while Emmett caught the woman running down the stairs. It seems they intended to rob us in our beds—whatever else they planned is but conjecture." He slipped a comforting arm about her shoulders and continued, "I confronted Grumm and his wife and they insisted at first that they were merely checking the locks before retiring, but then Timms explored the basement and found a vertible treasure trove of clothing, jewels, and money. When I suggested a visit to the local constable, they became quite agitated and offered to share everything with me."

She shuddered against him. "I told you I did not like the place."

"Let me finish. Dobbs inquired about, rousing people from their beds in the village until he found the constable. The fellow came over and examined Grumm's basement with a great deal of interest and arrested the both of them. He also commandeered my carriage to take them to jail in the nearest town."

"Oh, dear! And I suppose there will be an investigation and I will be discovered." She sighed regretfully. "And you will be embroiled in my affairs, won't you? I'm truly sorry, my lord."

"Ellen," he told her seriously, "you are looking at a man who's had to leave the country three times for killing a man in a duel. I can survive a scandal, but you cannot." He rubbed her shoulder reassuringly. "It won't come to that, however, I promise. I have already given my deposition to the magistrate—a veritable toadeater, by the by—and I have told him you are my sister. He is coming over; he expressed a certain interest in Grumm's robbery victims since none has come forward to complain. When he speaks with you, just remember that you are my sister and that I am bringing you home from school."

"At my age?"

"I thought it was rather clever of me, really," he told her with mock injury. "And you do not look your age, Miss Marling. I told him you were Ellen Deveraux."

"And I am Miss Smith to your driver and coacheys, Mrs. Smith to the Grumms. Do you not think he'll find that rather suspicious, my lord?" She stared into space for a moment. "No, perhaps you were right and I should have tried to stomach Brockhaven, but I just could not. I should never have embroiled you in this. Now, I will have ruined both our reputations, and my aunt will most likely disown me." She straightened her shoulders and added resolutely, "But I shall survive. I shall become a musician or a milliner, or something."

"My people will not contradict anything I tell them, Ellen. And you will not have to resort to anything so drastic, I am sure," he told her bracingly. "From all I know of Augusta Sandbridge, she'll read me a peal and take you in. My only fear will be that she'll try to make me offer for you."

"Well, she cannot. There *is* Brockhaven, after all."

They were interrupted by the sound of the carriage barreling into the innyard.

Trent stood up and pulled Ellen after him. "Come, my dear, let us get this over with. No doubt the estimable magistrate will be with them. Just remember, call me Alex as though you have done so for years."

The sunlight nearly blinded her as they stepped out to meet the carriage. Dobbs jumped down nimbly and helped an elderly man in old-fashioned clothing down from the coach.

"Mr. Langston, our magistrate," Trent hissed in a low voice.

"Your lordship." The old man bowed deeply in the marquess's direction and inclined his head toward Ellen. "I can understand your reluctance to expose you sister to this sordid business, but I am afraid I will need her to corroborate what you have told me."

Trent scanned the horizon before leaning over to whisper to her, "I do not like the looks of those clouds, my dear. Just humor him and say as little as possible that we may be on our way before the storm hits." Aloud, he told the magistrate, "She knows nothing of import."

"Eh?" The old man cupped his hand to his ear and frowned. "What's that?"

"She knows nothing!" Trent shouted.

"Oh." The magistrate turned his attention to Ellen. "Your sister, eh? I'd note the resemblance anywhere. Aye, she has the look of you. But you mark my words, young man, she'll give you grief if you let her wear gowns like that. Not at all the thing for a young miss— not at all."

"I know, but the hat she wanted was worse," Trent

responded loudly. A smile played at the corners of his mouth as though he were enjoying himself hugely.

"Don't know what gets into females these days," the old man muttered. "The missus and I had four of 'em, and not a one wore anything like that."

"Ellen"—Trent turned to her in an attempt to prompt the magistrate back to the matter at hand—"Mr. Langston is wishful of asking you about last night. I told him that you did not see or hear anything, but he would hear it from you."

"Aye, not so young as I was used to be. Let us go inside and get to the bottom of this. Unsavory business, it is—aye, unsavory. You, young fellow, d'ye think Grumm kept a decent wine cellar?"

They stood aside for him to lead the way in. Ellen leaned closer to Trent and whispered, "We shall be here all day if he discovers one."

"There you are wrong, my dear. I will procure some for him and mayhap 'twill keep him diverted from more delicate subjects. And there is, after all, nothing that says we have to tarry while he drinks it."

The magistrate found himself a table and pulled up a chair while indicating that he expected Miss Deveraux to do the same. Ellen sank warily into a seat opposite him as Trent disappeared in search of the wine cellar.

"Now, miss," the old man rasped, "you will be pleased to tell me what happened here last night, and do not leave out why you found it necessary to share your brother's chamber under an assumed name. Grumm says you both told them you were man and wife."

"That I did, sir," Ellen confirmed, "for as soon as I saw the place, I was afraid to be alone and I thought they would think it odd for a brother and sister to share a room in an empty inn." She smiled ingeniously at the magistrate and added, "Just look around you, sir—'tis enough to frighten an older lady than I."

"I see. Yes, well, your brother says you are but seventeen, and I suppose that explains it. You've still got your head full of fanciful notions, haven't you?"

"*I* don't think it was fanciful in the least, sir, not in light of what happened. Alex says they tried to rob us while we slept, and I believe it was only the intervention of our driver and coachmen that saved us from being murdered in bed.''

"Did you actually see or hear anything yourself?"

Trent had entered the room with a wine bottle and some glasses as Langston posed the question. Smoothly taking over the conversation, he shook his head and told him, "My sister sleeps like the very dead, sir. I could not even wake her sufficiently to tell her we were taking them to the constable. She had no notion of where we'd gone when she woke, and was so frightened when I returned that she nearly shot me with my own pistol."

"I did not! Alex, 'tis unfair. I did not plan to use it unless you were Grumm."

"Had I been Grumm, my dear, I should have expected you to shoot."

"You cannot be serious, my lord!" Mr. Langston appeared shocked to his very core. "Not at all the thing to give a female a pistol—she might have hurt herself."

Trent poured the magistrate a glass of rich red wine, diverting him momentarily. "Ah, but as a Deveraux, she is expected to know how to take care of herself in these unforeseen situations," he pointed out with a perfectly straight face.

"Deveraux? Thought you said the name was Trent!" Langston stared at the marquess, digesting this turn of events with distaste. "Deveraux, sir! I cannot credit it."

"You expected me to look positively evil, I suppose?" Trent prompted pleasantly.

"No, no—that is—"

"Alex, really! You have shocked poor Mr. Langston." Ellen joined in the spirit of it. Turning to the magistrate, she assured him, "We Deveraux are not nearly so bad as we have been painted."

"Dreadfully loose-living, if half the tales I have heard can be credited, miss." The old man caught himself guiltily and hastened to add, "But, of course, I should not be talking of your relations in front of you, I daresay. Besides, much of it must be exaggeration."

"Alex," she sighed, "have you been raking about again? Really, Mama will not like it if you cut up another dust like that last one."

"Really? What . . ." Mr. Langston leaned closer, his curiosity piqued.

"Our mother would like to see him settle down and get married," she continued conversationally.

"I daresay that might curb his excesses, but I doubt his suit would be welcome to most parents if he is a Deveraux."

"Nonsense, utter nonsense," Ellen dismissed airily. "My brother is, after all, a marquess, and I cannot think of many papas who would not welcome seeing their daughters a marchioness. The world is full of those who would sell their girls no matter how loathsome his reputation is."

"Ellen," Trent cut in abruptly, "I believe Mr. Langston is more interested in the Grumms than in the Deveraux."

Disappointed, the elderly magistrate sank back in his chair. Like many of his fellows, he found the ways of the *haut ton* far more interesting than the doings of a couple of thieves. Regretfully, he poured himself another glass of the wine and returned to the subject at hand. "Then we have established that you did not see or hear anything, Miss Deveraux?"

"I did not."

"It is probably just as well, child, for the story appears likely to get worse. My constable fears what he will find when the grounds are dug, for 'tis not at all likely that other robbery victims simply went on their way without complaint."

"Really?" Ellen shot a meaningful glance at Trent and muttered, "I told you we could be murdered in our beds when first I saw the place."

"But we weren't. Now, if Mr. Langston is quite finished with you, we had best be getting back on the road. By the looks of those clouds, we have tarried too long as it is. And I believe Dobbs has managed to procure some biscuits and sausages to eat on the way."

"Aye, you go on, my lord," Langston responded. "I expect the constable any time now with men and shovels, and it would not do to have the young lady here when they begin to dig."

No sooner were they safely inside the carriage than the

marquess burst into laughter. "Well done! Family resemblance indeed!"

"It probably was the dark hair that did it."

"Either that or the man was half-blind."

"Did you see his face when you called me a Deveraux?" She chuckled.

"I think it was the notion of you with a pistol that shocked him first, my dear."

"Would you really have expected me to use it? I mean, would your female relatives really have fired on anyone?" she asked curiously.

"Of a certainty, if there were any. By all accounts, my mother would have. And, by the by, if we are ever called on to continue this ruse, we do not have a mother anymore. Our mother passed away before you were born, if you must know."

"Well, I could scarce say that, could I? I should sound the veriest fool, my lord, for then how could we account for me? But," she added philosophically, "I doubt it shall be a problem, anyway, for we are surely not above another day or so from York."

"I don't know. It depends on the weather when we get there. We'll make good time if that storm passes, but since it is coming autumn, Ellen, we may not be so fortunate." He pessimistically eyed the dark clouds through the carriage window. "That looks like it is going to turn ugly, my dear. I think you are bad luck."

"I? And how do you know 'tis not your own misfortune?"

"Because I controlled my life until you dropped onto me at Brockhaven's."

"Well, I should not be proud of that, my lord," she retorted, "for no doubt your life to that point had been just one high flyer after another and a dozen gaming hells to squander your money in. Bad luck, indeed! 'Twas you who would come!" She caught herself and regretted her words. "I am sorry, I should not have said that. If the truth were admitted, I truly am beholden to you for your kindness."

"Since it is not too far from the truth, I'll let it pass."

She was silent for a moment and then changed the subject. "When you return to London, will the Mantini be very angry with you? They say she is very beautiful."

"She is." He shrugged. "But the world provides beautiful women every day to take a man's money in exchange for a few favors." His eyes met hers, and the corners of his mouth twitched with suppressed amusement. "You know something, Miss Marling? You are beginning to sound more like a jealous wife than a sister."

"Of all the conceited . . . I assure you that I have not the least interest in how you spend your life. My intent was to simply keep you from your tedious attempts to place the blame for being here on me. Certainly, I never wanted to stay in that awful inn."

"I despise females who have to be right."

"Really? I should have thought the Deveraux women to be infallible."

"There are no Deveraux women. I have one brother and a couple of wild younger cousins, all male."

"Thank heavens the world is spared more of you."

"Ah, but as you pointed out back there, I am accounted quite a prize, my dear. The *ton* is full of mamas trying to make their daughters Marchioness of Trent." He reached for his hat and leaned back, placing it over his eyes. "I did not get any sleep—unlike you—so if you are quite finished carping, I intend to remedy the situation."

"Your manners are abominable."

"Being a marquess, my dear, I do not need any."

5

THE SUN DISAPPEARED in the dark clouds, and the
wind came up, causing the carriage to sway even more as
it lumbered northward, but Lord Trent neither cared nor
noticed as he slumbered beneath the rakishly tilted hat.
Ellen, on the other hand, stared out her window at the
darkening landscape and felt her spirits sink. Try as she
might, she could not but think that her unannounced
arrival on the Sandbridge doorstep in the company of Alexander Deveraux would scandalize even her Aunt Augusta. And when it became known that she'd spent days
and nights in his company, she would very likely be
turned out in disgrace.

She glanced over at the dozing Trent and sighed. He
was a complicated man, to be sure, an unfathomable
mixture of unexpected kindness and insufferable arro-
gance. It was a pity that such blatantly handsome men
always seemed to be self-centered and disagreeable. Even
when he was doing a good turn, he could not leave it be,
but rather felt it incumbent to lash out in some way
before he became too pleasant. But then, perhaps it was
just as well, she reflected further, because even she was
not immune to such handsomeness and it would not do
for a plain Ellen Marling to entertain any romantical
notions about a man like Trent.

Apparently he was used enough to traveling on whim
in spite of what he'd said, for he at least kept a change of
clothing in the boot. Gone were the soiled and wrinkled
evening clothes, replaced now by buff-colored superfine
pantaloons tucked smoothly into perfectly polished boots
that reached almost to his knees, and a tan woolen cloak

draped rather than buttoned over a very masculine pair of shoulders. Where the cloak fell back, she could see he wore no coat, only a plain ivory shirt without ruffles or pleats that lay open at the neck. He looked no more like her image of a marquess than her brother Julian.

Shifting his hat back off his eyes, he met her quiet study. "Interested, ma'am?" he asked lazily from his slouch. "Can it be that you are no different from the rest of your sex?"

"No!" She jumped guiltily and her face flushed uncomfortably, but she managed to answer coolly, " 'Twas not my intent to stare, my lord. I was but wondering why 'tis necessary for one so handsome to behave so unhandsomely."

"Back to carping, eh? Very well," he muttered as he readjusted his hat to shade his face. "But pray do not stare so. Unlike you, I am quite a light sleeper and it disconcerts me."

"You cannot feel a look, sir."

"Obviously I can."

Scrupulously avoiding even a glance in his direction, Ellen turned her attention to the carriage interior. It was quite unlike anything she had ever been in before. The walls were lined with glossy mahogany panels trimmed out in brass; the coach lamps were small, square-chimneyed, and diffused with shell; the floor was carpeted with a finely printed Spanish wool and protected by a woven mat; and the seats were covered in a rich claret velvet. The rain began pelting at the windows intermittently at first and then washed like great sheets of water that obscured the outside world. A trickle of water seeped in at the top of her window and began its irregular path down the pane. With a quick, furtive peek at his lordship, she drew out his handkerchief and dabbed at the rivulet before it could reach the wood.

Poor Dobbs, Emmett, and Timms! It could not be a very good life for those on the box at any time, but in weather like this they must be soaked and freezing. And unlike their wealthy master, it was highly unlikely that they carried a change of clothes with them.

It seemed like hours that they careened through the blinding storm, with Ellen's face turned to avoid the marquess while he slept like a babe in spite of his avowed inability to do so. There appeared to be no lessening of the intensity of the storm, and no brightening of the sky ahead. A bolt of lightning struck precariously close by, and either it or its attendant thunderclap caused the horses to rear in fright. She could hear Timms yelling above the din of the storm at the team.

Suddenly they were no longer upright, and Ellen felt herself slammed across the seat against Trent and then they were both falling into one of the doors. The coach turned on its side and slid in the mud while glass shattered and showered them from above. Ellen tried to right herself only to be pinned down by the marquess's body.

"Lie still!" he shouted over her, "And let it come to rest." He flung a protective arm across her face to take the glass and buried his head in her breasts. It was over as quickly as it had begun, and an eerie feeling descended over them. For several seconds, the only sound they heard was the steady pelting of the rain.

Cautiously, Trent lifted his head and tried to get his bearings. Someone climbed over the side of the carriage and tugged at the door above them. The marquess pushed up in concert and finally it opened. Cold rain drenched them immediately.

"Thanks be," Dobbs muttered as he peered anxiously down at Trent. "Miss Smith—she all right?"

"I think so. Lend me a hand and we'll get out."

The coachey leaned over and pulled as the marquess braced himself against the side-turned roof with his boots and heaved his body upward. Clearing the doorway, he perched on the side and leaned down to Ellen. "Here, take my hand and try to swing upward when I pull. Come on . . . Good girl!" he encouraged as he lifted her through the door. "Are you hurt?" He pushed her hair back from a cut above her eyebrow that was already being cleansed by the rain. " 'Tis not too bad, my dear. You can be thankful it wasn't a shade lower."

"I am grateful to be alive, I assure you," she breathed shakily. "And I am quite all right." She looked up to where blood trickled down the side of his face. " 'Tis you who are hurt, my lord."

"A scratch from the glass merely."

Dobbs slid off the overturned coach and went to look after the others while Trent lifted Ellen down. A few moments later, the coachey came back shaking his head in disbelief. "Emmett's dead, mi'lor'—broke 'is neck—and Timm's hurt bad—'is leg."

"You'd best not look," Trent told Ellen as he stepped to shield her with his shoulder. "Death is not a pretty sight."

"No." She shook her head purposefully. "While there's naught to be done for poor Mr. Emmett, I can at least assist with Mr. Timms. You will find that I am not the least queasy in the stomach at the sight of blood." She pushed past him to slog through the mud toward the fallen driver, asking him, "Can you tell what you have done to it?"

"Dunno. Broke it, mebbe."

She bent over the outstretched leg and nodded. "Mr. Dobbs," she told the coachey, "we shall have to get his boot off before the leg swells. Can you cut it?"

"Aye, miss." Dobbs knelt and slit the driver's boot with his knife, then looked up for further guidance.

"Go on. It has to come off."

Timms winced and then went pasty white from the pain as Dobbs removed the boot.

"Let me see." Heedless of her wet gown, Ellen sat in the mud beside the driver and, with a total lack of fashionable modesty, began feeling along the bony ridge of the man's shin. "You are right—'tis broken and will have to be set." She looked up at Trent, who stood above her watching in fascination. "I think I can do it, my lord, but I shall require your assistance." She measured the driver's legs against each other and then tried to force the bone into place. The bulge under the skin moved but would not snap into position when she pushed. She shoved her wet hair back out of her eyes and shook her head in exasperation. "I know how 'tis done, my lord, but I have not the strength required. See if you can pull it into line by grasping his foot, and I'll push. Dobbs, if you will but get some of the wood from the coach for a splint . . ."

"Aye, miss," Dobbs answered promptly. "I think 'er's

got th' gift," he muttered to Trent as he passed. "Niver seen th' like fer a female!"

"You are supposed to be swooning helplessly, Ellen," Trent murmured as he knelt down next to her.

"Pooh. And what would that accomplish, my lord? Then you should have to tend to two people. Here—pull down like this . . ." She looked up and noted his reluctance. Mistaking the reason, she snapped, "Very well, if you are too exalted a personage for this, I'll ask Dobbs."

"You know, you are deuced cross, my dear," he complained. "And I know what has to be done, but 'twill hurt like the very devil."

"It will hurt less now than later."

"All right." He grasped Timms' foot, pulled it sharply while she pushed at the protuberant bone, and was rewarded by the sight of the leg moving back into line.

Dobbs returned with two shafts of wood taken from the coach's shattered body, looked down at the ashen driver, and shook his head. " 'E's fainted, miss."

"All the better. He won't feel it when we tie these on for support." She cast about for something to use for a wrapping and wished that fashion had not changed to where ladies no longer wore voluminous petticoats. "Can you use your knife to cut the traces, do you think? We'll have to bind these in place."

"Aye, miss."

They worked quickly, with Dobbs sawing the reins apart and she and Trent tying them around the broken leg.

In a short time, Timms was sitting upright in the mud and mire looking at her handiwork. He gave her a weak smile of approval. "All right an' tight it is, miss, but 'ow'd a lady like yersel' know it?"

"I used to help the doctor in our village"—she smiled—"until my papa found out. Alas, he felt it not an accomplishment for a female, and forbade me to continue."

"Can you ride, Timms?" Trent asked abruptly. "We'll have to boost you up on one of the team without a saddle."

"Yer lor'ship'll 'ave ter shoot one," Dobbs reminded him grimly.

"That still leaves three. You and Timms can ride back

the way we came and seek help. Ellen—Miss Smith—and I will take the one left and try to find shelter. I've got to get her inside before she contracts an inflammation of the lungs." He turned back briefly to Ellen and asked, "Can you ride pillion, ma'am? You'll have to sit astride because I cannot hold you on."

"I won't have any modesty left, will I?" She sighed. "But then, I don't suppose it makes any difference now."

"That's the girl," Trent approved. "Now, turn your back and cover your ears. No, don't argue with me." He waited until he was sure her head was averted, and then he walked to where one of the horses still lay tangled in the shaft and harness, its eyes wide and dilated with fright. Resolutely he raised his pistol and fired a ball into its head. Then he closed his eyes for a moment and leaned against the upended carriage. At least his powder had been dry enough still for the task and he hadn't had to slit its neck.

"Beggin' yer pardon, mi'lor," Dobbs interrupted diffidently, "but what's ter do 'bout Emmett?"

Trent exhaled slowly and straightened his shoulders. "There's nothing we can do for the moment. You'll have to get help and come back."

Dobbs nodded and went to fetch the horses he'd cut loose. When he led one back, he and Trent boosted the injured driver up on its back and then threaded a makeshift bridle around its nose and through its mouth.

"Can you make it, Timms?" Trent asked again.

"Aye, I think so."

Dobbs got another horse and pulled himself up by hanging on its mane. Leaning over to take Timms' rein, he decided, "Mebbe I better 'ave it. Yer looks queasy ter me."

"And you are chilled to the bone," Trent observed as he prepared to throw Ellen up on the last mount. "Here—take my cloak and wrap it around you. I'll get behind you and hold you on as best I can."

"No, you keep your cloak, my lord." The thought of his hands around her waist and under her breasts gave her pause. "And I think it would be better if I rode behind you."

"There's no time for argument, my dear. If you think

you can hang on better that way, I've no objection, but you will take the cloak." He gave her a boost up on the big black's back before removing the heavy woolen cape and handing it up to her. As soon as she had pulled it around her shoulders, he ordered her, "Hold him steady until I get up." And then he swung up in front of her. "Are you sure you've got your seat?" he asked as he reached for the makeshift rein.

"Can you handle him like this?" she asked anxiously.

"Aye, Deveraux are noted horsemen," he flung over his shoulder.

She arranged his cloak about her back and drew her exposed legs up against his, pulling the rest of the cloak to cover as much as possible of both of them. Leaning against his soaked back, she sought to give and get warmth.

Even as he nudged the horse forward, the rain came down harder again, forming sheets rather than droplets, and the wind increased until it howled. The temperature was falling from the early-autumn storm, and Ellen could not afford even a semblance of modesty. She hugged the marquess tightly and burrowed her face against his shoulder blades to protect it from the biting wind.

"Can you see anything?" she shouted against his shoulder.

"Nothing!" he shouted back.

They plodded along the sodden road until both Ellen and Trent thought they would surely freeze before finding any shelter at all. Her whole body ached from the chills that racked it, and her teeth chattered so hard that they clicked against one another. Then, as she straightened to ease the cramp in her shoulders, she saw it. She pounded his shoulder excitedly as the horse rounded a bend in the lane they'd turned into.

"Th-there's a b-barn or s-something ahead."

When they drew closer, they could see it was someone's hunting box, and it was apparently unoccupied. Ellen slid to the ground and held the horse while Trent dismounted and tried the door. It was securely locked. In desperation, he threw his weight against it several times in hopes of breaking the lock, but without succcess. Finally he walked around the box, testing each window until he found one that gave several inches.

"Here," he called out to her. "The ropes are frayed on this one. If I can but get it up a little higher, I'll push you through."

She looked at it in dismay. "I cannot squeeze through there."

He worked until he had it open about seven inches before turning back to her. "Aye, you can," he encouraged. "I'll put you up."

"You'll do no such thing!"

"Ellen, even if you are determined to freeze, you've no right to take me with you." Without waiting for her consent, he picked her up and lifted her to the window. "Bend over and I'll boost you through."

It was an effort, but they finally managed to get her inside with a considerable loss of dignity on her part. As she trailed her wet and utterly revealing gown through the box, she reflected momentarily that by now he must surely think her the veriest trollop. Thus far, he had seen her legs, had his hands on her buttocks, and had felt her breasts pressed against his back. If he made an improper advance after this, she could scarcely blame him. But then she caught sight of her face in a glass and had to be reassured: absolutely no one, not even a thoroughly dissolute rake, could be attracted to the dripping hag she saw. She opened the door to let him in.

"What a pretty pair we are, Ellen." He grinned as he entered. Thoroughly soaked himself, his shirt was transparent over his chest, his pantaloons were bagging with excess water, and his fine boots were thoroughly caked with mud. Water ran in rivulets from spiked ringlets that fell forward over his forehead. In short, the usually immaculate Marquess of Trent presented a picture that would have stunned his acquaintances.

"Aye." She grinned back. "Two drowned rats if ever there were any. But you are shaking with the chill, sir, and so am I. See if you can start a fire and I will look for something dry to wear."

She found the box to contain three small bedchambers, a kitchen with attached pantry, and an open area that passed for a combination sitting-drawing room. She could hear Alex puttering around in the latter as she rummaged shamelessly through drawers and wardrobes. She could find a supply of men's shirts and small clothes belonging to men of smaller stature than Trent. By the looks of it, the box belonged to a man who had some sons.

"I have lit a fire, my dear," Trent called from the other room. "Are you finding anything of use?" She looked up as his voice grew nearer and found him leaning against the doorjamb. "By the looks of it, I shall fare better than you."

"There's nothing else."

"Then you'd best take a blanket and wrap up while I dry your clothes. I'll hang them closest to the heat." He walked closer and selected the largest shirt and leather breeches to be had. "Hmmm—'twould seem the owner took his smalls with him."

Her face turned red and she looked away. He caught her expression and pointed out reasonably, "I did not mean to offend you, but surely you must have seen the laundry of your male relatives hanging on the line." Walking back to the door, he added, "Get out of those wet things and pass them through to me. You can use the blanket for warmth and modesty."

"I cannot run around with naught but a coverlet, sir," she blurted out.

He fixed her with a wry look. "I don't see why. You will be better covered than you are now. I have an excellent notion of your form through that wet gown. And if I am to continue being your self-appointed rescuer, I expect you to stay healthy." He went out, tossing back over his shoulder, "And if you do not hand out the wet things in two minutes, I shall come back for them."

Hastily, Ellen pulled a heavy woolen blanket from the bed and examined it for bugs and spiders. Finding none, she peeled off her wet gown, her petticoat, and her pantalettes. Pulling the blanket tightly about her, she cracked the door and extended the gown and petticoats out. He took them and draped them over a bench pulled up to the fire.

"You might as well give me the rest, Ellen. I've a fair notion of what is missing, since I have seen about every item of female apparel at one time or another." He came back to stand just outside. "And if you mean to wear them under the blanket, it won't do. You must get dry."

She opened the door wider, swallowed in embarrassment, and clasped the coverlet closer as she edged into the room. "I will hang out my own, sir," she told him with her chin held high.

Only her bare feet and her face and one hand were visible, and yet she felt utterly exposed. He faced her wearing a clean shirt and a pair of breeches that were too tight for comfort. With a jolt, she realized he must be embarrassed also.

"That should do, Ellen. Now, come warm yourself by the fire before your teeth chatter out of your head."

"You cannot be very warm, either."

"I am like solid ice," he admitted. "I don't suppose you found a comb or hairbrush in there, did you? We could both use one."

"On the chest." She edged closer to the warmth and found a bench. Stretching her toes to the fire, she did not think she would ever be comfortably warm again. She closed here eyes in exhaustion and leaned forward to huddle in the blanket.

"Ouch!" She felt a tug as her wet hair was lifted outside the coverlet and a clumsy attempt was made to drag a comb through it. "I can comb my own," she muttered ungraciously as she ducked away.

"That I should like very much to see." He grinned, unrepentant. "Most women of my acquaintance raise their arms to do their hair. To do that, you would have to let go of your wrap."

She turned around and found that he had combed his own hair until it lay ridiculously flat against his head, and she guessed he was like her brother, Julian, and did not appreciate the thick curls. She extended three fingers while maintaining a precarious grip on her cover. "Hand it to me and I shall go back and do my own."

"Have it your way." He shrugged. But as she retreated into one of the bedchambers, he added impulsively, "You have beautiful hair, Miss Marling."

"Nonsense, my lord," she called back. "And now is not the time to begin giving me Spanish coin, for I have no illusions about my looks. And I have not forgotten what you said when you found we were on our way to York."

"Well, I was wrong," he yelled through the door. "And I have revised my opinion. You are not nearly so thin as I thought. I think you would draw attention if you were properly gowned."

Squeezing the water out of her hair and pulling the comb through the dark tangles, she began to worry that he was trying to set her up for a flirtation that could only cause her grief. Admittedly, she found him exciting and attractive, but she was not foolish enough to think that anything could ever come of even the slightest flirtation. Men like Trent probably simply flirted with what they saw at the time, and certainly they did not really give an Ellen Marling a second look if anyone else were available. And even if he were serious, which he could not be, there was still the matter of Basil Brockhaven. Finally satisfied that she had done what she could with the hair, she pulled up her blanket and sought the fire.

They sat quietly for a time, savoring the warmth from the hearth. He appeared to be brooding about something— probably the loss of his coach and coachman, she decided— and she left him alone to his thoughts. Abruptly, he drew back and looked at her.

"I don't suppose you can cook, can you?"

"Of course not." She smiled as his face fell. "I have the accomplishments of a lady of quality: I do watercolors, play the pianoforte well, embroider with a fair hand, and sing on key."

"And set broken bones. You cannot say *that* is a lady's accomplishment my dear."

"Well, when I was younger, I wished to be a doctor rather than a lady," she admitted. "I have never wanted to be a cook."

"A pity. We are like to starve before Dobbs gets here, then." He rose and went into the small kitchen in search of something that would require little preparation. After an examination of the pantry, he returned in disgust. "Nothing but pork jelly, bags of flour, salt, and the like."

"Pork jelly? Ugh!"

"My sentiments exactly, though it is a restorative jelly,

whatever that is." He grinned down at her. "But if we are not discovered before the morrow, we may find that pork jelly has more appeal than we expected."

"Not for me."

"Then why don't you see if you can find anything? Surely you must have watched your cook make a muffin or something—even I did that."

"Then you be the cook."

He shook his head decisively. "No. 'Twas at least twenty years ago and I am sure my memory has failed me after so many years." He caught her look of skepticism and hastened to add, "Dash it, my memory is good, but not that good. However, I would be happy to assist you."

Reluctantly, she padded back into the bedchamber and got out one of the boy's shirts, pulled it over her head, and rolled up the sleeves. Then she pulled off a bedsheet, folded it in half and wrapped herself a long skirt, knotting the ends tightly at her waist. It was a trifle confining she admitted to herself as she hobbled into the other room, but it was a definite improvement over a blanket that wanted to slip off one arm or the other.

"Fetching, my dear. Does this mean you are ready to give it a try?"

"If you get the stomachache, do not be blaming me. I want it understood at the outset that I have not claimed to know what I am doing."

"Agreed."

He ducked outside with a bucket and found the well. Returning with the half-filled container, he set it on the table. "Thought you might need water," he explained. "And there are a couple of chickens out there if you need them."

"If you can kill one and clean it, I will try boiling it," she decided.

"I?" He raised an eyebrow. "In my home, 'tis the cook who does that."

"Yes . . . Well, I am not one of your ordinary cooks, my lord. I do not kill or clean chickens."

"I see. You are one of the temperamental ones. I suppose I shall have to attend to the matter." He left for a moment and returned with his pistol. She watched in fascination as he loaded the ball and checked it over. "I hope the powder's not too wet."

"What are you doing with that?"

"To kill the little beast."

"My lord, you do not shoot a chicken—you wring its neck!"

"Aha! You do know about it."

"Only enough to know that you pick the thing up by its head and twirl it around until the poor creature's neck is broken. And then you remove its head and pull out its insides. After that, I think you boil it to loosen the feathers and then pluck it. And when all's done, you can cook it."

"Sound's like a good program to me. I shall bow to your superior knowledge on the subject. I shall be happy to watch."

"I just resigned, my lord."

"All right," he capitulated, "but you will have to find me another set of clothes. I'll be damned if I am going to sit around in dead chicken feathers. And you had better get the water going, too. If we are to revert to the primitive roles of our ancestors, this hunter expects a cook."

Somehow, he managed to kill and clean a rangy rooster and she managed to cook it. As the aroma of boiling broth floated through the cottage, Ellen had an inspiration. "Alex," she confonted him, "were there any hens out there?"

"I am not killing another chicken today."

"Of course not. I did not expect you to. But if there are hens, there might be eggs."

"And I suppose you expect me to look," he sighed. "No doubt this cook does not venture out in the rain, either."

He was gone only a few minutes and returned with several eggs, which he deposited on the table in front of her. "There were more for breakfast, but right now I am most concerned about dinner. What are you serving up?"

"I shall try to make dumplings, but I have no great expectations of success."

By the time they sat down to eat, either would have been hard put to complain about anything. As it was, the dumplings were considerably on the heavy side and the chicken was quite tough.

Lord Trent gnawed off a piece and masticated it thoroughly before commenting, "Not bad, my dear. While it is not what we are used to, it is certainly not a total failure either." He watched her chew one of her doughy dumplings determinedly and added consolingly, "At least the flavor is good."

"Umm—well, no doubt we shall be considerably thinner if Mr. Dobbs does not reach us soon." She wiped her hands on a cloth she had commandeered for a napkin. "But for a couple of gently bred persons, I expect we have done fairly well."

After the meager supper, he went to explore the recesses of the tiny hunting box while she cleared the table and washed the dishes. Left alone finally to her thoughts, she listened to the steady beat of rain on the roof and her spirits lowered. Poor Mr. Emmett—left alone, his body lying by the roadside in the cold. And if it had not been for her reckless flight from Brockhaven's embrace, he would still be alive and warm somewhere in London. She brushed a tear that brimmed onto her cheek.

"What's this?" Trent came up behind her and reached to take the towel she was using on the dishes from her. "Ellen, you have come too far to feel sorry for yourself now."

"I—I was thinking of Mr. Emmett," she told him quietly.

"Oh. Aye." He sighed. "Emmett was a good man. I'll seek out his sister when I return to London and give her his pension." He hesitated a moment and then turned her around into his arms. "Poor Ellen," he murmured softly as he enveloped her. "Do not worry over what was not your fault. It was an accident caused by the weather and it could have happened anywhere."

"Even you said I was bad luck," she sniffed, and then stiffened to push him away, "and this is most improper."

"Here I offer you what I offer no one—the opportunity to cry on me—and you think of propriety." She looked up and saw him smiling ruefully. "Aye, Ellie, and I would offer something else I've offered no other female: I would stand your friend."

She could feel the solidness of his body and the strength of the arms that held her, and she could not deny the attraction she felt to him. Resolutely, she stepped back and managed a tremulous smile of her own. "Thank you, my lord," she managed. "I—I must be blue-deviled from the rain or something, but I will be all right."

"You have been through more in two days than any gently bred female ought to have happen to her in a lifetime, my dear, so I shouldn't wonder if you are in poor spirits." He pushed her toward the table where they'd eaten. "Here—you need a diversion, Ellen, and I have found some cards. What say you to a few games of faro?"

"Ladies do not play faro, my lord," she reminded him primly, and then let her face break into a watery smile. "But I am willing to learn if you have the patience to teach."

"I warn you that I am quite good, my dear."

"Then I might as well learn from a master." She looked up and caught the almost-boyish smile of encouragement that lit his blue eyes. It was no wonder he had such a way with women; she had seen none to compare with him. "Mayhap if my aunt rejects me, I can become proficient enough to be a female gamester on the Continent," she told him lightly.

"You would not like the life," he answered as he took the chair opposite and began to shuffle the cards. "And Augusta Sandbridge would not let a niece of hers sink to such depths, I promise you."

She proved an apt pupil and soon they were able to enjoy the game. While she shuffled, he rummaged through the closets and managed to find the absent owner's cache of wine and appropriated a bottle of burgundy to share over the cards. He poured them both a glass and then noted her hesitation.

"Go ahead," he urged. "It will ease your mind and body after all you have been through."

"Are you trying to ply me with drink, my lord?" she asked suspiciously as she eyed her glass.

"Lud, no! I had already told you on several occasions that you are not in my style, my dear, and seduction is the last thing on my mind now. But if we are to be friends, after all, I see nothing wrong with splitting a bottle over a few hands of faro."

"You know that I should drink ratafia."

"But I didn't find any of that, so burgundy will have to do."

After the first few sips, she had to own that it was really quite good. And when she won a few hands, she began to feel quite comfortable and cosy in the tiny kitchen. The thought crossed her mind as she watched him shuffle his turn that if anyone had told her only two days before that she would be alone and half-dressed in the company of a dangerous rake—a handsome dangerous rake, she amended—and that they would be playing cards, she would have thought the teller patently mad.

For his part, Alexander Deveraux studied Ellen under heavy lids and found himself thinking that she was the most unusual female he had ever met—a true Original, and certainly the first of her sex to keep him even mildly amused without providing him physical intimacy. Damn Basil Brockhaven! The fat pig had no business with a girl like her. Careful, a voice in his brain seemed to warn him, if you do not mind yourself, you are in danger of becoming softhearted. He watched her win yet another hand and threw down the rest of the deck in mock disgust. "You did not warn me you were a Mister Sharp," he reproached her.

"Mistress Sharp," she corrected him happily. "And I did not know it myself. Are you absolutely certain that you are not letting me win?"

"Word of a Deveraux," he pronounced solemnly while he poured them another glass.

"Are we getting foxed, my lord?"

"Not yet. Are you sleepy?"

"No, and if I go to bed, I will just feel sorry about this whole mess."

"You can scarcely be held accountable for a bad storm. Drink up and deal, my dear."

"If we were seen, what would people say, do you think?" she asked thoughtfully.

"Believe me, if we were seen sitting here like this, none of my acquaintances would trust their eyes and more than one would swear off drink. Your deal," he reminded her again.

"I suppose I could be a musician," she mused as she handed out the cards, "for I truly am quite good on the pianoforte, you know."

"No. If Augusta Sandbridge repudiates you, Ellen, you cannot become a musician, either, for they usually end up as rich men's mistresses—or worse."

"You make it sound as though all women who do not marry wind up as somebody's mistress. I cannot credit that, my lord, for not all unmarried females are immoral, do you think?"

He stared at her critically. In the soft candlelight, she seemed very innocent and vulnerable in spite of her brave words. It was an illusion, he told himself, for Ellen Marling had greater strength and more courage than all of the shallow misses of the *haut ton*. Almost without thinking, he asked abruptly, "Have you ever been in love, Miss Marling?"

Her violet eyes widened and she eyed him for some devious intent before she could bring herself to answer. "No," she decided positively, "I am sure I have not. And after this escapade I doubt I shall ever be."

"Why?" he asked bluntly.

"My lord, you have gone to great pains to point out to me that I shall never have the chance with any respectable gentleman. And in spite of what you might think, I cannot see myself as anyone's mistress." She made her points and laid down her cards. "And you, my lord, have you ever been in love?"

"Not even in my salad days," he admitted. "Every female, no matter what her station, always wanted to hang onto my purse rather than me."

"Your mirror ought to tell you a different story," she retorted.

"You know, you are the queerest female I ever met, Ellen Marling. You do not flirt, you do not faint, you do not throw tantrums, and you are devilish plainspoken. I swear I cannot see what Brockhaven saw in you except for your youth and your eyes."

"Well, thank you very much, my lord. You have again

reminded me that the Deveraux, for all their other estimable accomplishments, have no manners."

"My apology. What I meant to say, Miss Up in the Boughs, is that I should have thought he would have preferred a more biddable female. You require a man of more strength than Brockhaven."

"Are you sure you are not trying to set up a flirtation with me, my lord?" she demanded suspiciously.

"Word of a Deveraux. I told you, I consider you a friend."

"And I think I have had too much of this stuff." She eyed her glass sleepily. "I think I should retire, my lord." She pushed her cards away and rose, weaving unsteadily for a moment. "Yes, I believe I have definitely had too much."

"Do you need help to your room?"

"I shall make it by myself, thank you, but it will be an effort, I think," she murmured. Her speech was soft and slurred from the effects of the wine.

He watched her muster her dignity and make her way unevenly out of the kitchen, through the open area, and into the chamber she'd taken. He turned back to pour himself another glass and noticed that they had nearly drunk it all. Poor Ellen Marling! She was going to have a devil of a headache on the morrow, but for tonight at least, she would sleep.

He sat staring for a long time into the red liquid in his glass. Damn females, anyway, he decided, and the sooner he got rid of the violet-eyed Miss Marling, the better. The chit was beginning to give him a conscience.

6

ELLEN WOKE TO the sound of the marquess pounding on her door and asking if she intended to sleep away the entire day. She stretched reluctantly and became aware of the awful ache in her head. Pulling a pillow over her head to shut out the sound of the incessant pounding, she tried to ignore the noise.

"Aren't you hungry?" he called through the door.

"No," came the muffled reply. "Go away."

"Well, I am. So 'tis time for the cook to arise."

"'I thought dissipated lords slept all day," she muttered back.

"Only after dissipation, my dear, and I did not have enough wine last night."

"Well, I did. My head aches as though it could burst."

"Poor Ellie," he sympathized. "Now you have had but a small taste of what too many of us experience far too often."

"Then I cannot imagine why you drink the stuff. I can assure you that I shall not again." With a jolt, she realized his voice had come from close by. She rolled over and opened her eyes to see him standing expectantly by her bed.

"Well, do you get up or do I pull you out?"

"Oh, very well!" she snapped crossly as she swung her legs over the side of the bed before she thought. Wearing only a borrowed shirt, she exposed quite a bit of leg.

"You are longer of limb than I thought," he murmured appreciatively, and grinned.

"And you are insufferable, my lord!" She hastily pulled the covers over her bare legs. "What do you think you are doing in my room, anyway?"

70

"Very well." He shrugged good-naturedly. "I just thought you might be wanting these, unless, of course, you prefer to get up and get them for yourself. I would not particularly mind another glance at those long legs of yours." He deposited her dress, petticoat, chemise, and pantalettes on the foot of her bed.

She reddened and averted her face. "I can assure you that I am capable of getting my own clothing."

"All right. Let me but return them to the other room and you may come after them."

"Listen, you big boor, you unfeeling—"

"Cad?" he supplied with another grin. "Obviously you lack the training of the rest of your sex if that is the best you can do for a tantrum. Your choice of words is too tame by half. I am used to being railed at with far more color."

"Oooh!"

"Look, Ellen, my only intent was to spur you to making our breakfast. There is no need for us to fall into carping." He gave her a cheerful nod and then left, closing the door after him.

She scrambled from beneath the covers and dressed with remarkable speed, given the condition of her head. Only when the last button was safely fastened did she take her eyes off the doorway. Her sense of ill usage grew as she dragged her purloined comb through the tangles of her hair. The unfeeling Trent had dragged her out like a common servant merely to cook his breakfast.

"I have warmed some water over the fire so you can wash," he told her conversationally as she stalked in.

"You are so kind," she muttered sarcastically.

"Well, I intended to be, my dear, but if you insist on behaving like a spoiled child, I will be tempted to abandon you to your fate and set off on our only horse without you. After all, 'tis well past noon and I *am* hungry."

"Noon?" she retorted indignantly. "Eight, more like."

"Noon." He took out his watch and checked it. "See for yourself."

"And what am I to prepare for your lordship?" she capitulated with ill grace. "I do not think I could eat a morsel myself."

" 'Twill help your head if you do, word of a Deveraux. And I should like a seven-course meal, of course. However, knowing your limitations, I suppose I shall have to be content with a couple of eggs."

"Is there no sign of Mr. Dobbs?"

"None, I am afraid. So you will have to cook breakfast or we will starve."

"And has your lordship collected the eggs?"

"Well, under normal circumstances, I believe that to be the function of the cook, but since you have been pressed into service so recently, I will take on the task." With a parting smile that would have disarmed a bedpost, he sauntered toward the door. "But do be looking for a suitable pan while I am gone. I have a deuced nasty temper when I am hungry."

She hastily washed her face and hands in the water he'd heated before she bothered to search for a skillet. Finding one, she was about to look for some grease before another thought occurred to her. She put the skillet away and selected a cooking pot instead. Filling it with the remaining water, she placed it over the fire.

He returned and laid five eggs on the table before taking a chair to watch as she wiped them off and popped them into the water. She pulled up a chair opposite and leaned forward to hold her aching head.

"Boiled eggs? Dash it, Ellen—I could have done that!"

"Then why didn't you?"

"I don't like them boiled."

"Neither do I, but we must make some allowances for my limitations, my lord—and, besides, my head hurts."

"Then we had best hope that Dobbs gets here today before I have strangled you," he sighed, "for I cannot account for my temper when my stomach is empty."

"Really, my lord? I had supposed you to have a bad temper whenever you are crossed, so it is not entirely unexpected if you choose to show it."

They were interrupted by a knock on the cottage door. "Dobbs!" they breathed in unison. Trent nearly knocked over his chair on his way to answer it, but as he swung open the door, he was disappointed to find a young boy of scarcely ten or twelve standing on the threshold.

"Mister." The boy tipped his cap respectfully off his

bright-red hair. "I am Jimmy Bratcher from down the road. Me mum says to find out if'n ye be the new landlord here." He stepped in apologetically and added, "We saw yer smoke, and 'tis no secret that old man Chudleigh wanted to sell now that he don't hunt no more."

"Yes, we are the new owners," Trent told him baldly as he stepped back and gave Ellen a warning look before she could protest the deception.

"And who are ye?"

"Name's Trent."

A smile broke across the freckled face as he put out his hand in the most adult manner. "Mr. Trent." With a nod of recognition to Ellen, he added, "Mrs. Trent. Me mum'd like fer me to welcome you to Little Islip."

"Is Little Islip the name of the nearest village?" the marquess asked hopefully.

"Naw, 'tis only this cottage, ours, and the Raymonds', but they are gone to see her sick mum. Mebbe there used to be more, but I dunno 'bout that."

"I see." Trent's expression was grave, but there was a twinkle to his eye. "Well, Mrs. Trent and I are pleased to make your acquaintance, aren't we, my dear?"

"Delighted." Ellen joined in the spirit and decided to explain, "But we were not intending on staying here. We were only inspecting the property when that dreadful storm came up. We suffered a carriage accident on our way, and you find us without much in the way of clothing or food."

"I have sent for help, Jimmy," the marquess added, "but it has not arrived. Do you suppose your mother could be persuaded to sell us some meat, bread, and cheese?"

"She'd give 'em to yer, more like."

Trent pressed a couple of coins into the redheaded boy's hand. "Then see if she can manage something."

"Oh, yessir!" Clutching the coins happily, the child skipped out.

"Really, my lord, but one would almost think you had seen salvation," Ellen reproached him from her place at the table. "You ought to be ashamed for lying to a boy like that."

"Listen, Ellen—at this moment, I am perfectly willing to buy this place to get a decent meal. I'll have my solicitor look up this Mr. Chudleigh when I return to London if that will salve your conscience," he answered blithely as he rejoined her.

"What a whisker! And what will you say happened to me when you come back?"

"*If* I ever come here to hunt, I will tell them you died."

"I think I should prefer a divorce, if you do not mind."

"No. Too much of a scandal even for this rural setting," he told her positively. "You will have to be carried off by some mysterious illness and leave me nearly inconsolable."

"Well, I doubt you could even find this place again, anyway."

"I doubt it, but what's that to the purpose? I own dozens of places I've never seen, and at least this one looks like it has paying tenants."

She eyed the bubbling pot soulfully. "And I had just set my heart on eating a hearty meal of two boiled eggs."

"Now who's telling a whisker?"

Choosing to ignore the truth of that, she changed the subject. "Do you really think he'll come back? He could just take the money and keep going, you know."

"I fervently hope so. I do not relish the meal you have planned, but if he does not come back soon, I shall be forced to choke it down anyway."

He tapped his fingers impatiently against the tabletop as he watched the water in the pan bubble up and occasionally spray a drop or two into the fire. For a time, the bobbling eggs provided the only sound in the tiny kitchen while Ellen leaned on an elbow, her expression distant with thought.

"You know," he cut in, "I do wonder what it was about you that caught old Brockhaven's attention."

"I don't know," she murmured absently.

"Well, it must've been something. I think it could have been the eyes or the hair."

"What difference does it make? Not even Brockhaven would have me after this."

"I thought you did not care about that, Ellen."

"No"—she shook her head—"I never said that. I said I should prefer ruining my reputation to living with Sir Basil. It is not quite the same thing. Like most girls, I once dreamed of a husband and children of my own someday." She straightened up and squared her shoulders resolutely. "Never mind me, my lord. I should not be talking to you on the subject; the weather and my head have left me blue-deviled."

"Hey, buck up, my dear. Brockhaven cannot live forever, and once you are a wealthy widow, there will be someone come along who will not refine too much on an old story." He watched her thinking as he spoke. "Aha— there is someone!"

"Only Mr. Farrell, our vicar. He claims to have a *tendre* for me, and he would probably welcome the chance to save my soul. But he must be past thirty."

"Don't say it like that, my dear," he told her with a faintly injured air. "Thirty is not old. I will be there next year."

"I suppose it is not," she admitted. "In another seven years, I'll be there too."

"This Farrell—you say he has a *tendre* for you?"

"Definitely. He took every opportunity to pay me calls and to instruct me as to how I should go on, what I should wear, and how I should learn to curb my levity— you know, how I should strive to be like him."

"Egad! What a lover!" Trent muttered in disgust. "But I would not be one to tell another man how to conduct his courtship. Tell me, this Farrell—is he handsome enough for you?"

"Very," she told him definitely, "but his handsomeness is offset by his manner, which is conceited. Were I to ever marry him, with my usual luck, I would most probably be blessed with a dozen dull little boys just like him."

"I shouldn't think it at all likely. I'd wager they would inherit some of your spirit and daring."

"Ah, but you do not know Mr. Farrell. He is boring, prosy, conceited, and exceptionally strong-minded. Not even plain speaking on my part could deter him from thinking that I wanted to be Mrs. Farrell. He was as obtuse as Brockhaven on that head, the only difference being that Brockhaven's suit was favored by my father while Mr. Farrell's was not. No, I could not be a vicar's wife." She rose from the table.

"Where are you going?"

"To take up breakfast, my lord. Even I am hungry now." She managed a quick smile while nodding toward the cupboard. "And if I am to serve this elegant little repast, I expect you to lay the service."

His eyes glimmered with amusement at her recovery from low spirits, and he pushed back his chair to stand. "Well, would your ladyship require napkins? As for myself, I have need of nothing but my fingers and the saltcellar. 'Tis a little primitive, I admit, but then we should not need to wash anything but our hands."

"Put in such a way," she laughed, "I will have to bow to your suggestion, Lord Trent." She tried to pick up a hot egg she had removed from the water, and burned her fingers. Sucking on them to ease the pain, she managed to spoon the eggs into a towel, which she carried to the table. Rolling them out before him, she told him, "You get three."

"You aren't going to peel them?"

She took her seat again and rapped one of hers on the hard surface. Slipping pieces of shell off it, she looked up at him. "No, I do not think you completely helpless, my lord. But you may push the saltcellar this way before you begin, if you please."

They could hear the sound of voices in the lane and both lowered their eggs back to the table hopefully. "Surely that is Dobbs," Trent told her.

In that, they were destined for disappointment, for instead of the faithful coachman, Lord Trent opened the door to the Bratcher boy and a stout woman who bobbed her head respectfully and held up a basket laden with bread, fruit, and cheese.

"Jimmy says ye are stranded in Little Islip." The woman looked to his lordship for confirmation before proceeding. Trent nodded. "Well, I allus was one t' neighbor, sir, so 'ere's summat fer yer and yer missus." She handed the basket over to him and fished in her apron pockets to retrieve the coins he had given the boy. "And don't yer be thinkin' o' payin' fer what I'd be doin', anyways."

Ellen joined him in the doorway and smiled a greeting to the visitors. "Why, how very nice of you, Mrs. —Bratcher, is it? We should not dream of imposing on your generosity, I am sure. And as we will be needing other things until Mr. Dobbs gets back, we should expect to pay for them."

"And I would have young Jimmy get the money then." Trent grinned down on the flushed, freckled face. "If I remember anything of what boys like, I've no doubt that he can think of something he'd like—a kite, some spillikins, or something— right?"

"Oh, yessir!"

"Well—" the woman hesitated. "Yer sure? Don't think yer 'ave ter do it, 'cause yer don't."

"Oh, I want him to have the money." The marquess stepped back and held the door wider. "Do come in and sit while we breakfast, ma'am. Mrs. Trent is quite famished, so you'll have to pardon our haste to sample this."

Ellen shot him an indignant look as she followed him back to the table. "Your pardon, Mrs. Bratcher, for Mr. Trent's abominable lack of manners, but he has a bad temper when he is hungry."

"Oh, I know men, mum, so ye've no need to be excusin' 'im to me." The older woman nodded in understanding. "And me 'n' Jimmy cannot be stayin'—there's work waitin' ter 'ome fer us."

Trent was already busily unloading the basket and placing its contents on the table. "Do not think me unappreciative, ma'am, but we are hungry. And I would be pleased to purchase meals from you—my wife is inexperienced as a cook. You cannot know what we have endured since we arrived."

"Well, would yer be wishful o' 'avin' 'em brought up, sir?"

"Whatever is convenient. I am not so high in the instep that I cannot come for my dinner."

After considerable discussion, Mrs. Bratcher was persuaded to accept their custom, and it was agreed that she or one of her boys would send up baskets until the Trent servants arrived. Her eyes widened in amazement when she found he meant to offer her a pound a meal—a staggering sum to a woman whose family saw scarcely twenty times that in a year. It looked to her like the new owners of old Chudleigh's box were wealthy people indeed.

She and the boy had barely departed when Trent fairly fell on the food they had delivered. Ellen watched in fascination for a moment before pushing her boiled eggs off to one side and joining him. They ate in silence through an entire loaf of bread, half a cheese, and several thick slices of ham. It wasn't until he reached the apples that his lordship had anything to say.

"Your appetite seems to be failing you, my dear," he managed as he took a bite of the fruit.

"How can it be otherwise, my lord? You have eaten considerably more than your half."

"And I am considerably larger than you, but here, you can have all the rest." He rose from the table and stretched lazily. "And now that my good humor is restored, I shall bring in some more firewood. Who knows? Mayhap we could play cards again."

"I never want to see another glass of burgundy in my life," she told him with feeling.

"Still feel like cobwebs in the brain, eh?" He nodded sympathetically. "Well, it is brisk out, but a walk would probably do us both good, since it is not raining. Maybe we can determine more precisely just where we are and we can get a message out to my London establishment."

While he fetched the firewood, she set about to find something that could be used as a cloak, and when he returned, she was ready. He stared for a moment and she did not know whether to laugh or lash out. "Most original, my dear," he approved. "Of course, we can only hope that Chudleigh, or whatever his name is, does not return to discover you have cut holes in his blanket.

"It looks silly, doesn't it?"

"Not at all. At least, you will not be wearing my cloak while I trail after you with my teeth chattering. In fact, a look at my poor bedraggled garment tempts me to find a matching blanket."

"You are funning with me, my lord."

"I am not. I think you a very resourceful lady, Ellen Marling."

They explored the whole of Little Islip and walked through the bare forests nearby. The air was clean, crisp, and invigorating, and the leaves crunched beneath their feet. They found there was not much to see in Little Islip: three cottages some distance apart and nothing else except for the ruins of an old smithy's shop. And to make matters worse, in the light of day they could see they had strayed from the road and down a path that could not even in truth be called a lane.

"Do you think Dobbs can ever find us here, my lord?" Ellen shaded her eyes and turned full circle in search of some landmark, something that would draw attention to the fact that people lived there besides the three small buildings. "I mean, I cannot even see a real road from here."

"Maybe," he answered dubiously. "But if we do not hear from him by tomorrow, I shall have to leave you with the Bratchers and try to get out."

"You'll do not such thing! What if Chudleigh should decide to have a few days' shooting before winter comes? No—if you go, I go." Just as she spoke, she stepped into a hole concealed by the leaves and she pitched forward.

He caught her before she could go down. "Are you all right? You did not sprain it, did you?"

"No, my ankle is fine, I think."

"Good." He drew her hand into the crook of his arm and began to walk back. "You will be pleased to hold on to me, if you do not mind. I've no wish to look the veriest fool by carrying you back all the way to the box."

"Fiddle. As if you could do it, anyway."

"You do not think I could?" A mischievous grin spread across his face and deviltry lit the blue eyes as he looked at her. "As a confirmed gamester, I cannot let that pass." And before she could believe he intended to do it, he lifted her easily.

"Put me down this instant, else I'll scream!"

"Hmmm—should I carry you like a grain sack over my shoulder or like this?" he murmured as he adjusted her in his arms. "You know, if you do not hang on, it will definitely have to be the grain sack."

"Set me down," she tried more calmly, "or I will scream."

"You know, for a tall girl, you certainly do not weigh very much." He raised and lowered her as though to test her weight.

Startled, she clutched at him. "My lord"—she kept her tone reasonable in spite of the thudding of her heart—"if I accept that you could carry me, would you set me down before we make a spectacle of ourselves?"

"Miss Marling, I'll have you know that any number of females have gone to great lengths to be right where you are now."

"You cannot be serious, my lord."

"Oh, aye, you've no notion how plump my purse is, my dear. It has sent many a girl into a faint or a sprained ankle at my feet, I can tell you, in the hope that once I have felt her soft feminine form, I shall be obliged to court her. It doesn't work, of course, because I usually make Dobbs carry the chits."

"Of all the conceited, arrogant, self-important . . ." She stopped in midtirade and stared at him. "You surely do not think that I—"

"I do not," he continued to grin as he set her down finally, "for somewhere in all those lessons they gave you on how to be a lady of quality, they seem to have forgotten to teach you how to flirt."

"And you are an expert, of course," she retorted acidly.

"I think I am." He cocked his head to one side as though to get a better angle of her, and his expression sobered. "I have known a lot of women in the past ten years, Miss Marling, but I can truthfully say I have never met one quite like you. You could almost . . ." He caught himself and did not finish what he had been about to say. "Never mind," he finished abruptly. "Come on, we'd best get back before you take a chill."

He was strangely silent as they walked, but she did not seem to notice. Her own thoughts were in a jumble. He had held dozens, maybe even a hundred or more women, so he could be blasé about it, but she found the feel of his arms about her quite disturbing to her peace of mind. The sooner Dobbs showed up, the bettter, she told herself severely.

But whatever had sobered him seemed to linger once they'd returned to the tiny hunting box. Several times as she moved about the rooms tidying them as best she could, she looked up to see the marquess watching her almost thoughtfully, and there was something in his expression that she found somehow disquieting. At first, she tried to tell herself that it was her imagination, but then she looked up to catch him staring her direction again.

"Is there something wrong, my lord?"

"Hmmmm? Your pardon—I wasn't attending."

"I asked if something is the matter."

"No, of course not. Why?"

"Then I wish you would not stare at me. It makes me feel as though I look the veriest fright."

He managed a brief smile. "Is that how I am looking at you? If so, I must beg your pardon, for I can assure you that such was not my thought at all." He rose and stretched restlessly with his back to her. "I think I'll take a walk."

She was about to protest that they'd just come back from one and then thought better of it. If he were blue-deviled, it would be better to leave him alone until he came out of it. Instead, she picked up a cloth and began dusting the shelves and books in a corner cabinet. She could hear the door close behind her, and when she looked out the window, she could see him making his way to the Bratchers' cottage. Well, whatever had lowered his spirits was something he did not want to share with her.

There was not much to do in the box, but she managed to keep busy by making the beds, dusting, airing the curtains, scrubbing the small kitchen, and mopping the floors where they had tracked in the storm's mud. It was not what she was used to doing by any means, but she had watched the Marling maids often enough to know how it ought to be done. By the time Trent returned, she was up on a stool rehanging the curtains.

"Very housewifely, my dear," he murmured from the doorway behind her.

She was suddenly conscious of the picture she must present with her hair tied up in a rag and a sheet folded into an apron around her waist, and she felt almost foolish.

"Well, I had to do something, my lord," she snapped, and then shook her head. "I am sorry, it is not your fault that I was bored."

"Here, let me help you," he offered. "You are not quite tall enough to get that without risking a fall."

"I got it down."

"Then allow me to put it up." He took the rod and fastened it back into place above her. When she half-turned to look at him, he began to chuckle.

"I know." She made a wry face and began taking the rag out of her hair. "It looks ridiculous, but it would not stay out of my eyes when I was mopping the floor."

"No." He laughed. "I was thinking that we both look ridiculous, and that neither of us really cares."

"Speak for yourself, my lord. I was taught that ladies must go to great lengths to look presentable at all times," she told him primly, but she could not control the twitch at the corner of her mouth or the humorous sparkle in her eyes.

"Well, I am glad that you were a poor pupil in that," he teased, "for I find you ever so much more comfortable this way. Here, let me get you down before you fall and sprain your ankle or something."

"You seem to have an uncommon interest in the health of my ankles."

"Well, I am a miserable nurse, so it is in my best interests to keep you healthy. Put your hand on my shoulder and lean down." When she opened her mouth to protest, he simply caught her at the waist and lifted her. "You know, Miss Marling, you are far too independent for a female. You are supposed to take every opportunity to appear helpless, and you are supposed to exert every feminine wile at your disposal to entrap me."

"How very absurd! If I thought of you like that, we could not go on as we have, and it would ruin everything. Besides," she added sweetly, "whatever would I do about Brockhaven? No, my lord. I am far too aware of both your reputation and my circumstances to even entertain the notion of flirting with you. I suspect you could be quite a dangerous player of that game."

"The sensible Miss Marling."

"My lord, both my feet are on the floor now, and there is no danger to my ankles or anything else. You may safely unhand me."

He dropped his hands and stepped back to pick up the

basket he'd set by the door. "I have been to Mrs. Bratcher's and have brought back our supper. If you can get the plates, I can set out the food."

They shared a simple but substantial meal of cold chicken and roast beef, buttered potatoes and carrots, and bread. And packed in the bottom of the basket, Mrs. Bratcher had sent a freshly baked apple pie with cheese wedges.

When Ellen would have cut Trent a piece, he shook his head. "Not for me—I have had enough. Besides, I think I feel the beginning of a sore throat."

"I thought the Deveraux never suffered any illness."

"We don't. I daresay it will be gone by morning."

"And I had hoped we could play cards again. I think I was beginning to understand the game."

"If you understood it much better, we could open a gambling establishment, my dear." He caught her hopeful expression and shook his head. "But we won't. Really, I think I would just go to bed. You do not mind too much, do you?"

"No—not if you are unwell. I shall just read one of Mr. Chudleigh's books until I am ready to retire," she told him to hide her disappointment.

After he left, she cleared away the dishes and washed them before taking the lantern into the main room. A search of Chudleigh's bookshelves revealed absolutely nothing of interest, but she chose one anyway and drew close to the fire. In less than half an hour, she could hear his door open and his footsteps behind her. Resolutely she turned the page.

He reached over her shoulder and plucked the book out of her hands. *"Bingham's Treatise on the Merits of Merino Sheep,"* he read aloud. "Fascinating, I am sure, but I cannot sleep, after all. Do you think you might be able to tear yourself away from this and entertain me with a hand or two of faro?"

"Well . . ."

"Good. And if you could brew us some tea, it might help my throat."

7

SUNLIGHT STREAMED THROUGH her bedroom window as Ellen stretched lazily and then came awake. Sitting up, she realized that it must be midday and the marquess had not awakened her for breakfast, an odd circumstance, given his seeming attachment to regular meals. She kicked back her covers and slid her feet to the floor, still expecting to hear some sound of him coming from the main room. Yet when she opened the door a crack to look, the room was empty and the fire had died down completely. She dressed and went to his door, relishing the thought of dragging him out as rudely as he had her the day before.

Even as she raised her hand to knock, she could hear him coughing within. She beat a retreat to the kitchen and rummaged around until she found what she needed. Mixing it in a cup, she returned confidently to knock on the door.

"May I come in?" she called out.

"I am not receiving visitors today," he croaked back.

"But are you covered?"

"Yes."

She pushed open the door and found him huddled miserably beneath his blankets. She walked over to touch him and found him feverish. "I think you are ill, my lord," she announced flatly.

"Deuced clever of you to discover it," he muttered irritably as he rolled over to look at her. "Just leave—" His words were cut short by a paroxysm of coughing that left him nearly breathless. When he managed to stop, Ellen was perched beside him with cup and spoon. "What the devil is that?" he demanded.

"For your cough," she soothed. "It's something my nurse used to give me when I was a child. Here . . ." She poured a spoonful and leaned over.

"What is it?" he persisted.

"A syrup for your cough."

"No."

"Do not act like a child, my lord. I promise you it will help. Besides, if you do not open your mouth, I am likely to spill it all over you."

"Oh, very well," he snapped, and let her give him a spoonful. "Aaagh! What the devil is it?"

"Vinegar and honey. Here, one more."

"Very wifely, I am sure, Mrs. Trent," he managed. "But if you've no wish to wash it out of your hair, you'll take it away and leave me alone."

"Just one more," she coaxed.

"No!"

"All right, be a child then, but do not be blaming me if your cough gets worse."

"Leave me alone," he gritted before he was again seized with coughing. "Damn!" he managed when he finally quit. "All right, give me the nasty stuff and then get out of here."

Satisfied, she went to work on the fire in the main room, blowing on the embers until she got a few scraps of paper to ignite and then adding small kindling. Finally, she threw on a couple of logs and hoped for the best. Filling the kettle, she set it to heat over the hearth and drew on Trent's cloak for the walk to the Bratchers' cottage. When she opened the door, Jimmy Bratcher was coming up the path with his arms laden with breakfast.

"Mr. Trent told me mum 'e'd be up ter get it, but 'e ain't showed, so's I was ter bring it ter ye," he mumbled apologetically.

"Quite all right," she told him as she helped him unload the food. "I am afraid Mr. Trent is not feeling well today, so we shall require delivery anyway."

After the boy left, she ate a couple of the sausages and a still-warm sweet bun before she brewed the tea. The worst of her hunger satisfied, she made up a tray and took it to Lord Trent.

"I have brought breakfast, my lord," she announced as cheerfully as she could.

"Take it back and I'll come get it."

"Nonsense! You are sick."

"I am not. I have the sore throat merely, and I would not be babied, ma'am."

"You have a fever, a sore throat, and a cough, my lord," she corrected him, "and you are sick. You will be pleased to rest in bed and I will serve your breakfast." She picked up a towel and laid it across him. "Do you need help sitting?" she asked sweetly.

"If you leave, I'll get dressed and join you in the other room. It is unseemly for you to serve me like a servant, Miss Marling." He struggled to sit up and suddenly found the tray settled on his lap. "Oh, all right," he grumbled.

"I'll be back for the tray, my lord. Call if you require anything else."

"Managing female," he muttered to her retreating back. "A plague on all of you!"

By late afternoon, it became apparent that he was becoming very ill indeed. When she went to check on him, the bed shook with the violence of his chills and he was rolled up in his covers like a mummy. He opened his eyes when he heard her.

"I n-need m-more c-covers," he chattered from beneath the blankets. "I am f-freezing."

She reached to touch his forehead and found it so hot that she nearly drew back by reflex. "I'll get you some," she promised, and she ran to her room and dragged all the bedclothes off her bed to pile on him. He still shivered beneath the mound. "Could you drink some hot tea, my lord? Do you think it would help?"

"N-no."

Alarmed, she ran to the Bratchers' cottage and pounded on it until Mr. Bratcher, a thin, dour farmer, answered. She'd obviously caught him at his supper because his napkin was still tucked in his shirt neck.

" 'Ere now, mum, there be no need fer that," he told her sharply as he cracked his cottage door. "There's no deaf uns 'ere." He studied her suspiciously from beneath thick salt-and-pepper brows until he was satisfied. "Yer must be the Missus Trent," he decided finally as he threw open the door wider to admit her. "Mebbe yer wantin' Maggie—'appen she's still in back eatin' *our* supper, mum." He paused diffidently and hung back while she entered past him. "Now, I don't mind 'er cookin' fer ye, but I'd as lief eat first, ye know."

"I assure you, Mr. Bratcher, that food is the last thing on my mind just now. Is there a doctor in the neighborhood?"

"I dunno. A doctor?" He scratched his head thoughtfully. "Mebbe over 'n Tidwilly. There used to be an excuse fer one there—'if 'e ain't been run off."

Maggie Bratcher came out of the kitchen, still drying her hands on her apron. "A doctor, mum? Why'd yer be needin' one o' them?" She stopped at the sight of Ellen's worried expression and shook her head. "Niver say yer mister's taken sick—not a big strappin' man like 'im!"

"He's quite ill, ma'am, and in need of a doctor as quickly as is possible. I fear he has contracted an inflammation of the lungs—his fever is high and he keeps coughing. If you will but point the way to, uh, Tidwilly, is it?—I will take the horse and ride for help."

The older woman clucked sympathetically and shook her head. "We wouldn't think o' sendin' a lady like yourself over, would we, Sam? Yer go on back and take what care yer can. My Jimmy'll ride over. And let me send some barley water with yer—yer'll 'ave to 'eat it up some. 'Tis just the thing fer yer man, I know."

"Yes. Well, I am sure, uh, Mr. Trent will be most appreciative, but I need the doctor as soon as possible."

"I'll go meself," the farmer decided abruptly. "Yer know, 's possible 'e won't come fer no boy. Maggie, yer keep supper hot, mind yer." He put his coat and hat on and nodded to Ellen. "And don't yer worrit none, mum, if 'e won't come. Maggie's a fair 'and at nursin' 'erself."

"Oh, thank you," Ellen breathed in relief.

"I ain't got 'im yet, mum." Bratcher drew his hand back in embarrassment when she sought to pump it gratefully.

Returning to the box, Ellen found the marquess's condition unchanged. He was breathing with difficulty and chilling in spite of the mound of covers. She hastened to put the kettle of barley water over the fire and then sat down to wait for it to boil.

"Ellen—Ellen," came the croak from Trent's bedchamber.

"Yes, my lord?" she responded from the doorway.

"Damned thirsty," he muttered.

She went back and dipped a spoon in the broth to check its temperature. Satisfied, she poured some into a cup and took it into him. He struggled upright under the weight of the blankets and extended a bare arm out to take the steaming cup. He swallowed hugely, coughed, and choked. She pounded his back until he caught his breath.

"Egad, what was that? I've damned near burned my tongue out!"

"Barley broth. Here—'tis good for you, but do not take such a big sip this time."

"Barley broth?" He eyed the mug with disfavor. "It doesn't have much to recommend it."

"Mrs. Bratcher assures me it is just the thing for what ails you. Come on," she urged as she sat next to him and held the cup, "drink the rest of it."

Goaded, he reached for the cup. "At least 'tis hot," he muttered before he downed the remaining broth. As he handed the empty mug back, the covers slipped to reveal a bare chest. Red-faced, Ellen averted her gaze and rose to leave.

"No, sit awhile with me, Ellen," he coaxed before he was again seized with coughs that seemed to rack his entire body. When they passed, he put his hand out to her and clasped hers. "And I feared for your health." He smiled ruefully. "Next time, I shall keep my own cloak. You seem to be a deuced healthy girl."

"I am—I told you so. But you will feel better," she soothed, "once the doctor takes a look at you. No doubt he will be able to bring the fever down."

"A doctor? Dear Lady Brockhaven," he told her acidly, "I do not need one."

"Nonsense, my lord. You are quite ill and we both know it."

"Nonetheless, I do not want one." He paused for another spell of coughing to pass, and then repeated, "I do not want one. I have never met a doctor I liked."

"Liking is immaterial. 'Tis like a purge: it doesn't have to be pleasant to be effective." She loosed her hand and rose. "You need to rest and I need to get ready."

He started to protest and then lay back with a sigh before burrowing again beneath the covers. She moved briskly to setting the place to rights before Mr. Bratcher and the doctor arrived. Finally satisfied with the looks of the main room, she tidied herself up, braiding her dark hair and twisting it up into a knot on top of her head. She eyed her well-worn dress with disfavor, detesting that particular item of the Mantini's wardrobe. But at least, she had to admit, the rain had shrunk it up to the point where it was no longer necessary to stuff Trent's kerchief into the bosom.

It seemed like hours before she heard the approach of the farmer's wagon and then the sound of voices outside the cottage. She flung open the door before they could knock, and greeted Mr. Bratcher and the elderly man with him gratefully.

"I am so glad you came, sir. He's quite hot and has a dreadful cough."

"Most likely lung congestion." The old man nodded with authority. "Best let me see him. By the by, I am Doctor Cookson." He stood aside for her to lead the way, and Mr. Bratcher tipped his hat before escaping to the warmth of his fire and the rest of his supper.

"Ah, not quite feeling up to snuff, young man?" The doctor approached Lord Trent.

The marquess gave him a wary stare and refused to answer, but his lack of manners did not seem to bother the old man. He pulled up a chair by the bed and began taking out an evil assortment of instruments before leaning over to peer closely into Trent's face.

"Cough, if you please."

"I do not require your services, sir," Trent told him coldly before he was racked with another bout of coughing.

"Hmmmm—I thought so, but was not positive until I heard you, of course. You will have to be bled, else you will be carried off in your prime with a lung infection."

"Bled? I'll be damned if I let you!"

Unperturbed, the doctor turned to Ellen. "Do you have a basin, ma'am? It does not have to be large—just enough to cup him."

"I think so."

She left and returned with a bowl, which she handed over. "Is this large enough?"

"Excellent. You are not a queasy female, are you?"

"Not in the least," she assured him.

"Then, if you will just hold it right here, I will open a vein in his arm. And now, sir, you will be pleased to hold your elbow out straight."

"No," Trent growled.

"Alex, do not be such an uncomfortable patient," Ellen told him severely. "If I can hold the bowl, you can stand to hold out your arm."

"Easy for you to say—'tisn't your blood," he retorted peevishly, but he extended his arm.

"Very good, sir. You have most excellent veins," the doctor murmured as he drew out a small scalpel. "Now, just close your hand and this will be over soon enough."

Ellen's violet eyes met Trent's blue ones and locked. Neither was willing to watch the trickle of blood that drained into the bowl. It seemed like an eternity before the doctor pressed the vein closed and held it for several minutes, and then he ordered Trent to close his elbow tightly. Trent closed his eyes and sank back.

"Well, that should do it for today. I do not like to take too much—sometimes it weakens the patient—but it is necessary to restore the balance to the system. If you will step out into the other room, Mrs. Trent, I will leave you with some laudanum to make him more comfortable and explain the making of a poultice to break up his congestion. Beyond that, I am afraid you can only pray. But he is young and strong—perhaps he will recover."

Ellen's eyes widened, but she did not say anything in Trent's presence, choosing instead to follow the doctor all the way to the kitchen before demanding a prognosis. He sat down at the table and began writing out instructions for the poultice.

"How bad is it, sir?" she asked finally.

"One never knows when the lungs are involved. I have seen some cases where the patient is gone in less than two days," he answered quietly. "But I can tell you of a certainty that he will get considerably worse before he gets better, even if he recovers. I wish I could wrap it in clean linen, ma'am, but there it is—these things are quite serious." He handed her the paper and told her, "Onion poultice—be sure to prepare enough to apply hot every two hours until that cough loosens and he starts bringing up phlegm. Can you do that?"

She looked over the instructions and nodded. "If Mrs. Bratcher has the onions and the bacon grease, I can. It does not seem to be terribly complicated."

"It isn't. The problem will be weariness, ma'am. Every two hours becomes quite tiresome, but it must be done that often. And once you have lost a night's sleep, it gets harder to do." He gave her an appraising look. "But you seem to be a healthy young woman, so you will manage."

"I will."

He rose to take his leave and then stopped at the door. "Buck up, ma'am. I can tell you are but newly wed and I know the seriousness of the situation weighs heavily on you, but God willing, he will live to stock your nursery yet."

"I just hope he recovers," she managed back.

"Well, it is late and dark, Mrs. Trent, but I will return on the morrow to examine him again."

As soon as he left, Ellen hurried over to the Bratchers' and obtained the necessary ingredients for making the poultice. Then, back in the box, she prepared the evil-smelling concoction, stopping often to wipe her streaming eyes. As she stirred it over the fire, she wondered if Trent were indeed ill enough to stand for the application of the mess. When the mixture reached the desired consistency as described on the paper, she dished it up into another bowl. After tearing a bedsheet into strips, she advanced on the marquess with the steaming, strong-smelling poultice and several strips of cloth. He appeared to be asleep on his side, his covers pulled up around his ears.

"My lord," she called as she shook him awake. "Be pleased to turn over on your back."

"What the devil?" He opened his eyes as he rolled over, and he wrinkled his nose in disgust. "What is it?"

"Your poultice," she told him matter-of-factly as she rolled his bedclothes down to his waist. "Please do not cut up a dust, my lord, as this is necessary if you are to recover. And I find it as distasteful as you will, for I had to make it."

"Ellen," he warned, "if you do not take that nasty stuff out of here this instant, I will come out of this bed and outrage your sense of propriety. You are not putting that on me." He started up and fell back weakly as he gave way to another fit of coughing.

"I am sorry," she told him calmly, "but not even that would induce me to leave. If you do not care for your own life, you ought to consider me. I am stuck in this abandoned place with you—and you are my only ticket to York, sir. I cannot let you be carried off 'in your prime,' as the good doctor said. So if you have any wish to resume a life of raking about and chasing after the muslin company, you will be still and let me follow the doctor's orders."

"And what is that?"

"Laudanum. Perhaps after you have had some of this, you will not be so fractious about the other."

"I should have abandoned you to your fate when you jumped out that window," he muttered sourly.

"But you did not, my lord, and I will not abandon you either. Now, open your mouth, please."

Reluctantly, he did as she asked, and choked on the second spoon of it. When she was about to pour a third, he pushed her hand away. "Enough! Would you have me dead from the opium, Ellen? And if I am not mistaken, you are supposed to stir the stuff into water to make it more palatable. Ugh!"

"I don't know," she answered truthfully, "for he did not say precisely how to administer it or in what amount. He was much more interested in seeing that you were covered with this, if you must know." With that, she began to pour the hot onion mixture onto his bare skin, spreading it around with a large spoon. It plastered the dark hair on his chest with a thick slime that reeked with the odor of the onions. Once she decided she had put enough on, she applied a layer of sheeting strips over it and tucked them beneath his back. "There," she told him as she straightened up, "that will do it for a couple of hours. Now you should try to sleep."

"With this smell? I doubt I can."

But when she returned in half an hour's time, she found him sound asleep. And when it became time to clean off the slimy mess and replace it with fresh poultice, he did not even rouse. She touched his forehead then and worried—it was as hot as the mixture she had just heated over the fire.

All through the night and day and next night, Ellen scrupulously changed the dressings on his chest and gave him laudanum to ease his restless tossing. But instead of showing improvement, he seemed to be slipping. His fever seemed to climb even higher, and sometimes he cried out in feverish nightmares while other times he muttered incoherently.

By the dawn of the second day after she began treating him, he did not even appear to recognize her when she ministered to him. Yet, nearly dropping from weariness, she carefully spooned some broth into him, lifting him as best she could to keep him from choking. And she painstakingly dipped a cloth into water and dribbled it into his mouth in an effort to bring the terrible fever down.

At nine o'clock, Mrs. Bratcher came again and insisted that she watch while Ellen slept. Reluctantly, Ellen had to concede that she could not go on without rest, and she allowed the older woman to shepherd her to her bed. She lay down in her clothes and slept soundly for several hours, awaking finally to the sound of voices in the other room. Guiltily, she got up and went to check on Lord Trent. She found the Dr. Cookson and Mrs. Bratcher in earnest conversation, and by the sound of it, things were not good for the marquess.

The doctor looked up and shook his head discouragingly. "He does not seem to be responding, Mrs. Trent, and I am afraid we are approaching the crisis. By tomorrow, we should know if he will make it."

"But he *has* to make it," Ellen cried desperately as her eyes filled with tears. "You do not know the half—he has to make it through this!"

"There, ma'am," the doctor soothed, "you just take some of the laudanum yourself and go back to bed. I cannot see that the poultices are doing any good, anyway, and Maggie can watch him through the night."

"No!" She turned to Mrs. Bratcher determinedly. "If you can but stay the rest of the afternoon and keep trying the poultices—I'll pay you—I can take care of him in the night."

"Not to worrit, mum." Maggie Bratcher nodded. "I'll stay."

Ellen dragged herself back to her chamber and lay back down to endure nightmares of Trent abandoning her and Sir Basil chasing her. But when she awoke again, it was nightfall and the older woman was shaking her.

"Yer'd best eat summat, mum, before yer down yersel'."

"I am not hungry."

"Aye, yer are, if yer think on it."

Ellen forced herself to get up and follow Mrs. Bratcher into the kitchen, where a cold collation had been laid. Slowly filling a plate and pouring herself a cup of tea, she could not adequately express her gratitude.

"I can never repay you for what you have done for us, Maggie."

"As ter that, yer can remember sometime when th' rents comes due and we don't 'ave it."

Despairingly, Ellen realized that she would in truth probably never be in a position to help the Bratchers— her entire story to them had been a sham, and if Lord Trent died, he could not purchase Little Islip's hunting box and they would learn the truth. And Maggie would despise her when she found out.

Sensing Ellen's dejection, Maggie Bratcher laid a hand on Ellen's shoulder. "I 'ave t' be goin' now, mum, but yer can call if yer need me."

"No. I am all right, but I am so frightened, Maggie. Oh, he has to get well—he has to!"

"He will, mum. I can feel it."

As soon as she was alone, Ellen again began heating the onion mixture as the only hope of breaking up the tightness in his lungs. Then faithfully she began making the applications. In preparation for a long and lonely night's vigil, she filled the lantern and carried it to a bedside table.

About midnight, Trent became restless and knocked the mess off into the bed. Patiently, Ellen cleaned it up and reapplied some more. As she wrestled him to put clean sheets beneath him, she wiped her brow and allowed to herself that she had even ceased to be repelled by the odor of onions. At two o'clock, his breathing became more labored and she almost panicked and ran for Mrs. Bratcher, but then she calmed herself and tried to ease his breathing by pulling him up on more pillows. It was not an easy task, given that he was a tall man and almost all deadweight.

At four o'clock, there was no change, and she debated on whether to continue the poultices or not. He mumbled incoherently from time to time and was unable to drink the laudanum when she mixed it. She abandoned the attempt out of fear that he would strangle on it. Once more, she thought, I will try once more, and then I do not know what I will do.

As she unwrapped the dressings and prepared to sponge him off for the last application of poultice, it did not seem that he was quite so hot to the touch, but she was uncertain as to whether it was really so, or whether she wanted it to be so much that she imagined an improvement. She went ahead and smeared the mess over his chest and rewrapped him.

At seven o'clock he moved a little and it was not the restless tossing of before. She leaned over him and noticed that small beads of perspiration were forming on his forehead. She wiped him dry and murmured a hopeful prayer. In another fifteen minutes, he was drenched with a sweat of such magnitude that even his sheets were wet. Throwing maidenly reserve to the wind, she rolled him to the edge of the bed and uncovered him completely, pulling the sheet from beneath him as she rolled. Putting a dry sheet down, she rolled him back and then wrung out a cloth in a washbasin and began washing him down. She pulled his top blanket from the heap and covered him again to prevent a chill. Exhausted, she sank back into her chair and tried to stay awake.

"Ellen," he croaked as she was about to doze off, "I was wrong—you are quite beautiful."

Coming awake with a jolt, she thought at first that she had imagined he spoke, and then she saw that his eyes were open. "W-what?"

"You are beautiful," he croaked again.

To cover the overwhelming emotion she felt, she reached for the laudanum bottle as though checking its level.

"My lord," she told him severely, "I fear I have given you too much."

"Ellie, I am thirsty."

"That can be remedied, Alex. Let me get you some water. Wait right here." She brought back a cup of water and braced him while he swallowed it.

Weak from the effort, he leaned back and closed his eyes, smiling faintly. "And just where did you think I'd go, Ellie? I feel as helpless as a baby."

"I wasn't thinking, my lord."

"I know. I have been a sad trial to you, haven't I?"

"No, but you frightened me nearly to death, my lord. You were so sick and the doctor tried to discourage me." Her eyes began to fill with tears and she had to look away.

"I owe you a huge debt for this, Ellie. Nothing I could ever do would be enough to repay you."

"Just get better and take me to York and I am paid, my lord." Her voice was strained as she fought against the urge to cry in relief. He was alive and his fever had broken and she felt she had won an intense battle.

"You called me Alex earlier, Ellie. I much prefer that to Trent or my lord, my dear."

"I think your brain has been affected," she retorted, but she was smiling.

"Probably." He opened his eyes again and tried to turn his head to look at her. "But since we are to be friends, you might as well learn to use my name. Besides, I like the sound of it." He tried to pull himself up and found the effort too great. "You look hagged," he whispered. "Get some rest."

"Hagged? You have come to your senses, after all."

"Hagged—but beautiful."

"And you are too tired to talk so much. Close your eyes and rest, my . . . Alex."

"I will rest if you will," he promised. He watched as she rose to leave and then sank back again. "I'll never forget this, Ellie—word of a Deveraux."

8

"AUGUSTA! I KNEW YOU'D come."

"Of course, my dear. Where is he?" Augusta Sandbridge mounted the steps of the leased town house purposefully, her petite figure and her softly curling brown hair belying a woman of incredibly strong will. "And tell him it is nothing to the purpose to avoid me, Eleanor, for I mean to read him a rare peal over this." She drew off her fine red kid gloves and tiptoed to brush her sister-in-law's cheek with an impatient kiss. "Really, I cannot believe you allowed him to do such a shabby thing."

"You know him as well as I do," Eleanor Marling retorted. "So you know there is no reasoning with him where money is concerned."

"Bah! *I* shall reason with him soon enough."

"I doubt it, Augusta, because he is not here just now."

Lady Sandbridge gave the other woman a knowing look. "I see. Got wind I was coming, did he? You always were a peagoose, Nora. You ought to have let me surprise him with the music. Come to think of it, you should have warned me before he sold the girl. I'll warrant I could have stopped that soon enough."

"But, Gussie, there wasn't time! Brockhaven was so impatient that we did not have above two weeks to collect the bridecothes."

"Well, done is done, I suppose. Still, I could not credit your last letter about Ellen. Has no one heard from her since? I cannot like the story with a girl alone in a city like this." She stopped abruptly and nodded disgustedly at the tall, thin woman that had followed her in. "You remember Sandbridge's sister, Lavinia Leffingwell, I believe? She insisted on coming in spite of everything." She bent closer and murmured low, "Drives me to distraction—should never have told her she could live with me after Leffingwell died."

The object of her irritation did not seem to notice Augusta's remarks as she put forth her hand in the most affected manner. "Dear Mrs. Marling," she gushed, "of course you remember me. You and I were used to be girlhood companions, were we not, Nora? But I could not credit your letter to dear Gussie. What an ungrateful child your Ellen has proven to be. La! I remember Sir Basil from my Season—a fine figure of a man!"

"Cut line, Vinnie!" Augusta Sandbridge brought her up short. "That was a good twenty years ago, and you obviously have not seen the old roué since. Well, I have, and I daresay he weighs twenty stone or more and he is old enough to be the girl's father, if I may remind you. Not to mention that he's buried two poor wives already."

Lavinia Leffingwell lapsed into uncustomary silence, stung by her sister-in-law's sharpness. Eleanor looked uncomfortably from one to the other. She had heard that the living arrangement whereby Lady Leffingwell made her home at Greenfield was not an entirely cosy situation. Knowing that the two of them had never been particularly fond of each other, Eleanor had been surprised when the two widows had decided to share the commodious Sandbridge estate. That they were as different as night and day did not seem to occur to them until after the circumstance was effected. And then the sprightly, energetic, take-charge Augusta found the flighty, sour, and highly opinionated Lavinia a trial much of the time.

"As I pointed out to Gussie," Lady Leffingwell found her voice at last, "I could not but come to support you in this dreadful scandal. But how you are to fire off two more daughters after this, I am sure I cannot imagine."

That was too much for Eleanor. "Really, Lady Leffingwell," she retorted stiffly, "there is no scandal as yet. No one knows besides us and Brockhaven, and I am sure he is not telling. After all, it is scarcely a story to his credit, either."

"Not to mention that Amy is but seventeen," Augusta

added added comfortingly, "and has plenty of time on the Marriage Mart yet. As for dear Lucinda—or is it Lorinda?—she has years in the schoolroom before you have to give that a thought."

"Lucinda."

"Well, whatever. My point is that I doubt she will be much bothered by even a scandal, if it comes to that. My concern just now is Ellen."

"Oh, I don't know," Eleanor wrung out. "Gussie, we have heard nothing!"

"Now, Nora—she is a sensible girl—she'll come about."

"But if Brockhaven can be believed, she would have had to jump fifteen feet in the dark and then just disappear. I cannot credit it."

"Ten to one, she had it planned and is but waiting for news that Sir Basil intends to divorce her," Augusta soothed.

"Divorce!" Lavinia was scandalized at the thought. "But she could not want that. She'd be ruined and no one would ever receive her."

"There are worse things than being divorced, Vinnie— things like living with someone you cannot even like," Augusta reminded her grimly.

Newell, the Marling butler, coughed apologetically from the hallway. "I believe Lord Brockhaven's carriage is in the drive, madam. Shall I give out that you are not at home?"

"Oh, dear, and here we are standing like a flock of hens in the hall. No—yes—well, he is bound to see us, but I . . . Oh, dear me, I do so hate seeing that dreadful man."

"Show him in, Newell," Lady Sandbridge ordered briskly. "We shall be pleased to take tea in the drawing room with his lordship." She eyed her flustered sister-in-law with amusement. "And do collect yourself, my dear, for he will not do anything dreadful while I am here to support you."

The ladies barely had time to be seated and to arrange their skirts before Basil Brockhaven was ushered in. He surveyed the women with a scowl until he recognized Augusta.

"Lady Sandbridge, is it not?" he beamed. "I'd recognize you anywhere, even after all this time." After a portly bow, he got down to business with Eleanor Marling, demanding almost uncivilly, "Where's Marling? I would have a word with him in private, if you please."

"I think he has gone to Somerset, sir. He was not particularly precise in his direction," she told him doubtfully.

"What she means to say, Brockhaven," Augusta cut in, "is that Thomas bolted rather than face me."

"Nonsense," he scoffed. "Not a little thing like you." Turning back to Eleanor, he announced, "I shall wait, Mrs. Marling, for I do not believe he is not at home."

"But it is true," Lavinia chimed in, "for we came to see him and he was already gone."

"Eh? And who the devil are you?"

"You cannot say you do not remember Lavinia Rowell? For shame, Sir Basil," she tittered. "You stood up with me many times during my Season."

Brockhaven gave her a closer look through his quizzing glass and then shook his head. "Well, I daresay you must've changed, ma'am."

"It was in '95," she reminded him patiently, "and I was wed to Lawrence Leffingwell before my Season was out."

"Now, *him* I remember—quite plump in the pocket, I believe."

"That's the one," she encouraged, "and I was a blonde then, with blue eyes that you once complimented."

"Well, I daresay the gray hair has me confused now."

Newell interrupted to set a tray of glasses and a decanter of ratafia in front of the ladies. He bowed respectfully in the baron's direction and inquired, "Some Madeira for you, sir?"

"Yes, yes." Sir Basil impatiently waved him away and focused again on Eleanor Marling. "And now, madam, what is this nonsense about Marling being away from home? Damn it, er, dash it, I have business with the man."

"We know," Augusta told him matter-of-factly, "and that is precisely why we are come to town. We wish to salvage the situation if at all possible."

"Yes," Lavinia agreed eagerly, "we have come to help

you, Sir Basil. We cannot imagine what possessed that foolish creature to act in such a rash manner. I can only suppose that she did not recognize her good fortune."

"No doubt," Augusta agreed dryly.

"Then you will tell me what I am to do," Sir Basil responded in an aggrieved tone, "for I cannot forever give out that she is ill. You cannot imagine the gibes I've suffered in the clubs already."

"Brazen it out," Augusta encouraged, "and we shall support you. Tell me, do you drive out or go to the opera?"

"What's that to the purpose?"

"Well, if you are seen with her family, that should spike the tattlemongers' tongues. By the time we are through, you will be congratulated for your patience in coping with a wife suffering from consumption."

"What consumption?" he demanded suspiciously.

"Really, I had no notion you were a slow-top, my lord," Augusta told him in exasperation. "We must endeavor to save your reputation somehow. You said it was already becoming an *on-dit* that there is something wrong between you and my niece. Consumption is the answer. It is a disease that discourages visitors and certainly prevents the sufferer from attending public functions. You will be lauded for taking her under such circumstances."

"Dash it! People die from consumption."

"Well, it gives you time to wait for her to reappear. You can give out that you have sent her to the country, where the air is more salubrious. Then, when it is no longer of interest to anyone, you may divorce her and seek a more amenable wife," she explained practically.

"I do not seek a divorce," he told her stiffly. "I want my wife, and I believe that this family is sheltering her in her unlawful flight from my home."

"Nonsense," Augusta dismissed the notion. "I cannot imagine anything less comfortable than a wife who does not want to live with you. Of course, you will have to make up your own mind on that head. In the meantime, your mother-in-law, Lavinia, and myself will exert ourselves to appear publicly with you until the gossip dies down."

"Now see here—"

"No. *You* see here. We are as wishful as you about avoiding scandal. You will do it, or you will be the laughingstock of the *ton* when the real story is heard."

They haggled over her suggestion for several minutes while Lavinia and Eleanor looked on in shock. But when Basil Brockhaven took his leave, he was surprised to find that he had engaged himself to take all three ladies to the opera that evening. He was uncertain about Lady Sandbridge; she was either the most interfering busybody or a dear, and he could not tell which. But she was right about one thing: he could not continue to go about without Ellen unless the chit's family supported him, and he certainly had no desire to sit at home alone.

"Well, I never!" Lavinia sank back in her chair after he had left. "I repeat, I have never heard of such a tale, Gussie. Consumption! How could the wretched girl have done such a thing to that poor man when he is worried half out of his mind over her?"

"Is he, Vinnie? I rather think he is far more concerned about his own reputation. If he were truly worried, he would have called in the Bow Street runners by now. And you did not hear him say anything about her being alone and defenseless in a city like this, did you?"

"You do not think he has harmed her?" Eleanor asked in alarm.

"Brockhaven? Of course not! I was merely telling Vinnie that if I were a loving husband, I should be more concerned for my wife and less for what people would think. I believe he is merely piqued that she escaped his clutches before he had his way with her."

"Augusta, must you be so plainspoken?" Lavinia complained.

"Pooh. We are none of us green girls," Augusta snapped back.

Thus it was that Lord Brockhaven returned to the Marling residence with considerable trepidation some six hours later. The thought of spending an evening in the company of three middle-aged females was beginning to give him indigestion. And that thin thing looked dashed boring to him. It was no wonder Leffingwell had popped off.

"Hallo, Newell." He handed his hat to the butler with

blunt affability and asked, "Are the ladies down yet?"
Without waiting for an answer, he preened himself in an
entrance mirror. He was certain of one thing: he was fine
as fivepence. His yellow satin waistcoat gleamed beneath
his navy brocade swallowtail coat, and his yellow satin
pantaloons clung to his plump thighs without so much as
a wrinkle. And his valet had managed to find him a pair
of navy-and-yellow pin-striped stockings that set the en-
semble off perfectly. His pattens clicked against the marble-
inlaid entry as he followed Newell into the drawing room.

Augusta Sandbridge looked up coolly as he was ushered in and had to fight the urge to snicker. Mrs. Marling
took in his clothing and blinked to hide the fact that he
looked the veriest quiz. Lavinia Leffingwell, on the other
hand, beamed in admiration as he bowed stiffly over
Eleanor's hand.

"Ohhh, Sir Basil," she gushed, "you will cast all of us
in the shade tonight. Don't you think so, dear Nora?"

"Uh, yes, I think so," Eleanor managed finally.

"Quite, I am sure." Augusta nodded.

"But what of Miss Amy? Surely she would enjoy an
evening's entertainment," Sir Basil suggested.

"Amy is still in the schoolroom," Augusta announced
firmly. "And it would be most improper for her to appear in public before she is presented."

"But we are family. Surely—"

"No, I think not."

"But I cannot see the harm," Lavinia ventured, and
then quailed beneath the scathing look she received from
her sister-in-law. "But if she is not presented, I suppose
you are right," she finished lamely.

Once they actually reached the opera, the evening
passed fairly agreeably for all four of them. To Basil
Brockhaven, it was something of a credit to have *grande
dame* Augusta Sandbridge in his company. And if she
were a trifle distant in public, he decided it was because
she was dreadfully high in the instep. Mrs. Marling said
very little to him, but then she was kept busy explaining
her daughter's sudden decline. To his chagrin, Lavinia
felt it incumbent to entertain him at every lull in the
program.

"La! Is that not Maria Cosgrove over there?" she

chirped. "I have not see her in an age, but she looks a complete dowd now. I cannot fathom how she could let herself run to fat like that. Dear Sir Basil, do you suppose we could go over during the intermission?"

"I do not know the lady well enough to visit her box," Brockhaven told her happily, "but I shall be pleased to provide a footman to escort you over there."

"I think I should like that excessively," Lavinia tittered as she contemplated a reunion with an old friend who no longer had any claim to beauty.

"I believe I shall go with you," Eleanor added, "for there is dear Lady Dillworth with her."

"Egad, ma'am!" Brockhaven turned to Augusta after they left. "I wonder how you can tolerate such a prattlebox! Leffingwell must have been glad for the peace when they laid him in the ground."

"Oh, I shouldn't think so," Augusta answered coolly. "He was much older than Vinnie and he fairly doted on her—left her with an enormous fortune. She may rattle on, sir, but underneath her prattle, she is a very sharp female. I daresay she has improved on the inheritance in the years since he has been gone."

"You don't say! Then why did she not take a second husband to help her manage?"

"Why should she? She had the money, the houses, the land, and her children."

"She has children?"

"Two—Clarence is at Eton and Horace is at boarding school."

"Well, they will get the bulk of Leffingwell's estate, of course."

"No," Augusta mused slowly, "I should not think so. I believe she had their money arranged in trust. Of course, Clearence has the title, and I know she expects to purchase Horace a commission in his majesty's dragoons now that this unpleasantness with Boney's over once and for all."

"Dear me! And to think that I have not heard of Lady Leffingwell since her Season."

"Of course you have not. She is a veritable pattern card of propriety, my lord, and not given to squandering her fortune." Augusta was warming to an idea just forming in her mind as she added, "She's a perfect paragon, if you must know."

"Egad! I had no idea! But she looks too thin," Sir Basil decided as he looked at her across the loges. "She is most likely a chronic complainer—you know, one of those females with every conceivable megrim. I cannot say I envy you, dear lady, if you have lived with her these several years."

"Vinnie? Good heavens, no! she is never ill—never."

"Really?" He looked again with new interest.

Later, Augusta sat back in Sir Basil's opera box and watched as he conversed pleasantly with Lavinia. And for once in her life, Vinnie ceased her incessant chatter and listened. In fact, it was not until the third act that she actually focused her attention of the diva singing the lead and pinched at Sir Basil's coat for attention.

"What an incredibly beautiful woman!" she breathed. "And what a voice!"

"Sophia Mantini." Brockhaven nodded authoritatively. "She is the Marquess of Trent's latest flirt."

"La, what a pair they must make—if even half of what I have heard of him is true!"

"Shhhh!" Augusta hissed as she reached to tap Vinnie on the shoulder. "And *twice* what you have heard of him is fact."

"Very true," Brockhaven confided in spite of the quelling looks he and Lavinia were receiving from the adjoining boxes. "He is a cold and wild man, I can tell you—a devil when crossed, as he bears no slight. Excellent with pistol *and* sword, he was used to duel quite often, but now there's none to try him."

"Shhhhh!"

"Damme, Brockhaven, be quiet!"

The complaints from around him did not deter him as he continued to expound on the marquess. "He's a Deveraux, ma'am, and they are a wild and arrogant bunch—he's the worst, of course."

"Well, I am glad I have never met the gentleman," Vinnie murmured in shocked accents.

"Pooh." Augusta shook her head in disgust. "I have met him, and he makes me sorry that I am not fifteen or twenty years younger. Wild he is, but give me a rake any day."

"Madam!" Brockhaven drew back in shock.

"Gussie!"

"I stand by what I said." Augusta folded her hands in her lap and turned back to listen to the rest of the Mantini's performance.

Much later, after Brockhaven had returned the ladies to the Marling house and Lady Leffingwell had retired, Eleanor Marling faced her sister-in-law over a glass of wine. She lifted her glass and swirled it aimlessly.

"I do not know what you are about, Gussie, but I suppose you must know what you hope to achieve. Myself—I cannot stand Sir Basil."

"Repulsive as a toad," Augusta agreed.

"Then, what?"

"Leave it to me, my dear, and do not try to stick your oar in the water. I may just have found a way to solve both our problems."

"But I cannot quite like having him around here," Eleanor confessed, "because of Amy. Did you not note that he attempted to draw her into our little outing?"

"I noticed, and I supported you in your determination to keep her out of his way. Do but give me a week or two, Nora, to try my mad scheme, and then I've a mind to broaden Amy's education with a trip abroad. I have always favored Paris myself."

9

LORD TRENT'S RECOVERY from pneumonia was not without its problems. He continued to run a fever for several days after the crisis had passed, and he was a less-than-pleasant patient. Ellen continued to lose much sleep nursing him as she forced herself to rise several times each night to see that he remained covered. She feared a backset that would keep them from ever reaching Yorkshire, and she despaired of ever being found by Dobbs.

Maggie Bratcher assisted whenever she could, bringing food, gruel, and clean clothes to them. And being a short, ample woman, Maggie brought things that did not fit Ellen at all. Still, they were clean and Ellen was grateful to escape the Mantini's dresses.

"Egad, but you look a fright in that thing," Trent commented when she ventured into his room with a bowl of gruel on his tray. "If you gained ten stone, you could not fill it out."

"I am well aware of its lack of fit or style, my lord, but at least it is clean."

"Style? 'Twould have more if it were made out of a flour sack, my dear." He reached for the bowl and inspected its contents. "And what is this?"

She sat on the side of his bed and spread a napkin over his chest. "I would not mention the dress or the gruel around Mrs. Bratcher if I were you, Alex. You know we are quite dependent on her kindness."

"Gruel?" He sniffed with distaste. "I think I preferred the barley broth, for I at least had a notion of what was in it."

"Would you like a spoon, or would you prefer to drink it?"

He took a tentative taste and sat the bowl on the table by the bed. "I would have something with more substance, if you really want my opinion on the subject—something like roast beef, potatoes, carrots, peas, bread, and a bottle of wine—and I would finish it off with a peach or apricot tart."

"Dr. Cookson says it must be sustaining broths only, Alex."

"And he is a foot or more shorter than I. I warrant he could not sustain himself on this," he grumbled. "Oh, never mind!" He reached for the bowl and downed it in a several quick gulps. "Now, my dear, what else is there? I do not care for a second serving of this."

"I'll see if I can find something," she relented.

"Good girl! I know they have been feeding you something other than this pap. I am to the point where I would be grateful even for your crumbs."

She rummaged around the kitchen and pantry and returned with a dish of brownish gel and a clean spoon. "Here," she ordered, "open your mouth."

"Dash it! I can feed myself."

"I know, but 'tis merely a precaution to keep you from throwing it back at me. Now, open up and enjoy the luxury of having someone take care of your every need. It is not a circumstance that is likely to last long."

"If you think you are taking care of my every need, you are sadly mistaken," he told her wickedly. And then to prevent her from giving him a sharp set-down, he opened his mouth obediently for the spoon. She dumped it in and waited for him to swallow. Instead, he choked and grabbed for the napkin on his chest. Spitting into it, he managed to sputter, "Aagh! If you were my wife, I'd suspect you of attempting to kill me for my money. Taste that stuff before you give it."

She began to giggle in spite of her best efforts to keep a straight face. "Oh, Alex! You should see your expression—definitely not a recommendation for pork jelly."

"Pork jelly?"

"Panghurst's Restorative Pork Jelly, I believe it is called. And you do look as though you could use a restorative."

"I am not at all amused," he told her in disgust. 'I thought you sharp-witted enough to know that it is in your best interests to keep me alive. But, no, you would poison me with some damned stuff you have chanced to find on a shelf."

"Gentlemen do not swear," she told him primly.

"I am a nobleman, my dear. Sometimes there is a difference," he reminded her. "And do not be changing the subject. If you would ever have me recover, you will change your ways. Unless you wish to be stranded here, Miss Marling, you will find me something to support this body of mine." He glanced down at the outline of his body beneath the covers. "As it is, I'll warrant I have lost nearly a stone."

"I have done the best I could under the circumstances, my lord. A lady is not expected to be a cook, companion, nurse, and friend to an unmarried gentleman, or nobleman, or any man, for that matter."

"And don't be giving me that put-upon look, Ellie. You know I am damned grateful for your assistance. I would not be alive if it were not for you, but now you have to feed me," he coaxed, "if you would have me take you to York." He caught her hand and squeezed it.

"I'll see what I can find," she sighed.

She retrieved her hand and reluctantly went to get the remains of her own supper. Within the space of a few minutes, she was back with some cold meat, spiced apples, and soft buns. Behind her back, she held one of Chudleigh's bottles of red wine.

He grinned boyishly as he reached for the plate. "I might have known that mention of Yorkshire would be enough to get what I wanted. Say, what are you hiding?"

"Well, since we have stolen everything else from Mr. Chudleigh, I thought we might as well take his last bottle of wine."

"Ah, you darling girl! Nothing revives my spirits like wine."

He wolfed the contents of the plate and drank a couple of glasses of the purloined wine. When he was finished, he pushed the remains aside and lay back with his eyes closed. Ellen picked up the plate and started to leave.

"No, don't go, my dear. I am tired, but not so tired

that I do not want your company. Sit here and tell me what you will do when you reach your aunt's."

"I am not certain," she answered truthfully. "I suppose everything depends on how I am received. If she is bent on returning me to Brockhaven, I will run away again." She looked away and twisted the material of the skirt across her lap. "I guess I will invent some credentials and apply for a position somewhere. I should prefer to be a musician because I have some ability there, but if it will not do at all, then I suppose I will have to be a companion or governess. Surely they do not wind up as rich men's mistresses, my lord."

"Ellen—"

"Perhaps I could even open up some sort of a shop if you would but lend me a little money to start with. I have a good eye for color in spite of what you have seen, and I might try the millinery business. I would pay you back, of course."

"You are a very resourceful girl, my dear, but it wouldn't work. No, we will have to think of something else. If worse comes to worst—"

His words were cut off in midsentence as they heard the sound of an approaching carriage. She jumped up and ran to the window to see an elegant black equippage roll up the lane.

"Oh, no! Alex, I hope we are not about to face Mr. Chudleigh. Oh, how can we ever explain?"

She dashed madly from room to room, setting as much to rights as she could while Trent struggled into some clothes. Ellen came back and grabbed the dishes and the wine bottle and stashed them beneath a cupboard as someone began pounding on the door. She squared her shoulders and prepared to be evicted and disgraced in front of the Bratchers.

"Milord! Milord! " 'Tis me, Dobbs! And if ye be there, I've brought yer valet and yer things."

"Dobbs!" She threw open the door and fell into the arms of the astonished coachman. "Oh, thank heavens you are here! Lord Trent has been so ill that I have feared for his life."

" 'Ere, missy, no need fer that," he told her gruffly. "Bad time o' it, eh? " 'Ere, 'ere, don't be in such o' takin'—old Dobbs is 'ere," he tried to comfort as she gave in to long-pent-up tears.

"I don't believe it." Trent shook his head from the doorway where he leaned for support. "In all this time, I have not been treated to one single feminine weakness. Yet you arrive, and within two minutes, you have her weeping like a watering pot." He saw his valet standing behind the coachey, and he shook his head, "Behold, Crawfurd, what I have been reduced to enduring. As soon as you can manage it, I shall require a bath, a shave, and clean clothes that fit."

The valet took in his master's appearance and winced at the too-tight breeches and the open shirt. "Milord, cover yourself."

"You have obviously not inspected the drawers and closets of this place if you think that possible, my dear fellow. I cannot cough in anything we have found without splitting a seam."

Crawfurd turned disapprovingly to where Dobbs was handing Ellen his handkerchief. "And I might have known that there would be one of them here, but did you have to stoop to consorting with a local doxy?"

Ellen stared, but Trent's face went cold and his voice was like ice. "You will apologize to Lady Brockhaven this instant, Crawfurd. You may have been with my family since I was in short coats, but you can be turned off as soon as the next one. I will not tolerate any disrespect where she is concerned."

"Lady Brockhaven!" Dobbs and Crawfurd gasped in unison.

"Eh, yer went to 'is weddin'. Aye, there's where yer started this," Dobbs remembered.

"Surely you have not eloped with Brockhaven's bride, milord! Not even you can recover from this!"

"I am sorry, my dear," Trent apologized to Ellen, "but I tried to tell you how it would be. If my own people think the worst, you can well imagine what the rest of the world will say."

"But it is not true."

"I know." He turned back to Crawfurd and his voice lost its warmth again. "I have not eloped with Lady Brockhaven, chucklehead. I am—or I was—taking her to her Aunt Sandbridge's when that accident occurred. And if you have ever seen Basil Brockhaven, you will know that it was an act of compassion to do so."

"But—"

"But nothing," Trent snapped. "I repeat," he bit off the words with an icy precision that left little doubt as to his meaning, "I repeat, I will not tolerate any disrespect to the lady."

Crawfurd looked at the floor and mumbled an apology of sorts, but it did not satisfy the marquess. "Louder," he ordered. When Crawfurd finally looked Ellen in the eye and begged her pardon, Trent relaxed against the doorjamb. "That's better. Not even if you are in your cups will I allow you to say one word against her, do you hear? And you will not discuss her with any other servants if you wish to remain in my employ."

"Yes, milord."

"Now that you have understood me, you may see to my bath and bring in some decent clothes." He caught at the door for support and smiled weakly at Dobbs. "Do you think you could get me back to bed? I am still deuced weak from the fever."

Once he was again surrounded by his servants, Trent began to improve dramatically, and that improvement both cheered and disheartened Ellen. On the one hand, she was glad to see his lordship gaining strength, but on the other, she felt suddenly useless. She found herself taking a lesser role than the arrogant valet, Dobbs, or even the replacement driver, Mr. Leach. It was dispiriting to go from being so totally necessary to being merely an accessory to the situation.

Mrs. Bratcher came to call after Trent had had his bath and was elegantly dressed in silk shirt, buff kerseymere pantaloons, and mirror-perfect Hessians. She stared, stunned for a moment, at the transformation. "Why, Mr. Trent! Ye look ter be in a fair way o' recoverin', don't yer?"

When Crawfurd opened his mouth to set her straight, he received a swift warning kick from his lordship. Dobbs grinned at the valet's discomfiture, caught his master's expression, and quickly schooled his own face into impassivity.

"But where's Mrs. Trent? Poor thing's fair hagged out with tendin' ter ye. She ain't sick 'erself?"

"She is fine, thank you, but she is resting just now, ma'am," Trent replied before turning to his own servants. "Allow me to present Mr. Crawfurd, my valet, Mr. Dobbs, my coachman, and Mr. Leach, my driver."

The woman bobbed a hasty little curtsy to the obviously stiff-necked valet, and the man snorted derisively at her lack of knowledge about how to greet servants.

"Well, sir, no doubt yer got all th' 'elp yer need now, so I'll be goin'. Tell the missus I called."

"I assure you, Maggie, that you are still quite necessary to us. None of these fellows can cook any better than Mrs. Trent." He picked up the leather purse that had been refilled with coins brought by Crawfurd. "Here—with five of us to feed, you will be put to considerable expense."

"Oh, I couldn't sir." She shook her head. "Like I told yer missus, there might come a time as we didn't 'ave the crops fer the rent."

"No, I insist, Maggie. We can talk about the rent later."

They appeared at a standoff until Crawfurd could stand it no longer and snapped irritably, "You'd best take anything Trent offers, woman. I can assure you his generosity is seldom noted."

"No. We'd be poor tenants if we could not share with the landlord, especially as kind as Mr. Trent 'as been. And what with 'im so sick and 'is wife so worrit, I just couldn't." She looked up at Trent. "Yer understand, don't ye, sir?"

"Yes, Maggie, I do."

"I 'spect I'll 'ave ter 'ave 'elp, so's Jimmy'll carry. Now, if yer was ter want ter give 'im a mite, I'd understand."

She had no more than left when Leach smirked knowingly to Crawfurd. "I knew it was a hum. *Mrs.* Trent, she says! Yer had th' right o' it!"

Exhausted from being up so long, Trent leaned heavily on a chair back and fixed his new driver with an icy Deveraux stare. "Mr. Leach, you are discharged," he told him, "And you will leave this house immediately."

"Naw—yer wouldn't—not fer a bit o' muslin," Leach scoffed in disbelief until he met the cold blue eyes. Then, as it sank in that his lordship was indeed quite serious, Leach paled. "But—my lord—," he wavered uneasily, " 'tis mistaken yer are—I—I—"

"No," Trent bit off precisely, " 'tis you who are mistaken, Mr. Leach. Despite my express warning to Mr. Crawfurd, you have chosen to slander a lady under my protection."

"Alex—" Ellen interrupted from the doorway of her chamber.

"And you will stay out of this, Ellie," Trent ordered brusquely. " 'Tis between Leach and myself."

"But it concerns me!"

"No, it does not. Go back and lie down, my dear, for you need your rest if we are to press on to your aunt's on the morrow." Turning back to the discharged driver, he continued, "You may ride the black horse in the shed, but I am afraid that I cannot accommodate you with either saddle or bridle. When you reach London, you will be pleased to return the animal to my establishment there."

"But—yer lor'ship—" Leach appealed desperately. " 'Tis days to Lunnon!" Turning toward Ellen, he sought support. "My lady—"

"You will be pleased to address me, Mr. Leach," Trent cut in sharply. "It is decided, and I shall brook no interference."

Ellen looked from the white-faced driver to the cold face of the marquess and realized that Trent's mind was set. Apparently, Leach came to the same realization, for he suddenly lost his pallor. Impotent rage sent a flush of color to his face as he snarled at her, "Turned off fer a bit o' muslin—yer can't do thet to ol' Leach—naw, yer can't! Tell yer summat, Miss Fancy Piece—yer ain't seen th' last o' Leach, yer ain't."

"Leach!" Trent's voice was like a knife, and his blue eyes blazed as he released the chair back and stepped toward the driver with raised hand. He swayed slightly, sending Ellen, Dobbs, and Crawfurd forward all at once while Leach backed away.

"Alex, please—you'll have a backset!" Ellen cried out

as she slid a supporting arm around his waist. "You cannot fault Mr. Leach for thinking what anyone would think under the circumstances."

But Trent was not in the mood to be mollified. In spite of breathing heavily from the sudden move, he managed to grit out a warning sufficient to chill Leach's anger. "Understand this—if you so much as utter her name to anyone, Mr. Leach, you are a dead man. D'you understand me?" he demanded. "Speak of this at all and there's not a place in England to hide you."

"My lord—" Crawfurd laid a placating hand on Trent's arm only to be shaken off.

"*Do* you understand me?" Trent repeated.

The driver refused to meet his eyes but muttered, "Aye—ol' Leach unnerstands all right—been turned off fer 'er."

"I'd do what he says," Crawfurd interposed hastily. "If I was you, I'd leave while I still had a whole skin."

Dobbs, not wanting to chance further demonstration of the famed Deveraux temper, grasped Leach firmly by the elbow and propelled him out the door and into the small yard. " 'Ere now—'tis empty in th' loft yer are if yer mean ter cross 'im. Best leave it—I kin tell yer 'e means it."

"Naw—'e'd niver catch up wi' me."

"Dunno 'bout thet—yer can't be sure. Besides, she ain't what yer was thinking—she's a lady."

Inside, Crawfurd had reached the same conclusion. As he helped his master back to his bed, he unbent to soothe Ellen. "Do not be worrying over Leach, ma'am—I can assure you he's no loss to any of us." Leach's abrupt departure had brought home quite plainly that Trent regarded this girl differently from the others. Besides, Dobbs had maintained all along that she was different, and sometimes it paid one to listen to the lowly coachman. By the time he'd tucked the marquess up for a nap, Crawfurd had convinced himself that Ellen Marling was no high-flyer, after all. As a result, he came out determined to treat her with the deference reserved for true Quality.

When Trent arose, somewhat revived from the rest, he and Ellen dined alone in the small cottage while Dobbs and Crawfurd shared the Bratchers' table. Her spirits lowered by the impending departure, Ellen was unusually quiet and withdrawn into her own thoughts. Mistaking the reason, Trent finally leaned over and squeezed her hand across the table. "Do not be worrying about what Leach said, my dear—he'll not tell the story."

"I don't know—he certainly took a dislike to me," she sighed.

The return of the servants precluded any further discussion of the departed driver. As Crawfurd condescended to remove the dishes and covers from the table, Ellen was startled to hear Trent suggest that they all amuse themselves with a game or two of silver loo or whist. She looked up to meet his rueful smile. Dobbs and Crawfurd exchanged confused looks, but Trent shook his head to remind them that they would have to play something suitable for the lady.

"Perhaps we could teach her faro, my lord," Crawfurd suggested almost timidly. "I am no hand at all at whist."

"Aye. Who's to know?" Dobbs brightened. "None o' us'll tell."

"And I do not mind learning in the least, my lord," she told Trent with a wicked gleam in her eye. "I'll wager I could learn it quite quickly if I put my mind to it."

"We could let her try," Crawfurd urged hopefully. "I daresay she will find it more amusing than whist, and I certainly would never say a word to anyone."

"Well . . ."

"You could let me try—and if I cannot master it, we can then play whist," she argued.

"I have the distinct feeling that you will master it," Trent murmured in capitulation.

She tried to cover that she had been playing the game with his lordship by asking a variety of idiotish questions while the rules were being explained. And for the first few hands, she made some rather foolish stands. Finally, Trent nodded to Crawfurd.

"Fetch my purse, and we'll make this more interesting. I shall stake all of you and we will play it the way the game is intended. Crawfurd, you will be the house."

They played for about an hour and totaled their money.

The big winner was the marquess, who managed to nearly beggar the two servants, and the surprise was Ellen, who was the smallest loser. Even Crawfurd conceded in good grace, "You are uncommonly sharp for a female, ma'am."

Trent rested his head on his elbows. "I am sorry to end this, but I find myself quite tired. Perhaps we can continue this on the morrow." He tried to rise and the effort made him shake.

"You have overdone it, my lord," Ellen chided as she lunged to catch him. "Dobbs!"

Between them, they were able to support him until he steadied himself. "I am as weak as an infant," he muttered in disgust. "Leave me be a minute and I can make it on my own. Crawfurd, if you will but let me lean a little, I think I should like to retire."

"Aye, my lord."

Both servants managed to help him back to his room while Ellen cleared the cards off the table and soaked the dishes from the supper. Her spirits were unusually low, given the fact that they had been rescued at last, and she felt an urge to cry. She ought to be glad that help had arrived, she chided herself, for now they could press on to Yorkshire as soon as his lordship mended. But somehow she already missed the close, easy relationship she had established with Trent in those days they had been alone together. It almost seemed as if the arrival of help had changed everything yet again.

The next three days passed swiftly, and Trent gained strength. His fever no longer came up even at night and his cough was improving. He decided almost abruptly that he was able to withstand the rigors of a carriage ride, and he ordered everything packed. It was an easy task for Ellen, who had only the Mantini's ruined dress and the few ill-fitting garments Mrs. Bratcher had given her. She folded everything she was not wearing and sighed. In clothes like those, she would not even get past the servants into her aunt's house. No butler worth his salt would let a young female whose ankles showed in the front door.

Trent confronted his valet as he came out of his chamber, still tying his neckcloth with careless but expert hands. "Where is she? About to set out, do you think?"

"Packing, milord, but she's naught to wear. You cannot take her to her relatives dressed like a milkmaid, sir."

"I know. We'll have to procure some things for her in York itself before we try to beard her aunt, I suppose." He stopped a moment as though suddenly struck with an awful thought. "Make sure that she does not lay by a few jars of pork jelly for my health."

"Pork jelly, sir? Never heard of it!"

"Be thankful that you have not. Just the same, be on the watch, and consign any you find to the trash heap."

Thus charged, the valet caught Dobbs as he was putting the last of the boxes onto the coach. He pointed to the food hamper and told the coachey, "Make sure there is no pork jelly in that—his lordship's orders."

"Pork jelly? Ugh!"

"Yes, well, I have gathered his lordship is not especially fond of it, either."

"I hope them starchy relatives o' 'ers don't turn up their noses at 'er," Dobbs confided to Crawfurd as he strapped the final box on top. "She ain't in th' common way fer a lady, but 'er's a good un."

"I admit that I thought her like the rest." Crawfurd nodded. "But she isn't. Now I would not say her name in the same breath with any of the others. I don't know how or where he found her, but I wish he would keep her."

" 'E can't—she's Brockhaven's, yer fergit." Dobbs straightened up and surveyed the top of the carriage. "All right and tight," he decided as he checked the straps. "Eh, we ain't got no driver."

"Do not look at me. I am cow-handed when it comes to driving. And do not be complaining to his lordship, either. He's wild enough to take the reins himself and he's just up from his sickbed."

"I dunno what's ter do."

"I expect you will drive. With a little good fortune, you might even get promoted."

"Lud!"

10

"YOU CANNOT BE serious, my lord," Crawfurd sputtered indignantly. "I am a gentleman's gentleman—not a lady's maid! What would I know of such things?"

The carriage was stopped in front of a dressmaker's shop in the city of York. A sign in the window indicated, "A large selection of the latest stuffs, twills, satins, and bombazines executed in the French style." A card below proclaimed further, "A good variety of pelisses, dresses, millinery, flowers, and feathers of adornment."

The marquess gave him a decidedly pained look. "Have I ever imposed on you before, Crawfurd?"

"Frequently. But I simply cannot do this."

"Do you remember Leach?"

"Alex, do not tease Mr. Crawfurd. *I* shall choose my own gown, thank you." Ellen reached for the door handle and started to twist it before Trent caught her arm.

"Goose! Would you have everyone see you like this? No, I did not think you would," he noted smugly as a flush crept into her cheeks. "Just so. We cannot take you to Augusta Sandbridge's dressed like a gypsy beggar, but we cannot openly take you shopping either."

"And how am I to fit her, I ask?" Crawfurd continued to protest. "I have no experience in such things. Would you have me go in and say as nice as you please, 'I should like a lady's gown and whatever else 'tis necessary, but I am not precisely sure as to the size'? They should laugh me out of the place, my lord."

"Oh, very well!" Trent snapped irritably as he owned the truth of the aggrieved valet's complaint. "I suppose I shall have to see to it myself."

Dobbs swung down and opened the carriage door with a flourish. "And would yer 'ave us walk th' horses, yer lor'ship?"

"No. I shan't be long."

"Ellen wished she could have seen the expression of the modiste's and shopgirl's faces when the Marquess of Trent swept in and demanded a complete toilette for a lady of fashion on the instant. She was denied the treat, however, and he returned some twenty minutes later trailed by a manservant carrying two boxes. Trent took them and thrust them into the coach in front of him. "There—that should take care of everything, I believe," he told her as he settled in across from her. "I have instructed Dobbs to seek a secluded lane where you may change."

"I cannot dress in the open, Alex," she told him flatly.

"Well, you certainly cannot dress in her drive either, can you?" he responded reasonably. "Crawfurd and I will get out while you dress. You will find everything you require in those boxes, I even thought of a hairbrush."

"But there is not room. I cannot even stand to straighten my skirt, much less twist to do my buttons in such a narrow place."

"Do you have a better notion, my dear?"

"No," she admitted reluctantly, "but I shall feel the veriest fool."

"It is a simple gown, Ellie, and should not require much help. And when you are done, Crawfurd will help you with your hair."

The carriage rolled to a halt a short distance out of town, and Trent looked out the window before nodding. "Aye, this appears deserted enough for our purposes, I think. Come on, Crawfurd, let us step down and give her some privacy."

"I should not think of doing otherwise," the valet muttered. "But I take leave to tell you, sir, that I have not the least experience with female hair."

"I should think it all to be the same," Trent shot back as he jumped down.

"Alex—"

"Ellie, I have not come the length of England, faced highwaymen and robbers for you, fought off pneumonia, and stolen poor Chudleigh blind just so you can turn missish on me in the last instant. You will open that box and get into that dress, if you please."

"But 'tis broad daylight."

"Alas, I have no control over the sun, else I should put it out for you. Now, do you change your clothes or do I change them for you?" He flashed her a wicked grin and added, "I could, you know."

She waited until she was certain that they were out of sight before even untying the cord on the biggest box and lifting out a simple pink muslin dress of very demure cut, a creation more suited to a schoolgirl than a runaway bride, and a chemise, white silk stockings, and beribboned garters. With a wary eye on the window, she stripped out of Maggie Bratcher's homely gown and worn-out underclothing. Fishing deeper in the box, she found the pink silk pantalettes and the zona, and her face flamed to think he'd selected such things for her. Hastily, she threw everything on and was surprised to find that it all fit.

The other box yielded toilet articles—hairbrush, comb, mirror, and pink flowers for her hair—as well as soft pink kid slippers. It was there that he'd erred, for the shoes were so long they would have to be tied on. But that was of little consequence, she decided.

"Dressed, Ellie? Let me help you down and straighten out your gown for you." Before she could answer, he'd opened the coach door.

"Much good it would do me if I weren't!" she retorted sharply.

Grinning, he reached to circle her waist with his hands and lift her out. Setting her on the ground, he twitched the narrow skirt in place and straightened the high-banded waist under her bosom before she could protest. Turning her around, he deftly did the small satin-covered buttons while calling out to Crawfurd, "Come tie the sash, will you?"

"I? I've never tied a bow like that in my life."

"Neither have I," Trent admitted, "but between us we'll have to."

Somehow, they managed to get it into a semblance of order. Trent stood back and surveyed her with amusement. "None would mark you for a married lady, Ellen. You look like you cannot be a day above fifteen. Crawfurd, throw out that rag she was wearing, if you please, and dispose of the empty boxes. I would not have the fortune she is wearing crushed."

"Fortune? Alex—"

"Aye. You are wearing the only hundred-pound muslin I ever heard of, my dear, and I had a devil of a time getting it, I can tell you. 'Twas being made for a Miss Fenton, and the dressmaker made me ransom the damned thing."

"But you shouldn't have! Alex, I have to repay you and I never—"

"Nonsense. 'Tis a parting gift to a rare lady who saved my life." He stared at her for a moment with an unusual warmth in his blue eyes and then he turned away abruptly. "Crawfurd, do something with her hair."

"Really, my lord"—Ellen shook her head—"I shall just brush it and wear it down. 'Twill be all of a piece with this dress."

Everyone in the coach was strangely silent the rest of the way to Greenfield, the Sandbridge estate, each apparently given over to his own thoughts. Trent stared determinedly out the window while Ellen studied him for the last time. His hat was pushed back and a black curl fell rakishly forward as his face was profiled against the pane. A heavy sigh escaped her and she had to look away. It was time to say good-bye to a man she'd grown to respect in spite of his awful reputation, a man she truly liked—nay, loved, she had to admit to herself in these waning moments with him. No doubt, once he returned to London, she'd hear more of his amatory exploits, but she had to own that he'd been exceedingly kind and good to her, expecting absolutely nothing in return. She'd had that rare chance to look beneath the rakehell and see the man. What did Trent really think of her? she wondered. Would he have treated her differently had she not been Brockhaven's bride?

"Something amiss?" he asked gently as he became aware of her downcast mien.

"I don't know. I shall miss you, my lord, although I expect you will be heartily glad to wash your hands of me. I was thinking that I very likely will never see you again."

"Ellen . . ." He reached to take her hands in his, and his face was uncharacteristically sober. "Once you get to your aunt's, knowing me will be nothing to your credit, I am afraid. I am not fit company for a lady like you." He waited for her to look up and meet his eyes before continuing, "But if you ever have need of me, I will give you my direction and you can send word to me. Word of a Deveraux, I'll not stand by and let anyone send you back to Brockhaven."

A lump formed in her throat that threatened to suffocate her. "I—I cannot thank you enough for all you have done for me, my lord," she choked out. "And I thank you, but—oh, dear friend—I shall miss you!"

The carriage was already slowing as it entered the long, tree-lined drive, and the huge house loomed ahead of them. Crawfurd cleared his throat to hide his own sadness at the parting. As far as he could see, Ellen Marling had been nothing but a good influence on Alexander Deveraux.

"Your aunt keeps a large house," Trent observed to break the gloom that was descending over them.

"Yes, and there is but Aunt Augusta and Lady Leffingwell to share it. You will like Aunt Gussie, but I fear you will find Lady Lavinia a sore trial."

"No, I won't," he told her as he released her hands, "for I cannot stay. Besides," he added lightly, "entertaining elderly females is not just in my style. Once you are safely delivered, I mean to leave."

When Dobbs finally opened the door, Trent gave her a wry smile and handed her down. Following her, he leaned to whisper, "Buck up, Ellie—after what you have been through, 'twill be easy."

He stepped up and banged the knocker loudly. She hung back, afraid of what her aunt would say when she saw her. He turned and caught her elbow and held it for reassurance. It seemed like an age before an elderly retainer finally opened the double doors.

"Be pleased to inform Lady Sandbridge that the Marquess of Trent awaits her," Trent ordered imperiously.

"Madam is not at home, my lord."

"Very well, we'll wait, but be so good to send some sherry 'round to the library—and some ratafia for the lady. By the by, where *is* the library?" Trent walked in with the authority of a man rarely denied anything.

"I am afraid Lady Sandbridge is in London, my lord— gone to visit the Marlings. And Lady Lavinia has gone with her."

Ellen sank into a reception chair in the hallway and covered her face with her hands to prevent Trent's seeing her cry. Her shoulders shook noiselessly and her whole body seemed to go limp with despair.

"A devil of a coil, my dear," he soothed as he bent over her and clasped her shoulder. Seldom moved by feminine wiles or bouts of tears, he was touched that she would still try to control herself in the face of the devastating news. She gulped and nodded.

The butler stared at her in fascination. "Is she all right, sir?"

"Of course she is all right. She is merely overset that we have missed Lady Sandbridge. Come, my dear."

"But—"

"Would you be wishful of leaving your card, my lord? I cannot tell when she might return, but I collect it will be several weeks."

"No. My sister and I were just in the neighborhood."

"Ah, then perhaps you will see her in London."

"Perhaps."

They took their leave and Trent held her arm tightly as they stepped back outside. "Careful, Ellie—just hold together a little longer and then you can turn into a watering pot with my blessing."

"I am together," came the muffled reply, "but I need to think what I am to do now. I cannot go back and throw myself on Papa's mercy—I cannot!"

"Ellie," he murmured softly as he slid his hand down to hold hers, "I am tired of running all over the countryside. I have been ill and I have no wish to face Sir Basil either. We are going to my home in Berkshire."

Mortified, she looked at the ground. "I cannot go home with you."

"We are going home," he repeated. "My house is your house."

"I cannot live with you." She pulled back awkwardly and looked up through wet lashes. "I've no claim to you, my lord, and besides, think of the scandal."

"We've been together for weeks, anyway, Ellen, so what difference will a few more weeks or months make now?"

"But you do not understand! It was all right because we were coming here. It was the means to an end. There was no impropriety between us, and we both knew it was just until I got here. No one had to know about it except Aunt Gussie."

"I'm afraid you'll have to make the best of it. I'm taking you to the Meadows."

"But think what people will say—think of the scandal!"

"Look, Ellie, there are worse things—you said so yourself. You do not want to return to Brockhaven, do you?"

"No, but this isn't a *carte blanche* offer, is it?"

"Lud, no! Ellie, a man does not take a mistress home with him."

"But—"

"We are going home," he repeated firmly, "and I will do my damnedest to see you are not hurt by any of this. Come on, you'll like the Meadows and you'll like my brother Gerry."

11

LORD TRENT'S ARRIVAL at the Meadows was a surprise to everyone. His hasty note to his younger brother offered no explanation for his sudden decision to rusticate in his country home. If he had again quarreled and dueled, he would have gone to France rather than returned to the Meadows. Gerald Deveraux reread the tersely worded missive and puzzled over it. It was most unlike Alex to leave the delights of London before the absolute last event was over. And it was more than six weeks until Christmas. Besides, several weeks before, a friend had written that Trent was involved with a new opera singer.

"Well, Biddle," he told the butler, "ask Mrs. Biddle to remove the holland covers from the main drawing room. As best as I can make out from this, Trent will be home today or tomorrow and he will be bringing a guest."

"A hunting companion, perhaps?"

"No, Alex does most of his hunting in London. But I gather that it is a rather important personage. He asks that we reopen Mama's rooms for him."

A younger son, Gerald Deveraux cheerfully accepted his lot in life. It never occurred to him to curse a fate that gave him a brother nearly five years his senior, a brother to whom both title and estate passed when they were both still boys. But having been left with a generous allowance and a princely portion himself, he found jealousy an unnecessary vice. Nominally a captain in the dragoons, he was frequently afforded the opportunity of a few weeks at home, something he'd been unable to enjoy before the previous year's Waterloo.

"It's him! It's him!" A servant shouted from the wide porch at the front of the house. And from all over the huge mansion, people scurried to be a part of his welcome. Alexander Deveraux was immensely popular with his own servants, and they took relish in recounting his wild exploits among themselves. The boy—never mind that he was nearly thirty—was a handsome devil, and they were sure there was not another like him anywhere. His looks, his easy grace, his aristocratic bearing, even his famed exploits with his rapier—all were things his people admired in him. That he was a Deveraux would have been explanation enough, that he had been a marquess when in short coats, unhampered by the restrictions of parental discipline, was but icing on the cake. They delighted in hearing about his reckless carriage races, his conquest of one beautiful mistress after another, his fantastic gaming successes, and even his duels. In short, he provided them with pride in their own.

"He's got a lady with him!"

"A lady? Let me see."

"Gor! 'E does."

"Naw, he wouldn't bring no lady here."

"Well, you look at her. She ain't one o' them Lunnon doves."

"No, it's a lady, all right."

Biddle pushed his way to the front of the servants to get to the door. "His lordship knows what is due his ancestral home," the butler sniffed, "so you can be assured that he is *not* bringing a member of the muslin company."

Mrs. Biddle craned her neck to watch Lord Trent lift Ellen down from his carriage. "Unnuhhh." She shook her head knowingly as she reached the obvious conclusion. "She is plainly Quality, I can tell you. Not a beauty, mind you, but she's pretty enough. He's brought his bride home to us."

"A Lady Trent?" was the doubtful murmur around her.

"Thought he was raking around with some foreign singer."

"Sophia Mantini."

"But that would not keep him from getting married."

"Naw, 'ee'd not get shackled—'e's a Deveraux."

"And 'ow'd ye think they get 'em—Deveraux, I mean—if they don't marry?"

Gerald hung back aloof from the uproar caused by Alex's arrival. He did not know who the chit was, but he'd lay money that it wasn't any Lady Trent.

Everybody moved back when the marquess entered his hall with Ellen on his arm. He nodded cheerfully to all of them while taking her into the drawing room. She had the uncomfortable feeling that every servant there was looking her over very carefully, a feeling that did not lessen even when a tall, immaculately dressed man bearing an uncanny resemblance to Trent followed them in and shut the door.

"Hallo, Alex."

"Gerry. I'd like to present Ellen. Ellen—my brother, Captain Gerald Deveraux."

"Ellen." The captain bowed gracefully over her hand. "Charmed to make your acquaintance, my dear. That army out there would have it that you are Alex's bride."

Ellen's hand stiffened in Gerald Deveraux's clasp.

"Not my bride, Gerry. Brockhaven's."

There was a stunned silence as Trent's brother digested what he had heard. He turned loose of Ellen and stared at Alex for some sign of a jest.

"It's true, I am afraid," Trent sighed. "But it is a very long story."

"If you have run off with another man's wife, I cannot fathom why you have brought her here," Gerald told him stiffly. "It will be the first place anyone will look."

"It isn't like you think at all, Gerry. Can you not just look at her and tell this is no light-skirt I bring home? Even I am not totally lost to propriety."

"But if she is Brockhaven's wife—"

"I told you it was a long story!"

"Then tell it."

"Listen, she is tired and hungry. Wait until she is settled and I will tell you the whole."

"Alex," Ellen spoke up, "perhaps it will be easier if we all sit and we explain it now. He may not believe us, but we at least owe your brother an explanation."

"You'll have to meet Brockhaven over this, Alex, and

it will not look good—killing an old man for his young wife."

"Take a damper, Gerry." Trent's temper was rising rapidly until he glanced down at the white-faced Ellen. "Look at her. Does she look like anyone I would run off with?"

"No."

"Then be quiet and let us explain."

Ellen fixed her gaze on the carpet pattern while Alex Deveraux proceeded to enlighten his brother with the whole story of their arrival at the Meadows. He began with the wedding and omitted almost nothing in the telling. She flushed to the roots of her hair when he spoke of their stay at the Grumms' awful inn, but she did not miss the pride in his voice as Trent told of her setting Timms' leg and the saving of his own life. To her, the telling seemed ever so much more sordid than the living, and she tried to prepare herself for Gerald Deveraux' censure. Instead, he broke out laughing when Alex finished.

"Gad! Only you could do something like this! Your pardon, ma'am, but you have to admit he is game for anything. I can see almost every part of it."

"I could not leave her standing on the ground underneath Brockhaven's window, Gerry."

"Neither could I, had I been there, I daresay," Gerald admitted. "But what are we going to do now? She cannot live here—not that I mind the idea, but think of the scandal."

"I suppose it will just be said that I am our father's son." Alex looked up to the portrait that hung over the mantle, a portrait of a man very like himself.

"What he means, my dear," Gerald told Ellen, "is that our father took a fancy to our mother and made off with her. But it cannot be said to be the same thing—our mother was only betrothed."

"I meant that we are an impetuous lot, Gerry. This was not a very romantic elopement, I assure you."

"It was not," Ellen agreed emphatically. "There was not the least romantical thing about that awful inn or about trying to cook and care for a man who would not cooperate. There were times I despaired of our survival."

"You did not. Gerry, do not let her tell you such a whisker. She was as calm as Mama through the whole thing."

"But it was awful," she insisted, "when you were sick."

"And you were not even the one who was bled, and you were not fed pork jelly either," he reminded her with feeling.

Fascinated with this glimpse of his brother's suffering, Gerald could not resist asking, "And what is pork jelly?"

"You do not even want to know," Trent answered with a visible shudder.

"A restorative—at least that's what the label said, my lord," Ellen reminded him with a perfectly straight face. "And you cannot say that it did not help. Before I gave it to you, you were lying about in the greatest lethargy, but after, you were inspired to rave and rant almost like you would usually."

"I did not 'rave and rant' nearly enough during the whole escapade, my dear girl. You cannot know how close you came to being abandoned when you lost us lodgings that first night."

"But, of course, being a Deveraux, you simply could not do it." She smiled. Turning to Gerald, she could not resist adding, "You have no notion, sir, how very sick I was of the Deveraux in one day. I had to listen as to how Deveraux excel in virtually everything."

"Including conceit, I would suppose." Gerald grinned. "Aye, we do have a surfeit of that."

They were interrupted by Biddle announcing that a small supper awaited them in the dining room. Ellen looked at her travel-creased dress in dismay, but Trent shook his head.

"You are fine as you are. Just rinse your hands in the fingerbowl—Gerry and I will promise not to notice." He moved closer to add *sotto voce*, " 'Tis but a small country supper, but you'll like it." He gave her his hand to pull up with, adding, "Besides, I am famished."

His definition of a small country supper was misleading, she decided when she surveyed the table. The Meadows' cook had obviously been to pains to provide his returning master with the best to be had in the kitchen.

There were no fewer than four meat dishes consisting of roast, ham, squab, and a pork pie, four vegetables, a fruit compote, and a delectable fruit cake with rum sauce, in addition to the usual breads and wine. And after diner, there was brandy for the men and an arrack punch for Ellen.

Thoroughly stuffed, Ellen leaned sleepily toward Trent and murmured, "Would you mind very much if I retired, my lord? I should like to discuss what I am to do, but I cannot think just now. I do promise, however, that I shall not impose on your generosity any longer than necessary."

"You are not to worry on that head, my dear. You will stay here, of course. Biddle!"

"Aye, milord?"

"Have Mrs. Biddle show Ellen up to m' mother's rooms, if you please."

As she followed the housekeeper up one of two staircases that branched off either side of the open entry hall, Ellen reflected that it would not be difficult to get lost in Trent's country house. Her father's home had once seemed grand, but it absolutely paled in comparison and probably would fit in its entirety in one wing of the Meadows. The walls and floor of the entry were of shining marble, as were the stairs and the balustrade, while the upper walls were plaster outlined with gilded moldings, and the ceiling over the whole open area was crossed with the same moldings and decorated with gilt rosettes. Upstairs, the hallway floors were wood polished to the gloss of lacquer, with fine Aubusson wool runners in the center. Still, even after such opulence, she was unprepared for the scene that greeted her as the housekeeper opened the door proudly to the rooms that had belonged to the last Marchioness of Trent. The front sitting room was as large as the Marlings' small drawing room in the house they'd leased during the wedding preparations, and it was fitted in a style that could only be described as truly regal. Two sofas covered in a delicate rose-and-green matelassé flanked a marble-faced fireplace, where a fire had been laid. Cherry-wood and marble-topped tables holding fine brass candelabra sat at either end of the sofas while a high-backed Queen Anne chair done in a rose velvet faced the fire. The rug that covered the center of the room carried out the soft rose and green in a floral pattern, and the walls were covered with green French moiré silk. Even the ceiling was decorated with white plaster and gold rosettes like the entry hall downstairs.

Ellen almost could not tear herself away to follow Mrs. Biddle into the bedchamber and dressing room as she stood stunned by her surroundings. She managed to collect herself finally and allowed the woman to guide her into the dressing room, where a large gilt-splashed *poudre* table with a marble top held every item imaginable for a woman's toilette. A Louis Quinze chair with a green velvet seat had been drawn back invitingly, and a brace of candles glowed in front of the gilt-edged mirror. Off to one side, a marble washbasin rested on a gilt-washed stand, and a brass pitcher sat on the ledge above it. A rose velvet wrapper and a white silk nightgown lay across a low, velvet-padded bench.

Mrs. Biddle nodded and managed a pleasant smile. "I laid out your nightclothes, miss. As yet, we have no dresser, but one of the maids has some skill with hair if you would wish her assistance tonight."

"No." Ellen shook her head slowly, still in a state of shock to find that Trent lived in such luxury. "I would just go to bed, if you do not mind."

"Your bed is already turned down, miss, and Marie will bring up some warm milk to help you sleep. I hope you do not mind it, but we are quite informal here. I do not know what you are used to, but we call most of the servants by their first names, except for Biddle and myself."

Ellen looked up to see if the woman intended her remarks as a set-down and saw nothing but kindness mirrored there. "Thank you, Mrs. Biddle. We were not particularly formal in my home either."

"Do you require assistance before bed—I mean, do you need help with your undressing?"

"No. If you will but get the top few buttons, I can take care of everything, thank you."

The little housekeeper reached up and undid the buttons as requested with a smile. "There. Well, if that is all, I will be going. There is a bell pull by your bed that rings in my room, miss, so if you need anything in the night, do not hesitate to use it." She hesitated a moment before adding, "And if you cannot sleep, there are some books in cases in the bedchamber. Nothing recent, of course, but the marchioness was quite a bluestocking, as scholarly as his lordship and the captain."

"I am sure that I will be able to find everything I need," Ellen assured her as she walked her back to the sitting-room door.

"Good night, miss."

"Good night."

Ellen turned around and made her way into the bedchamber to find that everything indeed had been prepared. Another fire was laid in another marble-faced fireplace and it gave the entire room a very pleasant glow. Again, there was the thick floral rug, the silk-covered walls, the gilt-trimmed ceiling, and a sense of overwhelming elegance. This time, the furniture was of highly polished cherry wood and consisted of a four-poster bed covered with a rose satin coverlet and pillows, a small settee upholstered in cut velvet, two chairs, and several small tables. Bookcases flanked double French windows that opened above a small garden turning brown with autumn, and twin mirrors hung over a pier table across from the bed. And as Mrs. Biddle had said, the bed had been turned back to reveal ivory linen sheets edged in lace.

Ellen looked around the room as she finished her buttons and then moved back to the dressing room, where she removed and hung up her gown in one of the two large chifferobes. She finished undressing and put on the gown and wrapper. A faint odor of cedar permeated the garments, indicating that they had been stored and probably had belonged to his lordship's mother. She must have been a tall woman, since both the gown and the wrapper were long enough for Ellen. If so, it was no wonder that Trent and his brother were so tall.

A timid knock sounded at the door, followed by the entrance of a girl bearing a tray with steaming milk and a piece of cake of the sort served with afternoon tea. The girl set down the tray on a table by the fire and dipped a slight curtsy.

"Thank you, Marie."

"Anything else, Miss Ellen?" The girl seemed to want to linger, but did not know how to go about it without Ellen's permission. Finally, she blurted out, "Are you going to be our lady, miss?"

"What?"

The girl flushed and looked at her feet. "I'm sorry, miss, but there was betting belowstairs, and I was told to ask."

"I see. No, I am merely visiting."

"Oh. Well, you are the first lady his lordship has ever allowed to visit, so some of us thought . . ." Her voice trailed off in uncertainty.

"No, I . . ." Ellen started to say she was already married before she thought and then realized how it would sound. Besides, married or not, she was definitely not in his lordship's style, anyway. "I am afraid I am just visiting for a little while."

Belowstairs, in the library, Gerald was speculating in much the same vein over his brandy. He refilled his glass and Trent's and carried it to where Trent lounged easily before the fire. He handed one over to his brother and took a chair opposite. They both stared into the flickering flames in silence for a while until Gerry set his glass aside and leaned forward to stare at Trent.

"What are you going to do with her, Alex?" he asked quietly.

"I don't know," Trent answered slowly. "Believe it or not, I have given it a lot of thought, but I don't even know what I want to do. I do know that I have promised her that she will not be returned to Brockhaven."

"Why?"

"Have you seen him?" Trent asked in disgust. "A fat pig—an *old* fat pig—he has no business with a girl like Ellen."

"But she married him," Gerald reminded him.

"She had no choice! Marling starved his daughter, Gerry, and then threatened to give Brockhaven her sister, a child not yet out of the schoolroom, unless she agreed to marry the old roué." Trent stared absently into his glass, swirling the brandy in it, before shaking his head. "She never even had a Season, if you can believe it, so what chance did she have? Her father was too clutch-fisted to put her out on the Marriage Mart, where she would have been snatched up in weeks by a better prospect if Marling had been but smart enough to know it. She's a head above the rest of 'em, I swear."

It was so unlike Trent to express any admiration for a respectable female that Gerald's curiosity was whetted. He reached for the decanter and refilled both glasses again. "Tell me about her, Alex."

"What is there to tell that I have not already said? She is different, that's all." He sipped his wine thoughtfully, his eyes still fixed on the fire. "No, do not ask me, I don't know what it is. She could be pretty if she had decent clothes and a good lady's maid, but there is more to her than that. Despite the way I found her, there is nothing even remotely fast about her. You can just look at her and tell she's Quality, but she's not empty-headed and selfish like the rest of 'em. She's calm and resourceful and honest." He looked up and met his brother's skeptical eyes. "Believe it or not, she's not hanging out for a man's purse, Gerry. She worried about what I spent on her. Look at this!" He held up his hand to show the narrow band of rubies and diamonds that circled his little finger. "She paid me with her wedding ring."

"You sound almost besotted."

"Do I?" Trent appeared surprised and then nodded. "Aye—maybe I am."

"And if Brockhaven divorces her, are you prepared to marry her?"

"I'm not a marrying man, Gerry. I'd be a poor bargain for her when she wants a respectable, worthy husband. No. I mean to protect her, that's all."

"If it gets out that she has stayed here, one of us might be compelled to offer for her to avert the scandal of the divorce."

"Gerry"—there was a note of warning in Trent's voice—"don't even think it. She's no more up to your weight than mine. She deserves better than either of us."

"Oh, I don't know. If she's such a paragon, I might not mind making the sacrifice. Save me the time and trouble of going to the damned balls and routs, you know," he teased lightly.

"I forbid any flirtation—*any* flirtation, Gerry, and I mean it. She's a green girl in spite of what she's been through, and I won't see her hurt by your *or* me."

"Coming the puritan a bit strong, aren't you?"

"I mean it, Gerry."

"All right, Alex, but what are we to do with her? Two bachelors—two very disreputable bachelors, in fact—and a young female of Quality? 'Twill give the tattlemongers a month of gossip if it gets out. Devil of a scandal, brother."

"I mean to give it out that she's Ellen Deveraux, Mademoiselle Deveraux, to be exact, sent to us from the French Deveraux, since her family fell upon death and misfortune in Napoleon's late wars. Well"—he looked across at Gerald—"what do you think? Can we pull it off?"

"The truth? I think 'twill be a difficult tale to tell—I mean, the French Deveraux are dreadfully loose living, but they aren't such loose screws that they'd send an innocent female to live with us. For one thing, they're Catholic—they'd send her to a convent."

"We know that, but does anyone else? But if you have a better idea on the subject, I am all attention."

"Put that way—no. Does this mean she's going to stay?"

"It does. I owe her my life, Gerry, and I will not stand idly by and see her returned to Brockhaven. Here at least I can keep her safe."

"For how long? Days? Months? Years?"

"I don't know . . . until something happens."

"All right," Gerald sighed, "I can see your mind is set. You know, Alex, this is the first time I have ever seen you go to so much trouble for anybody. Maybe your fever addled your brain."

Above them, Ellen tossed in the four-poster bed, her mind in turmoil over what she would do. She could not stay dependent on Trent's generosity indefinitely, no matter what he said, and yet she quite literally had nowhere to go. While he might think he owed her some sort of pension for saving his life, she could not accept it. She simply could not live in the same house with him, not just because of the danger of scandal, but because she recognized that she was in love with him. She already was in danger of wearing her heart on her sleeve. It was becoming impossible to hide the fact that she was irresistibly drawn to those very blue eyes, the ruffled black hair, the perfect patrician countenance, and the man behind it. There was no way she could see him come and go, hear of his latest mistresses, and stand it. Yet she would miss him unbearably.

When she finally did manage to sleep, she lapsed into restless dreams where Basil Brockhaven's pudgy fingers squeezed her flesh and his wet lips smacked against her throat. Bone-weary still, she was nevertheless grateful when Marie wakened her in the morning to tell her that her bath was drawn.

After the maid left, she bathed, luxuriating in the lavender-scented water, and then dressed in the other gown that Trent had procured for her in York. It was little better than the first and certainly unsophisticated, a high-waisted schoolgirl frock of lavender sprigged muslin, trimmed around the modest neckline in ecru cotton lace, with leg-of-mutton sleeves that came demurely down to her wrists. As she sat before the *poudre* table and brushed out her thick hair, she reflected wryly that everything Trent had seen her in was either too daring or too childish. Resolutely, she twisted her hair and knotted it on her crown: at least today she would not wear it down like a chit in the schoolroom. By the time she descended to breakfast, she was moderately satisfied.

"Hallo, Ellen."

Below her, Gerald Deveraux flashed a friendly smile and waited. By the light of day, his resemblance to Trent was even more pronounced than she'd thought. He drew her arm through his as she came off the last step and indicated the rows of portraits that flanked the staircase on either side of the hall.

"Quite a bunch of fellows, aren't they? Our ancestors— and each one of them believed he owned the world, by the looks of 'em. That last one is my father as Sir Thomas Lawrence painted him. Quite a good likeness, really— you can tell just by looking that there was a bit of the devil in him, can't you? Quite a shocking profligate until he met my mother." He turned her to look at the companion portrait across from it. "Lady Caroline—also done by Lawrence—and you can quite see why he risked everything for her, I think."

Ellen looked up at the tall paintings and nodded. It was obvious that the Deveraux brothers got most of their handsomeness from the late marquess, a tall, imposing figure in satin coat and kneebreeches who seemed to be looking down on her with a faintly mocking smile. Aye, he looked the dangerous man with his dark hair merely tied back without the conventional powder of the time, and his hand resting suggestively on the dress sword at his side. She turned to study Trent's mother, a breathtakingly beautiful girl when she'd been painted, as fair as her husband was dark, with intelligent eyes and a lovely smile.

"They're beautiful—both of them."

"Aye. I've looked at them often hanging there, for I can barely remember either of 'em, but Alex says they were a prime pair. There was a devil of a scandal at the time. She was betrothed to a worthy gentleman, but he just carried her off straight out of her parents' house like Scott's Lochinvar. I often wondered if Scott got the idea from the scandal, you know—not that Papa actually rode his horse into the house or anything like that. Still, it set the *ton* on its ears. Married her out of hand at Gretna and did not come home until Alex was on the way."

"How romantic," Ellen sighed as she looked again at the two beautiful people above her. "Did her parents ever forgive them?"

"Alas, no," he admitted, "but I doubt they cared. By all accounts, they were deliriously happy until Mama died of a fever when Alex was eight and I was four. Papa died soon after in a riding accident."

"I see. I'm sorry."

"It was harder on Alex than me, for he was old enough to know what had happened. He came into the title then and was much spoiled, although Button tried to dampen his sense of self-consequence. But," Gerald changed the subject abruptly, "we tarry when you must be famished, my dear." He stood back at the dining-room door and waited for her to pass in. "I'm told that ladies take chocolate in the morning, but we don't have any as yet. Biddle is sending to London for some, though, and I expect you'll have it by the end of the week." He held out a chair for her and then seated her before taking the place across the table.

"Tea is fine, Captain Deveraux. Indeed, I will take anything." She placed the napkin on her lap and smiled. "You will find me given to picking at what I am offered, sir, for it is better than what I am used to. My father is rather clutch-fisted and once ordered Cook to save the tea leaves and use them twice."

"Now that is a pinchfarthing," he murmured sympathetically.

"Yes, well, Papa will die a rich man because he cannot be brought to part with a groat once it touches his hands. He even made Brockhaven pay for the wedding."

"Shhhhh. Make no mention of the baron here. We have given it out that you are our French cousin come to live with us."

"I beg your pardon?"

"Well, you can speak French, can't you?"

"Of course, but—"

"Just sprinkle it into your conversation from time to time, my dear, and no one here will be any the wiser."

"Captain—" She tried hard to keep a straight face. "He cannot be serious. I speak French with an English accent."

"We'll tell everyone you are from one of the provinces, then."

"I thought Lord Trent said you did not have any female relatives, sir."

"We don't, but who's to know what's over there in France? I mean, what with Boney cutting up a dust all those years, there's not been that much discourse between us. Besides, here at the Meadows, people will believe whatever Alex chooses to tell them." He leaned across the table and lowered his voice, hissing, "Shhhh—there's Edward."

The footman appeared with a silver teapot and poured for each of them. Moving the sugar and creamer closer to her, he asked her pleasure for breakfast.

"Sausage and porridge, if you have it, please."

"Of course, miss. And you, Captain?"

"I haven't had porridge since Button stuffed it down

me," he admitted, "so I might as well see if it has improved. I'll have the same."

"I heard about Button."

"And I suppose Trent told you I was her favorite? A hum if there ever was one, but we used to fight over it. I know now that she loved us both equally." He spooned a dollop of heavy cream into his tea and leaned back to look at her. "Trent tells me you are an Original."

"Must've been the fever if he said that. No. I am quite unexceptional, Captain, and you can take that from one who knows me best."

"If you have restrained my brother's wilder propensities for three weeks, Ellen, you have succeeded beyond what anyone else has done."

" 'Tis hard to be a rakehell when one is abed with a raging fever and miserable cough." She smiled. "And, of course, I doubt the onion poultices were exactly inspiring either."

"You know, Ellen, I did not think so at first, but I find I quite like the prospect of having you here. 'Twill be rather like getting a sister when one is old enough to enjoy one."

"I cannot stay here. I am quite determined to earn my own bread."

"Nonsense, my dear," he dismissed flatly. "Trent is so plump in the pocket that he will not even note the expense, I assure you. Best let Alex take care of it."

"I could be a governess, perhaps," she mused aloud. "Perhaps you would know of someone with a position?"

He raised an incredulous eyebrow and shook his head. "No—and neither does Alex, I'll wager. Lud, but could you not see the face of a matron if you arrived with a character from either of us?"

"Oh."

"Just so. But here is Edward with the porridge, and by the looks of it, I shall most probably regret having ordered it." He wrinkled his nose at the bowl set in front of him. "I fear it is as I remembered it."

"You will not deter me by changing the subject, Captain."

" 'Twas not my intent. Speak with Alex if you would leave."

It was useless to argue with either of the Deveraux brothers, she decided, when she did not even have a plan of her own. Resolutely, they fell to eating, and by the time they were done, the discussion had been dropped. As Edward began removing the covers, Gerald gave her an engaging smile.

"Well, my dear, are you ready to explore the barn?"

"I'd scarcely call it a barn, Captain Deveraux, when it looks more like a palace."

"But then you have not lived in it all your life. Some of it is as cold and drafty as a stable, particularly when you get into the older parts. There are rooms that have been under holland covers for years because they are so difficult to heat. You'll think that the early Deveraux must have been a hardy lot to have survived the winters."

"Nonetheless, this house surpasses everything in my limited experience. I think it quite beautiful."

He tucked her hand in his elbow and proceeded to give her a tour with the thoroughness of the director of the Elgin exhibit, stopping to point out pictures of this ancestor or that, and to repeat some of the moderately lurid tales of them. They walked through rooms that had been occupied as far back as the sixteenth century, when the early Deveraux had had the foresight to side with the Lancastrians in the waning days of the Wars of the Roses and been rewarded by Henry VII with confiscated Yorkist lands. To Ellen, it was fascinating.

"You really ought to talk to Trent about the house, of course," Gerry told her, "for he is the scholar in the family when it comes to history. Before he was sent down from Oxford, he was an excellent student."

"Trent?"

"You seem surprised."

"I *am* surprised. His more exciting exploits seem to have hidden or overshadowed his bookishness. Brockhaven told me only that he was a notorious rake and a high-tempered duelist, but somehow he forgot to mention he was a scholar."

"Oh, make no mistake, Ellen. Alex is everything you have heard of him, good *and* bad, but if I ever had to put all my faith in anyone, I should choose him above all others."

"And what of yourself, sir? Do you admit to being a scholar too?"

"Well, I am not so well-versed in history or the classics as Alex, but I do like Shakespeare and poetry. Between us, I am probably the more romantic one." He stopped to open the door to a spacious music room large enough to accommodate guests for a musicale.

Her face lit up almost immediately when she saw the highly polished pianoforte, and she could not resist taking a seat before the keyboard and fingering it lightly.

"My mother's," he told her. "She was quite accomplished, I think, and I can remember her playing when I was quite small."

She tested a note or two tentatively. "It seems well-tuned."

"It is. We use it for parties when Alex is in residence, particularly for the area gentry at Christmastide. We usually bring a musician from London to play it."

She cocked her head absently and began picking at the keyboard until she got the feel of it, and then she fingered a melody with her long fingers until she was ready to launch into a fast-tempoed country song. After several minutes, she changed to a soft, lilting melody of surpassing and haunting beauty.

Alex was coming down the stairs when he heard it, and he stopped to listen to the sweetness and clarity of the song. Following the sound to his music room, he stood in the doorway and applauded when she finished.

"Bravo, my dear!" He came into the room and stood behind her, smiling his approval. "I thought you were funning when you said you played rather well, but I have paid to hear far worse."

"Oh, Alex, do you think I could earn my living with my playing?"

"No, I do not." The smile had left his face and he was frowning. "It is out of the question, Ellie. I do not mind if you play here, but you will not appear publicly as a musician."

"That is not for you to say, my lord," she reminded him. "It is for me to decide how I am to live."

"I will not have it said that I abandoned you to the boards," he snapped before he abruptly started to walk out.

"I would rather have it said that I earn my money honestly than have it said I am your mistress when it becomes known that I have been living here," she flung after him.

He stopped but did not turn around. "There is no question of your doing either, Ellie. I have given it out that you are our cousin from France, but you have been in school in England. Since your parents are both dead, you have come to live with us."

"But I cannot live here forever."

"It is the only way I can keep you safe from Brockhaven."

"I have to earn my way, Alex."

"You saved my life, Ellen, and that is sufficient."

"But it isn't!"

"Practice your piano, my dear, and I will talk to him," Gerald told her before he left to catch up with his brother. "Alex!"

Trent waited. "Back off, Gerry. This is not your affair."

"Careful, Alex. You sound like a damned tyrant."

"I thought I told you I'd tolerate no flirtation, Gerry."

"Flirtation? Dammit, I like her!"

"Let me remind you, brother, that there is Brockhaven, an impediment even in these lax times."

"Is that the way you see all females?"

"Gerry, I am your brother," Trent managed evenly, "and I know you are no better than I am when it comes to the fairer sex. You are not to prey on her foolish desire for an independence that she cannot maintain. It is incumbent on both of us to see that she does nothing indiscreet until we can think what is ultimately to be done. Had Augusta Sandbridge been at home, she could have given it out that Ellen had been with her these past weeks, but she was not. I have not yet determined how to save her from the scandal, but I do know one thing: until I can get her out of this mess, she must not be allowed to even think of leaving to earn her bread."

" 'Tis mad, Alex! What about Crawfurd? Or Timms? Or Dobbs?"

"They all fairly worship her, they'll not give her away."

"I don't know, Alex."

"Neither do I, but I cannot get a decent night's sleep for thinking about it. I have to leave—there'll be less talk if I am gone. And I should think you'll be getting back to your regiment soon. 'Twill not be so remarked when she is but here with the servants."

"Actually, I have been thinking of selling out, been thinking of it for some time now."

"Since this morning?" Trent asked sarcastically.

"No, since the last time you had to flee the country and I had to look after the Meadows."

Alex stared hard at Gerald and then shrugged. "You will do what you want to do, of course. Do not let us be quarreling over the girl, Gerry. You look after things and I will be back for Christmas."

"That's almost two months away."

"I can use the time to think. Besides, the Mantini is still in London and I do not know if I am through in that quarter or not." He hesitated and then shook his head. "But while I am gone, Gerry, I expect you to keep your amatory instincts in check where Ellen is concerned."

12

"DEAR LADY LEFFINGWELL," Lord Brockhaven teased, "if I did not know how the other ladies looked forward to our rides in the park, I would suspect you arranged other engagements for them."

Lavinia colored guiltily, as that was exactly what she had done. After three successive mornings of driving in the park with his lordship, she had found Gussie and Nora reluctant to accompany them again. Propriety required that she demur also, but she managed to invent an important errand. And when Augusta had been on the verge of capitulating and accompanying her, Vinnie had lied and said she was taking a maid.

"La, Sir Basil, how can you say such a thing?" she tittered as she fanned herself nervously in spite of the cold weather.

"Well, it is not a bad idea, anyway," he admitted generously as he waved to a gentleman wrapped up in a passing carriage. As they neared, the other driver reined in, and a middle-aged man leaned out the window to inquire of Ellen.

"Ah, Rockingham—howdedo! Ellen? Not much better, I am afraid. The doctors are beginning to despair of a cure. May I present one of her relatives, Lady Leffingwell?" After the appropriate nods, the gentleman signaled his driver to go on, and Brockhaven turned to Vinnie, "You'd think they'd forget to ask, wouldn't you? It's a deuced nuisance keeping up with the questions."

"You poor man," she clucked sympathetically. "It is beyond me how the ungrateful girl could have behaved so shabbily to you."

"Aye. And I am a flesh and blood man, I need a wife."

"I understand perfectly, Sir Basil, but you must proceed with caution. Once the story has died down, you can get an annulment on the grounds that her health is bad."

"Hadn't thought of that," Brockhaven owned thoughtfully. "I suppose I could say that I did not think her health sufficiently good for childbearing, couldn't I? Hmmmmm . . ." Abruptly, he reached to pat Lavinia's hand. "And how old are you, my dear?"

"A gentleman never asks a lady her age," she simpered.

"But you ain't above forty, are you?"

"La, but I shall never tell."

"But you ain't?"

"No, not quite."

"Good."

In spite of the cold, Lavinia had to own that the rest of the drive went rather well. Sir Basil bent himself to be all that was accommodating and polite, and she was pleased with the attention. Since Sir Lawrence's death, she had lived at Greenfield almost as a recluse, emerging only when it was necessary to support dear Augusta through something, and now she was restive with yearning to return to a more active life.

Mrs. Marling was standing at the window when they returned. She could not help her lack of manners—she had to stare when Sir Basil clambered out and assisted Vinnie down. While Vinnie was quite colorless, the baron was quite something else.

"Augusta, will you look at that?" She held back the curtain for her sister-in-law.

Augusta looked out and had to suppress a chuckle. "Looks like a fat robin. Really, Eleanor, would you tell me why a man of Sir Basil's proportions would be seen wearing a light suit with a red waistcoat, especially a suit so tight that he cannot possibly breathe in it?"

"Lavinia does not seem to notice."

"No, she doesn't, does she?" Augusta agreed.

"I thought I should have died of mortification yesterday"—Eleanor shuddered at the memory—"when he arrived to take us out in a puce suit with yellow stockings."

"He has no taste."

The object of their amusement was already reentering his carriage, blissfully unaware of their comments on his sartorial splendor. He settled back into his seat and placed his fingertips together over his well-rounded belly while he mulled a new and intruiguing prospect. He was still engrossed with the idea when he alit at his home and mounted the steps to his town house.

A man darted out and touched his coat sleeve. Unused to being accosted by members of an inferior class, Brockhaven raised his cane to show the fellow a thing or two.

"Now, guv'nor, ye don't 'it Leach," the man told him with an injured look. "Yer missin' yer lady, ain't yer? 'Appen I know where 'er is."

"I have no idea what you are talking about," Brockhaven told him stiffly, and pushed past.

"Pretty thing 'er is—dark 'air, big eyes—got an aunt in York—"

"Get out of here!"

The man shrugged. " 'Ave it yer way, guv'nor. Mebbe there's others t' listen t' Leach."

"Wait!" Sir Basil's mouth was dry as he glanced furtively up and down the street. "What do you want?"

"Ter restore yer lady ter yer." He doffed his hat with a wicked grin and added, "Fer a price."

"I see." The street appeared deserted as Brockhaven made up his mind. "Come 'round to the back and I'll have someone let you in."

"Thought yer would."

Later, in the safety and privacy of his library, Lord Brockhaven listened to Leach's strange story. He paced restlessly while the driver watched from the comfort of one of his chairs.

"But Lady Sandbridge is here. My wife cannot have gone there."

"Thet I don't know fer a fact, guv'nor, but I do know 'er was with milord Trent. Mebbe 'e took 'er 'ome wi' 'im."

"Trent? You are mistaken—he would not want a woman like her."

"They looked friendly enough ter me."

"No, not Ellen."

"Thet so? 'E discharged me fer talkin' 'bout 'er."

"I do not even know Lord Trent's direction."

"I do. Yer fergit—I was 'ired t' work fer 'im.'"

Brockhaven closed his eyes and pictured Ellen—her slender young body, those purple eyes, that youth. Trent! That could be unpleasant, but not even Trent would dare to cut up a dust over another man's wife. Besides, even if the story were true, he would probably have tired of the girl by now. If rumor could be believed, he'd not been constant to anyone above two or three weeks, anyway.

"How much do you want?"

"Five 'undred pounds."

"Ridiculous!"

"I can allus tell 'er family."

"Three hundred—payable when she is returned. After all," his lordship reminded the driver peevishly, "I do not even know you are telling the truth."

"Five 'undred, guv'nor, when 'er comes 'ome."

"Oh, very well," Brockhaven capitulated finally, and then set about formulating a plan whereby Leach and another man were to meet him the next morning and set out for Trent's country home first and then go on to Augusta Sandbridge's estate in York if Ellen proved not to be with Trent.

"Yer can trust Leach," the driver promised confidently, and took his leave.

Brockhaven poured himself a good-sized drink and sat down before the fire to mull over this strange turn of events. The Marquess of Trent! Unthinkable! And yet there had been the ring of truth in the strange little man's story. A slow smile crept over the baron's jowled face. Well, if it proved to be true, he bet the chit knew a thing or two now.

Committed to taking Mrs. Marling, Lady Sandbridge, and Lady Leffingwell to the theater for the evening, he considered sending around a note of cancellation and then thought better of it. After all, if he were successful in retrieving Ellen, he would still need the good offices of those ladies to pull it off without a scandal. No, it was best to keep the engagement. But to think he had been contemplating offering for the Leffingwell woman! He must have been on the verge of insanity. She might still be young enough to provide him with an heir, but she certainly could not compare with a young woman.

Later, while dressing with his usual care, he hummed happily at the thought of having Ellen back. This time, he would not have to bother with the subtleties; he'd bet that Trent had already taken care of that, and the girl would know how to please a man now. A thought stilled him momentarily: what if she were increasing? He'd have no bastard Brockhavens—never! Well, he could wait to see on that one. He began to hum again as he tied his starched neckcloth under his full chin. He glanced in the mirror and ripped off the offending piece of linen with an oath, cursing the day that stocks went out. His valet stepped forward with a fresh cloth and draped it around his lordship's neck, twisting it deftly into the Oriental, a style that Brockhaven himself never cared for—too plain by half. The baron stood to shrug himself into his lavender swallow-tailed coat, a creation that had even given his tailor pause, for it was lined in a purple-and-green-striped nankeen that matched his trousers. To set it all off, he wore a green silk waistcoat. When he left his house, he was certain he would impress the ladies.

It seemed to him that his choice had been perfect, for when he led the three women into his box, Lavinia, herself attired in bright parrot-green satin with dyed-to-match ostrich feathers in her hair, was on his arm. He noted with satisfaction that all heads turned to watch them. Behind them, Augusta Sandbridge and Eleanor Marling trailed as far as was polite in their rather subdued silk Empire gowns. To acknowledge what he was certain was the admiration of those around him, Brockhaven bowed smugly to the occupants of the boxes around his.

He was in high spirits at the thought of reclaiming his young wife, and he set about to entertain Vinnie with the latest gossip before the candles were doused and the curtain rung up. He put his glass to his eye and worked through the crowd looking for interesting pairings.

"There's Rockingham"—he pointed—"with Lady Marlow." Catching sight of the earl, he waved brightly before moving on with his glass. "And over there is Mrs. Farmington—Moreland's mistress, you know."

But Lavinia's attention was already caught by the people in the box directly opposite them. She tugged at the baron's sleeve to gain his attention. "But is that not Madame Mantini over there? And, good heavens! Who is that arresting man with her?"

"Eh?" He strained to follow her direction and saw the raven-haired beauty pouting next to the marquess. " 'Tis the Mantini—and Trent!"

"La—is that the Marquess of Trent? My, 'tis no wonder he is so remarked." She turned her pale eyes back to the baron to observe, "But he dresses rather plainly for a marquess, don't you think?"

Brockhaven seemed frozen in his seat as he stared across the pit and tried to make sense of Trent's presence in London. Either Leach was a complete liar or Trent had already abandoned Ellen somewhere. "Hmmmm?" he finally caught himself and acknowledged Lavinia's insistent tugging.

"Are you quite all right, Sir Basil?"

"Yes, but I am surprised to see him here. I had thought him in the country."

"You do not look at all well."

"I am fine," he muttered half to himself, "but I intend to pay his lordship a call at first intermission, you can be sure."

His agitation was so great that he could not have repeated anything that occurred in the first act. He knew it would be risky speaking with Alexander Deveraux, given the man's high temper, but Brockhaven meant to make the attempt in hopes of gleaning some information as to Ellen's whereabouts. He'd paid enough for the chit that he did not intend to be cheated of his rights even by the likes of Trent. As soon as the candles were relit, he excused himself and made his way around to the other box.

"Your servant, my lord," he told the marquess as he pushed his way into the closed area. "I would have a few words with you, sir—in private, if you please."

Trent shrugged and nodded a curt dismissal to Sophia Mantini, who stood up, rustling the skirt of her red silk gown, and tried to hide her irritation. "I see Leonie, Alex, so I shall pay her a call." She brushed past Brockhaven without a word and ignored his appraising stare.

"Egad, sir! The luck is all yours!"

Trent ignored him and adjusted the sleeves of his dark-blue coat over the snowy cuffs of his silk shirt with a detachment that the baron found disconcerting. Brockhaven stared at him in fascination, amazed that anyone dressed so plainly could make him feel so dowdy by comparison. It must be the man's height, he decided. He cleared his throat to regain Trent's attention, and tried to screw up his courage to ask about Ellen. Trent, for his part, leaned back in his chair and lifted his long legs up to rest his feet on the polished brass rail before clasping his hands over his flat stomach. His blue eyes were very cold and forbidding when at last he looked up at the baron from heavy lids.

"Well?"

A wiser man than Brockhaven would have heard the challenge in the icy voice and backed down, but the baron chose to interpret that single word as an invitation to sit. He dropped heavily into the chair beside the marquess and mopped his sweaty brow. After taking a furtive look around them, he leaned closer.

"An interesting story came my way today, my lord," he began.

"I never listen to interesting stories, Brockhaven, for I find they are usually incorrect and therefore a waste of my time." Trent turned his head slightly to his unwanted guest. "But you may go on, if you find it necessary."

The baron again wiped his wet forehead and licked his dry lips. "There was a man by the name of Leach who came to my house today, sir." He waited impatiently for a reaction and got none. "He said you had my wife." There was not even a flicker of interest as Trent sat there with a bored expression still on his arrogantly handsome face. Finally, Brockhaven could stand it no longer and blurted out, "Well, do you?"

The marquess raised a black eyebrow. "You have lost your wife, Brockhaven? How careless of you. I never favored having one myself, but I doubt I should misplace her if I did." His whole body was a study of indifference, as he added casually, "But do go on. What else did—I am sorry, I am afraid I did not get the name—but what else did this person allege?"

"Leach. He said you was taking my wife to her Aunt Sandbridge."

"But I seem to be here, Sir Basil, and if I am not mistaken, that is Augusta Sandbridge in *your* box. I would suggest you approach her before you come to me with the tale." Trent swung his legs down and straightened up. He vaguely indicated another box with a sweep of his hand, and the light caught the ring on his little finger. "If you are quite finished, sir, I believe I see Brummel over there—ah, yes—and Prinny, too. I believe I'll pay a call."

"But I am not through. Dash it, sir. Is Leach telling the truth?"

"That your wife is at Lady Sandbridge's? How the devil should I know that?" Trent asked irritably as he heaved himself up to tower over the dumpy baron.

"But have you seen her?" Brockhaven persisted recklessly.

"Lady Brockhaven? I believe I once had the distinction of spilling champagne on her wedding gown."

"But have you seen her since?"

"Really, Sir Basil, I tire of this ridiculous discussion. You have insinuated yourself into my box with some farradiddle about my having taken your wife somewhere. Now, if I remember the chit, she is rather plain, and I do not consort withh plain females, Brockhaven." There was an edge to the marquess's voice.

"You have not answered my question, sir," Brockhaven snapped as he lost his temper.

Trent's hand snaked out to lift the baron until he dangled in midair by his chin. Brockhaven's florid face grew redder as he wriggled helplessly. "I choose not to dignify such a sordid story with a reply. If you persist in this nonsense, I shall conclude that you are calling me out. Certainly, I know that if I thought someone had my wife, I should be issuing a challenge rather than asking silly questions." He set Sir Basil down with deceptive gentleness. "Well?"

"Your pardon, my lord." Brockhaven's face paled now to a sickly gray, and his eyes bulged. "Of course, I did not credit the story, my lord. Heh, heh. I did but think to amuse you with the tale. I quite see I was mistaken."

"I should not repeat it anywhere, if I were you. I believe I should stay with the rumor she has consumption."

Brockhaven strained to catch another glimpse of the ring on the marquess's hand, but the light was faint. He was positive that Trent had begged the issue, but he dared not push it. He bowed stiffly and turned to leave.

"Oh, Brockhaven . . ."

"My lord?"

"You may tell Mr. Leach that he is a dead man when I see him." Trent inclined his head slightly, and a faint smile played at the corners of his mouth. "Good night, Sir Basil."

13

ELLEN SAT CURLED up in a chair before the fire in the Meadows' library with a book open on her lap as she listened to Gerald read Trent's letter. It was but a brief message telling that he'd posted an anonymous letter to her parents in London assuring them of her well-being, that he expected Gerald to see that she had whatever she needed in clothes and pocket money, and that he'd be home Christmas week.

Gerald finished reading and looked down to where she sat with a faraway expression in her eyes. There was a wistfulness on her face that touched him, and he felt compelled to drop a consoling hand on her shoulder.

"Do not be pining for him, Ellen," he advised her gently.

She gave a guilty start. "I am not pining!"

"You would have better luck in getting me into parson's mousetrap than Alex, my dear—and that's not saying much."

"Gerry, please, I am not up to even the mildest flirtation."

" 'Twas not my intent, Ellen. I was but telling you that neither of us is husband material, when it comes down to it. And while there have been dozens of women who thought to bring Trent to heel, not a one has even come close to managing the trick."

"Captain Deveraux," she sighed, "I was not even thinking of Alex, if you want the truth. His letter did but remind me that I've no right to be here hanging on his sleeve and letting him spend his money on me. I am not your poor relation, after all."

"If neither of us minds, my dear, I cannot see why that should worry you."

"But it does! Can you not see? I've not the least claim to either of you."

"Ellen, you saved his life—'tis enough. And to tell the truth, I like your company: you make intelligent conversation, you play more than a credible hand of faro, and I could listen to your music all day. Moreover," he added with feeling, "you ain't given to megrims and freaks of temper—except when you get this maggot in your brain about being beholden to us. I find myself wishing we were related, my dear, for I've no wish to have you leave." He dropped to his knees beside her chair so that he could reason face to face. "You know what?" he confided. "You remember my friend Allendar who was her yesterday? He's quite taken with you, too—went so far as to ask if I thought Alex would entertain his suit."

"What a hum, Gerry. He did no such thing." A hint of a smile crept to the corners of her mouth.

"He did—said you don't fan and flirt and preen yourself like a peacock in a man's presence, that you've got some ideas of your own in your head."

"And what do you think he would say if he knew about Sir Basil?"

"I don't know," he admitted, "but I'm telling you that you lighten this place up enough that you earn your bread here. When we have Christmas, the whole neighborhood will admire our lovely cousin."

"Now I know that is a whisker, Gerry"—she laughed in spite of herself—"for I had it from Trent himself that I was not a beauty and would not even rate a second glance were it not for my 'unusual eyes.' "

"Must've been drunk when he said it."

"No. 'Twas the morning after."

"Ah! See, that explains it."

She closed her book and set it down carefully on the table. "I have been thinking, you know, and I am convinced that I could earn my way with my music. I could go to the Continent under a false name and become a musician with an opera house in some place like Milano."

"No. Worse than being a rich man's mistress," he told

her positively, "for you'd wind up having to share your favors with a string of men to keep you fed. They don't pay much in places like that. I mean, look at the Mantini: a prime singer and—" He caught himself at the strange expression that came to Ellen's face, and then he remembered the gossip about Trent. "Well, what I am saying is that even someone like that has protectors."

"Thank you, Gerald Deveraux, for your confidence in my moral character," she muttered with unwarranted sarcasm. "You and Alex would have it that any female who tries to earn a living winds up in the muslin company."

"Didn't mean it like that, my dear, but 'tis about true. There ain't any money in playing the pianoforte." He stood up and stretched lazily. "Tell you what—let's not worry about it and take a walk in the village instead. The air's chilly, but not miserably so, and the sun's shining for a change. And since I cashed in, I am growing as fat as a toad from sitting."

"Now, that, Gerry, is a capital idea. Let me get my cloak. I promise not to keep you waiting above five minutes."

She met him in the vestibule and they walked the half-mile or so to the small village situated on the Meadows land, stopping briefly here and there while he pointed out various spots of childhood sport to her. Just before they reached the row of cotters' cottages, he stopped at a small wooden bridge. Leaning over, he pointed to the bank beneath them.

"Down there, Alex and I used to play knights. We were awful—challenged poor villagers who would cross the bridge. Alex used to take pride in his ability to knock even the most strapping lads into the water."

"And you?"

"Oh, I admit I knocked my share off also, but my specialty was the small sword. It was the only weapon I could ever best Alex with, for he was always quicker with the rapier, more accurate with the pistol, and handier with his fives."

"Poor Gerry," she sympathized.

"No, we were much like any other brothers, in spite of the title. I actually liked him—still do, as a matter of fact."

He slipped his hand to cup her elbow and steered her off the bridge and across the narrow lane to where an elderly woman swept her stoop. "Ah, Mrs. Wallace." He smiled. "Allow me to present our cousin, Mademoiselle Deveraux, come to stay with us this winter—French, you know."

"I'd a knowed she was Deveraux anywheres—got the look of ye." The old woman bobbed respectfully and gave Ellen a toothless grin.

"Thank you, ma'am," Ellen managed politely, school-ing herself to keep a straight face until they were out of the old woman's hearing. "Gerry," she murmured as she leaned closer to keep from being overheard, "do they truly not know?"

"Aside from Cousin Dominick, they've never seen an-other of us and can only guess as to the family. You forget that there is still a vast social difference between marquess and tenant."

They continued along the entire row until he stopped her again, this time to knock at the door of a small cottage much like the hunting box at Little Islip. "Button!"

"Quit your pounding, boy! I do not move so quickly as I once did," the small sprightly lady with thinning white hair admonished as she opened the door a crack. She threw it wider, and her old face lit with pleasure at the sight of him. "Gerald!"

He enveloped her in a hug and then stood back to present Ellen. The old nurse beamed at her and, before he could make the introduction, clasped her hand warmly. "So you've brought me your betrothed at last, my boy."

"Not quite." He grinned. "But I have brought a cousin, Miss Ellen Deveraux, for a visit."

The old woman looked sharply at Ellen for a moment and then nodded. "Ah—Miss Deveraux it is, then."

"I have heard about you from both Alex and Gerry," Ellen told her.

"We told her you were responsible for the ruffians we have become," he teased.

"Don't believe it, miss. 'Twas the blood. I tried to make them behave when I had charge of them." She cocked her head to look up at Ellen with renewed interest, and her old eyes twinkled. "So you know Alex, do you? I hear the tales, but he never behaved badly as a boy, I promise you. He was always truthful—even when the truth hurt him."

"He spoke of you with great affection, ma'am."

"Aye—and one of these days he'll settle down again just like his father did after he brought Lady Caroline home to the Meadows. Never was such a change in a man, I can tell you for the truth." She turned to Gerald. "You know, this one reminds me of your mother. Oh, she don't look like her, but there's something."

"Her highest compliment," he murmured in an audible aside to Ellen.

"But I forget my manners," the old woman continued brightly, "and I do go on. You'll be staying for tea, of course. Naught's baked today, but there's jam and bread and the water's hot."

"Strawberry jam?" Gerald asked hopefully.

"And what else would I be keeping, Gerry?"

They stayed nearly an hour drinking tea and listening while the nurse rattled on about the exploits of the Deveraux brothers as boys. Finally, Gerald checked his pocket watch and rose to leave. Ellen stood reluctantly and watched as he stooped to brush a kiss on the old wrinkled cheek.

"She's a fine one, Gerald," the nurse hissed wickedly. "I hope you mean to come up to scratch soon so I won't be too old to hold your babes."

"Alas, Button, but Alex has forbidden the flirtation."

"Then tell him to make an offer. I cannot be waiting forever."

Ellen colored uncomfortably and hastily mumbled her good-bye before slipping out the door. Gerald caught up with her in the tiny yard and held out his hand. She clasped it and they began the slow walk back down the lane.

"Button—Mrs. Allison—is the closest Alex and I have to a mother. I suppose that since I could not remember much about Mama, I depended more on Button than he did. She's a good soul, but she's blind to our faults."

"But why is she not still at the Meadows?"

"She left two years ago to care for an invalid sister, and then she refused to come back, saying there was no one at the big house to need her anymore. I think she just wants to see us settled."

"As though you did not have any time left. How old are you, anyway?"

"Twenty-five."

"Scarcely into your prime."

"The problem is, Ellie, that I've never found a female I thought I could live with. I took the usual trips to London for the Season and looked over the Marriage Mart, sipping nasty lemonade and eating stale cake at Almack's, but I never saw anything but empty-headed beauties. I could hear their mamas whispering to them, 'Trent's brother—he's got forty thousand at least.' It was obvious that they expected to take my money in exchange for sitting around looking fashionable at my expense. It's no wonder men turn to opera dancers and actresses and the like—they only expect part of a man's purse."

"You and Alex seem to have met the same young ladies," Ellen responded dryly. "And I cannot believe that all were like that. I'll warrant that somewhere in the background there was a papa telling them to keep their tongues and just try to marry money."

"Well, I never was inspired to look that far."

"What you need to do is to go to town next Season, Gerry, for my sister Amy is out then. She is *very* beautiful and not the least empty-headed."

"Is she like you?"

"She is much, much prettier than I ever hoped to be."

"She could not be."

"Spanish coin, Gerry," she dismissed. Suddenly, she gave a start and her fingers tightened in his. Her violet eyes widened and her face lost its color.

"What is it, Ellie? Is something the matter?"

"No, I don't think so," she answered slowly as she regained her composure. "But I thought I saw Mr. Leach over there. No, it cannot be."

He followed her direction and saw nothing. "Probably just a villager that resembles him. Who is he, anyway?"

"He was Trent's driver when we were at Little Islip

and he was discharged. You must be right—I thought Mr. Leach went to London."

"Well, you look as though you had seen a ghost. Come on—'tis time I got you home, anyway."

They returned to the Meadows in time for a light nuncheon, and then Gerald left to ride out with Trent's bailiff to visit tenants and collect the rents. Ellen watched him go and then settled in to give her novel another try. Less than fifteen pages into the story, she was interrupted by Mrs. Biddle, who announced that there was a gentleman to see her. Knowing that none knew her whereabouts except for Trent and Gerald and Gerald's friend Allendar, who had already departed for London, she decided it must be a mistake. Aside from her brief foray into the village that morning, she'd kept close to the house and none had seen her.

"Pray tell whoever it is that I am not in, Mrs. Biddle, for I know of no one who should be received when Captain Deveraux is not at home."

"I'll tell Biddle, miss."

Ellen turned back to her book thoughtfully and then dismissed her concern as she became absorbed anew in the story, a rather gothic romance Gerald had ordered for her from Hookham's. But as the heroine of the tale allowed herself to be victimized again and again by her unscrupulous relatives, Ellen finally set it aside in disgust. How very like a male author, she decided, to assume that a woman was a helpless creature. But then her thoughts brought her up short—aside from her daring escape and her care of Trent, what had she herself done to change her own destiny?

With that lowering thought, she rose and stared at the late-afternoon sky. The days were short and the sun was already fading. Her spirits declined further as she turned again to her own dilemma, and she longed to confront the marquess to resolve her situation. She missed him so terribly that sometimes she actually ached in her breast. Stop it, she chided herself severely, you cannot look to him to take care of you no matter what he says. But none of her very limited options was inviting in the least, and both Gerry and Trent had made the life of a musician sound so unappealing that she was almost ready to abandon that idea. Perhaps she would have to invent some credentials and become a governess.

Outside, the wind was coming up and the bare tree branches were rattling against the many-paned windows. There was something about the wildness, the freedom of that wind that drew her as she abandoned yet again the attempt to resolve her problems. She took her cloak from the hall closet and decided to clear her mind with a solitary walk. As she stepped out into the empty garden, now devoid of greenery, the dead leaves and small twigs crunched beneath her soft slippers. The cold air was fragrant with the smoke from the mansion's many chimneys rather than from summer's blossoms. She pushed her hood back to let the wind whip her hair, and bent into it.

She rounded the curve of the long drive and was surprised to see a coach parked on the side while the occupants argued. Since she was certain that Gerald had invited no guests, she instinctively started back toward the house. Running footsteps sounded behind her, and she began to run, too, as they drew closer. At the last minute, she turned around and saw Leach bearing down on her. Her scream was lost in the wind as his hand closed over her mouth and he wrestled her to the ground.

A coachman caught up, and together he and Leach carried her kicking and fighting back to the waiting coach, where they threw her up in the open door. She righted herself and came face to face with her despised husband.

"Basil!"

"Surprised, my dear?" he asked nastily. "I'll warrant you are not nearly so shocked as I when I found you to be Trent's latest." He smiled unpleasantly and leaned to grasp her wrist painfully with pudgy fingers. "But you find me willing to forgive this lapse on your part if you do as you are told."

"You cannot. Trent—"

"Is consoling himself with the Mantini, my dear, and I doubt he has any interest in you anymore."

He was disappointed that his news did not inflict the desired pain in her, but then perhaps the chit concealed her feelings better than most. He began to stroke her hand possessively and moved closer.

"Yes, my dear, I think I shall enjoy having you back in spite of this," he chortled, "for I have not the least doubt that now you know how to please a man."

"I would not wager on it," she answered evenly.

"You ain't increasing, are you?"

"Why?"

"I'll have no one's bastard inherit from me, Ellen. But then that's simple enough to know, isn't it? I shall just have to wait to take you until I am sure." He leaned back, quite pleased with himself for thinking of the obvious, and released her hand.

"What if I told you that I have not been Trent's mistress?"

"D'ye take me for a fool?" he snorted derisively. "There's not be another reason in the world for a man like him to look at the likes of you."

"I suppose not."

"But do not be fretting over it, my dear. Since the story is not known, I'll not repudiate you. I shall, however, expect the utmost in correct behavior in the future. And," he added significantly, "I shall expect you to give him the cut direct if you ever chance to see him."

"Given your circles, Basil, I doubt I shall encounter him."

"Aye—and he is not given to hanging after his discards, either."

Her mind worked feverishly while she tried to follow his conversation. "How have you managed to conceal my absence?" she asked suddenly.

"Your Aunt Sandbridge did that for me—gave out that you was suffering from consumption."

"I have never been ill in my life," she told him flatly.

"Nevertheless, my dear, you will be pleased to appear fatigued until a recovery is effected."

She eyed the rotund baron with distaste, mentally comparing him to the tall, muscular marquess like night unto day. Finally, she favored him with a contemptuous shrug. "Well, I daresay that if you insist on appearing in clothes like those, I shall be fatigued."

He looked down on his coat and waistcoat in alarm and demanded to know, "And what, pray, is wrong with them?"

His aggrieved tone told her that she had found her weapon in repelling her odious husband. She managed to laugh as she allowed her eyes to sweep over the offending garments. "But, my lord, they make you the veriest quiz—they accentuate your roundness, I assure you."

"Roundness?" he fairly howled in indignation as his florid complexion darkened to the shade of a cooked beet. "Listen, you ingrate," he seethed as he slapped her hard across her face, "you ought to be grateful that I am willing to take Trent's leavings."

"Grateful?" she scoffed. "And why should I be grateful for that? If the story were common knowledge, you'd divorce me. I should like to shout the tale from the rooftops, if you must know." She could feel the sting where his hand had hit her, but she refused to acknowledge the blow at all. "No, Sir Basil, I am not grateful at all."

He leaned closer to her and hissed, "One day, dear wife, I shall be teaching you a lesson that you'll not soon forget. Until then, I have nothing else to say on the subject." He drew back and turned to stare in sullen silence out his window.

The entire journey back to London was spent in cold silence, with neither party deigning to speak to the other as the hours and the miles rolled by. Occasionally, Brockhaven allowed himself to steal a glance at his wife's proud profile. Damn the chit! Didn't she know she would be disgraced if he repudiated her. She ought to be on her knees pleading for his understanding, but she was far from that. He fairly seethed with a sense of ill usage. She was the Marquess of Trent's cast-off, and yet butter wouldn't melt in her mouth. Well, he'd teach the chit a thing or two—once he was certain she was not increasing. And he'd drag her out into society under close guard and show her off.

As Brockhaven's carriage sped down the London road, Ellen's disappearance was being discovered back at the Meadows. Captain Deveraux returned and dressed for dinner while thinking Ellen was doing the same. But once in the huge dining room, he waited patiently for the always-punctual girl to appear. The ever-present Edward hovered expectantly by her empty chair ready to begin service of the meal. Finally, after nearly twenty minutes, Gerald nodded to the footman.

"You may tell Miss Deveraux' maid that we are waiting dinner for her mistress."

A few moments later, the maid herself appeared cautiously at the dining-room door. "Beggin' yer pardon, sir, but she ain't here."

"Dash it! It isn't like her to miss a meal."

"She went out—one of the downstairs maids saw her," Edward explained.

"Out? It's dark!"

"As to that, sir, I believe she left several hours ago. I think we should send out a search party," the footman offered. "Had I been informed earlier, I would have done so on my own."

"Well, now we all know," Gerald muttered tersely. "Set up a hue and cry, though what we'll find in the dark, I don't know. And send someone to the village, take lanterns and walk down the road, do what you have to do. No one eats in this house until she is found." Gerald flung himself into the hall while calling for his cloak and pistol.

Biddle shook his head and looked at his wife. "Never seen him so upset. It begins to look like he's thrown his hat over the windmill for the gel, don't it?"

"The marquess'll never stand for it if he has," she murmured cryptically before turning her attention to her own tasks. "We'll have to have a cold collation laid to feed them when they come back, I daresay."

The search party combed the entire drive, the lane into town, the fields on either side of the road, and finally the village itself. Gerald was becoming frantic. Alex had left the girl in his care. He stomped into the local pub, scattering people and chairs before him.

"The devil's loose—look at 'im!"

"Naw, 'tis the Cap'n—th' Devil's in Lunnon."

The red glow of the fire and the cheap tallow candles gave an eerie aspect to Gerald Deveraux' face as he demanded the attention of the assembled drinkers.

"My cousin, Miss Deveraux, is missing!" he shouted above the crowd to be heard. "I need your help." He lofted a purse that clinked with coins. "This to the man who finds her."

They all looked at one another. Quality missing? Whoever heard of a missing lady? Something bad must've happened to her, but it was going to be hard to find anyone in the chill darkness. Gerald lofted the bag of gold higher. Well, for the size of the purse, they'd give it a try. The men began casting about for wood to use as torches and then moved out into the deserted lane to start the search.

Only the blacksmith hung back for a word with Gerald. Almost diffidently the burly man approached until he caught Gerry's attention by calling out, "Sor—yer pardon, sor, but 'appen a gent arst fer 'er just t'day."

"Who?"

"Dunno. A fat'un, qualitylike, but queer."

"Queer? How?"

"Niver seen none t' wear nuthin' like hit."

Gerald racked his brain for anyone who could have resembled the big fellow's description and came up empty. None knew her whereabouts to ask about her. They'd been too careful to keep her sheltered at the Meadows. But someone had given her a start in the village that very morning. What was the name she'd murmured—Leach? Damn! He should never have chanced taking her out of the house. He hesitated and then tossed the bag of coins at the smithy. "Here."

"Here yersel', Cap'n." The fellow threw it back neatly. "Don't like fer nothin' ter 'appen t' a lady."

Gerald's heart sank with the cold realization that Ellen had met no accident. There could be only one person who would find it necessary to abduct her from Trent's protection. "Brockhaven," he half-whispered to himself. "Damn his impudent eyes," he yelled aloud as he broke his riding whip over the nearest chairback. "If Alex doesn't kill him over this, then by God, I shall!"

Within the hour, he was riding hell-bent for London, accompanied by the still-mending Timms and two man-servants. That it was November and cold did not seem to be a consideration for the captain or Timms, and the others had the good sense not to grumble openly. By carriage, they were some six hours from London, but the ride could be cut to less than four on a swift horse. And both Trent and his brother kept horses at post houses on the way.

By three in the morning, they were rousting out the household at Trent's town house in St. James's. The affronted butler was about to turn them away when he caught sight of Gerald Deveraux in the lantern light.

"Captain! A fine time to be calling, sir. Thought you was at the Meadows."

"I was, Crabtree. Where's Trent?" Gerald demanded brusquely.

"He's out, sir."

"Where?"

"I am sure I do not know, Captain."

"Damn! I have to find him! Now!"

Crawfurd, still clad in his nightshirt, with a wrapper clutched to his chest, appeared over the stair railing to see to the commotion. "Sir, thought you was at home!"

"Where is he, Crawfurd? I have to reach Trent. Ellie's missing!"

The valet came down the stairs two at a time. "Miss Ellen? His lordship'll have a fit." He caught Gerald's impatient expression and hastened to answer, "I should look to the Mantini, sir."

"Lud, is that still going on? No matter. Her direction, man, out with it!"

"Half Moon. Down by the end." Crawfurd nodded. "But wait, I am going with you."

"You're a valet, man."

"And I can carry a cudgel with the best of them, sir, if the need be. Besides, if anything has happened to Miss Ellen, there'll be the devil to pay where my lord is concerned." Without waiting for Gerald to refuse him, Crawfurd disappeared back into his chamber.

"Devil a bit!" Gerald muttered. "I have not the time to wait. Timms! Have you the Mantini's direction?"

"Aye, sir!" Trent's driver limped up behind him.

"Leg still paining you, Timms?"

"Don't mind it, sir."

"We'll take the second coach. You can drive better than you can ride, I daresay. Come on."

"I am ready, Captain," Crawfurd announced from the stairs above with as much dignity as he could muster while still tucking his shirttail into his pants.

"Captain Gerry," the butler remonstrated, "you cannot mean to intrude on his lordship!"

Without answering, Gerald, Timms, and Crawfurd pushed past the scandalized Crabtree and back out into the night.

"Gor!" a footman breathed behind them, "they mean to roust the Devil!"

14

SOPHIA MANTINI STUDIED the magnificent ruby necklace before raising her eyes to the marquess. At first, the high-tempered beauty had been unable to believe that she held his parting gift to her. Her mercenary mind debated whether to make a scene or to accept the fact that their liaison was at an end. He'd been different since he returned to London the week before—inattentive, distant, and preoccupied—so much so, in fact, that he'd shown no interest in sharing her bed. No, it was over and it was time to admit it. Besides, something in his expression told her it would be useless to plead. Well, he'd been generous enough with his money that she had no complaint. She stared a long moment at the handsome, impassive face and sighed.

"There's someone else?"

"Yes."

"She must be very beautiful, Alex."

"Not in the usual way, Sophie, but I find her attractive."

"And so the dashing Marquess of Trent mounts another mistress," the singer managed through twisted lips.

"No, Sophie . . ." He hesitated, picking his words carefully. "You cannot pretend that you expected it to last, my dear. You are no more constant in your affections than I have been." He gave her a brief, wry smile. "My salad days are over."

"Am I to wish you happy, then?"

"No. I would it were so simple, but it is not. Goodbye, Sophie."

He bent to kiss her one last time, brushing his lips

chastely against the artfully rouged cheek. Behind him, the door burst open to admit Gerald, Timms, and Crawfurd. Trent spun around, his hand instinctively reaching for the rapier he'd left in his coach.

"What the devil—Gerry!"

"Madame, I tried," Sophia Mantini's butler explained from behind the captain, "but they would not listen!"

"Signor! I demand an explanation," she flashed indignantly. "You have invaded my house!"

Ignoring everyone but Alex, Gerald blurted out, "It's Ellie—she's been abducted."

The color drained from Trent's face and the room spun around him crazily. Time stood still until he exhaled slowly to master the rush of emotion he felt. "When?" he demanded tersely.

"Before dinner, but we did not miss her until we sat down. I set up a hue and cry, but 'twas too late. The smithy said someone had asked about her in the village earlier and she saw someone called Leach when we walked down to Button's."

"Brockhaven," Trent muttered succinctly. "Damn! I should have known. He asked about her the other night. I should have sent warning." The color flooded back into his face and his blue eyes blazed. "I'll kill him—I'll kill the bloody beast! I swear if he has touched her, I'll carve him like a fat pig," he shouted as he brushed past the stunned Mantini.

The night air was like a cold bath when it hit him. Gerald caught up with him before he reached his carriage and told him, "I brought the other coach, Alex, and the horses are ready. Do we roust Brockhaven at his house and see if he dared bring her here? He could have taken her to the country, you know."

"Either way, his servants will know his direction."

"Are you armed? I brought pistols in the coach."

"When am I ever not? Aye, I've got my pistol, and the rapier's in my carriage—it discourages impertinences." He turned and barked to Dobbs, "Hand me my sword and take home the carriage. Alert the household that we must be ready to travel. Crawfurd, go with him and see that all is packed in case I have to flee. And, Crawfurd . . ."

"Aye, my lord?"

"See that we have enough money to support us in France." Turning back to Gerald, he was all business now, and his anger had cooled to that deadly calm that inspired awe and fear in his fellows. "I mean to take her away this time, Gerry, and be damned with the consequences. Are you with me in this?"

"You know I am."

"Then let's go. Timms, do you remember Brockhaven's address?"

"Aye, yer lor'ship."

Trent swung up into the carriage and Gerald followed. Settling himself opposite, Gerry shook his head. "There'll be a devil of a dust over this, Alex. You cannot kill him to get his wife."

"She's not his wife!" For a moment, his temper flared again.

"The *ton* won't see it that way."

"She cannot go to that fat toad, Gerry. I cannot let her!"

"Aye." Gerald nodded in the darkness. "You promised her."

"I love her, Gerry—I cannot deny it. I have but come to my senses and realized that I don't want to live without her. I mean to have her if I have to kill Brockhaven to get her, and then live out of the country for the rest of my life." Trent's anger had faded, replaced by a sober determination. "But I will not tell her until I can get her free of him. I have to offer her more than a slip of the shoulder."

"The scandalmongers won't know the difference."

"I will. Gerry, if I don't have to kill him to gain her freedom, I mean to stay here until I can make the arrangements to marry her. If I do, if for some reason I have to make her a widow, I'll be coming with you. Otherwise, I leave it to you to see that her arrival in Paris is unremarked."

"I'd tell her, Alex. I'd tell her what you mean to do."

"No. She must be free when I make my offer."

The coach came to a jarring halt in front of the darkened Brockhaven residence. There was no sign of life without or within, but Trent was not to be denied. He leapt down from his coach and began pounding on the baron's door.

"Open up! Open up! 'Tis the watch," he shouted.

In a matter of several minutes, lights began flickering at windows as people stirred inside. Finally, the thick panes by the door lightened and grumbling servants could be heard muttering oaths inside before the door swung open.

"Here—here! The watch, you say?"

The still-dressing butler peered out at Alex. Trent pushed past him into the foyer and waited for Gerald and Timms to follow.

"You are not the watch!"

"How very observant you are," Trent murmured almost apologetically as he leveled his pistol to point it at the man. "But then, I could scarce expect you to open the door if I used my name, could I?" He gestured with his other hand toward the maids and footmen who peered cautiously around corners. "Fetch Sir Basil!" His mouth curved in that strange smile of anticipation, chilling the cowering servants. "Tell him Trent is come to settle accounts."

"At this time of the morning, my lord?" the fellow protested incredulously. "Can it not wait? Besides, his lordship is not at home.'

"Where is he, then?" Trent tapped the toe of his dress shoe impatiently. "Out with it—where?"

"I believe him to be at his club, sir."

Trent cocked his pistol and waited while the man squirmed under his cold-eyed stare. "I don't believe you."

"I-I am t-telling the truth, I swear! He and Lady Brockhaven had a row and he left some three hours ago! For the love of God, sir, do not point that at me!"

"She is here, then? Where?"

"She is asleep, my lord. But if you were wishful of waiting for his lordship, I will procure some Madeira for you, and you may wait in the book room."

"Not this morning, I am afraid. No, I have a rather more entertaining reception planned for him." Turning again to Gerald, his exhilaration at having found Ellen was obvious. "Gerry, you and Timms escort the servants to the cellar and lock them up. And see that the lights in the front of the house are doused in case he should return before I am ready."

"The cellar?" a maid squeaked in alarm. "There's rats down there."

"Then take candles," Trent snapped. "Come on, there's little time."

"You heard him," Gerald prompted, his own pistol trained on a nearby footman. "Move! Alex?"

"I am going after Ellen."

As he mounted the steps two at a time, he could hear the protests of Brockhaven's servants behind him. It was pitch-dark in the upper hall, so much so that he could not see the last few treads. Gaining the hallway, he found it so dark that he couldn't make out the doors. With a curse muttered under his breath, he groped his way around a corner and stumbled against some sort of bench or table. A candlestick fell of and the candle rolled against his foot. He bent, felt around on the floor, and found it. Fumbling in his pocket for his flint, he drew it out and sparked the wick of the taper several times until it caught at last. Then he held the flickering flame up to faintly illuminate the hall and moved slowly from door to door trying to remember the approximate location of where she'd jumped. He picked one that he judged to be in the right area and nudged it open to reveal an empty bed-chamber. A glance into the shadows told him what he wanted to know: the valet stand draped with a man's coat gave proof he'd found Brockhaven's chamber. He edged over to the window and looked down to the bushes below, marveling at the courage it must have taken for her to have even attempted such a jump. He tried the doors that led off the main bedchamber, discovering an assortment of closets and a dressing room, until he found one locked. Carefully setting the candle in a holder, he turned his shoulder and threw his weight against the door with such force that the casing splintered and the lock gave way, sending him staggering into the tiny room. He righted himself against a bedpost and looked down where a sliver of light from the broken door fell narrowly across the bed.

Ellen turned over at the sound and then readjusted her position in her sleep. Her dark hair spilled over the pillowcase and into the shadows, and her closed lashes lay like black fringe against white cheek while her bared arm cradled her head. He stared reverently for a moment before reaching to touch her face lightly and trace its contour with his fingertip. "Sleepyhead," he murmured affectionately. "Ellie."

Instead of opening her eyes beneath his touch, she recoiled and shut them tighter, screaming out, "Aiiieee, aiiiieeee!"

"Shhhh, Ellie, it's me! It's Alex! You are safe!" He shook her awake and dropped down beside her to cradle her against him. "You are all right, Ellie. I've come for you."

Her eyes opened wide to stare in disbelief before she let out a sob and turned her head into his shoulder. It was no dream. She could feel the heavy wool of his cloak against her cheek and the pressure of his strong arms about her. He was there in the flesh, cradling her, rocking her gently, and making soothing sounds into her hair. She began to cry with relief.

"Ellie, Ellie, it's all right, love." He smoothed her hair against her head and held her close. "Gad, girl, but you gave us a fright. I should have stayed at the Meadows with you and he'd not have dared to be so bold." Slowly, her shaking subsided, but she made no move to push away from him. "He didn't hurt you—I mean, he didn't . . ." He could not bring himself to ask outright if Brockhaven had forced his attentions on her.

She shook her head against his shoulder and gave a watery chuckle. "No. He said he wanted to be sure I was not increasing first. He thought I—that I have been your mistress."

"Filthy swine!" He ruffled her hair to hide the intense emotion he felt for her. "Listen, Ellie, I am taking you to a safer place."

"I cannot stand him, Alex."

"I know, I know." He was loathe to release her, but time was short. "Come on." He eased off the bed and pulled her up with him. "You've a long way to go before you are missed again. Here . . ." He pulled out his handkerchief and began dabbing at the tear streaks.

Her eyes filled again and she threw herself against his chest again. "Oh, Alex, I am so very glad you came for me. I cannot repay—you cannot *know*—"

"Shhhhh, Ellie, I understand," he murmured low. "It's

all right. I have you safe." He gently disengaged her arms and tilted her chin up to look at him. "I'll not let him have you, I promise—word of a Deveraux." He frowned slightly and dropped his hand. "You know, don't you, that I'll do what I can to stop the scandal, but things may get unpleasant. I can take you away, but I may not be able to stop the gossip."

"I can bear it," she sniffed. "Brockhaven thinks I am your mistress anyway."

"Well, we know differently, and that's what really matters, isn't it?"

"I see you have found her," Gerald observed as he walked in with a branch of candles, "and by the looks of it, you've turned her into a watering pot." Ellen moved self-consciously away from Trent and wiped her eyes with the back of her hand as Gerald drew closer. "Hallo, Ellie. A devil of a time you've given me, my dear. I have not yet had my dinner."

"Oh, Gerry, thank you!" Heedless of her nightdress, she hugged him gratefully. Trent watched with an arrested expression as his brother's arms closed around her tightly.

"Enough of that." His voice sounded unusually harsh even to his own ears. "There's no telling how much time we have, both of you. Gerry, you will take her 'round by the house and get whatever funds Crawfurd has collected and then you will take her to Dover and catch the packet to France." His eyes traveled to Ellen and his gaze softened perceptibly. "And this time, my dear, I think you should have a decent wardrobe. Gerry will roll up the contents of the closets in the bedsheets and drop them down to Timms, who waits outside. They'll be more than a trifle creased, but I expect we'll find a French maid to press them."

Gerald nodded. "And you, Alex?"

Trent fingered the rapier he'd brought with him. "I intend to wait for Brockhaven."

The gesture was not lost on Ellen and she paled. "Alex—no! You cannot force a quarrel on him for my sake. You'll be disgraced and have to flee."

"It wouldn't be the first time, my dear. Either way, I mean to join you at Dover and see you off to Calais. It's my quarrel now, Ellie. The cur came to *my* house to get you." He caught her hand and lifted her fingers to his lips, brushing them lightly. She drew back as though burned. "Best get dressed, unless you plan on traveling in that fetching but rather chilly nightdress." He stepped out into Brockhaven's chamber and listened for a moment. "I think 'tis safe to go out by the stairs this time, my dear."

"Alex," she tried desperately, "I despise Brockhaven, but I cannot let you do this for me. I would rather stay here than bring scandal to your name."

"How very noble of you, Ellie"—he smiled wryly— "and how very ridiculous. The Deveraux are no strangers to scandal, and my own reputation is beyond repair in spite of that farradiddle I told you on the road to York. You'll go with Gerry if I have to throw your clothes on you and carry you out to the carriage myself. And whether it is general knowledge yet or not, we are scandal-bound already, and have been since that night you dropped into my arms. Now, unless you want to see the pig carved before your eyes, you'll get ready." To prevent further protest, he turned on his heel and stalked out.

"Gerry, what am I to do? Surely you see that he cannot, that he *must not* suffer for his kindness to me."

"I'd advise you to get dressed, unless you favor 'twould being dressed by a man, my dear, though I admit 'twould be the reverse of what he is used to," Gerald told her with a grin. "Oh, come on, Ellie. Alex does not do anything he does not want to. Buck up, girl! I can think of dozens of females who'd give anything to be going off with Trent." He threw open a wardrobe door and began stripping gowns off hangers. "Here"—he shoved one at her— "this looks passable, but you'd best wear a petticoat in addition to the pantalettes, for it gets deuced cold in the coach this time of year."

They were impossible, the both of them, she decided with a sigh as she shook out the dress. "Gerry, I cannot put this on with you here," she reminded him.

"I'll turn my back," he promised while he deposited several more gowns on the bed coverlet and bent to tie them up. Moving to a bureau, he opened a drawer and dumped its contents on a blanket. "But if it bothers you, my dear, you can go behind those doors."

"Gerry—"

He finished tying up that bundle and directed his attention to removing the contents of the other wardrobe. "But if you insist on being missish about it, I suppose this will be enough, anyway." A blast of cold air blew in as he opened the French windows and threw out her clothes. "There. I'll wait outside if you will hurry," he murmured while reshutting the windows.

As soon as the door closed behind him, she had the blue gown pulled over her head even as she divested herself of the night rail. In a matter of seconds, she was twitching the hem down to cover her legs before stepping into a pair of lace-trimmed pantalettes.

"Decent, Ellie?" Trent asked as he pushed the door open.

"Much good it would do if I weren't! Alex, can you never knock and wait?" she complained.

He watched the blush creep becomingly into her cheeks and grinned. "Can't do the buttons on this one either? Here, turn 'round and I'll have you done up in a trice." He reached behind her and began fastening the back of her dress. "But first let's get your hair out of your gown before it gets all tangled up." He lifted the thick hair up and let it fall down her back, but did not remove his hand. Almost involuntarily, his fingers traced a line from the nape of her neck to her earlobe and then tipped her chin up. She had the oddest sensation that he meant to kiss her, and her pulses raced at the thought.

"Ahem," Gerald cleared his throat diplomatically behind them. "We need to be going and I need to eat something, Alex. *I* did not spend my night dining and flirting."

Trent watched Ellen stiffen, but he silently thanked his brother for interrupting—Brockhaven's bedchamber was scarcely the place for a declaration. He chucked her under the chin in a brotherly gesture. "Quite right, Gerry. Do not forget warm bricks when you stop by the house."

"And you, Alex, if both carriages are gone—"

"I'll purloin one of Brockhaven's nags and ride it home."

"All right. Come on, Ellie. I mean to raid the larder while the bricks are warming." Gerald took her by the arm and propelled her purposefully toward the hall. "If we are fortunate, Trent's cook will make us up a basket to take along."

Alex watched them from the window as they left the house below, and then he turned back to Brockhaven's bedchamber. Divesting himself of his coat, his neckcloth, and his shoes, he pulled a wing chair up to the window and helped himself to a decanter of the baron's Madeira. Sipping pensively, he waited for the London sun to come up. His head was remarkably clear for his having been up all night, and he felt at ease for the first time in weeks. An odd smile played at the corners of his mouth as he let his thoughts wander to Ellen Marling. If anyone had told him three months before that he would be caught by the merest dab of a female . . . No, not true, he decided—she was not a mere anything, she was a truly extraordinary female. Still, it was hard to credit—he'd certainly fought admitting it—but it was true. Neither the Mantini nor any of the other pleasures of London had been able to keep her out of his thoughts since he'd returned to town. Not even the most reckless pursuit of bachelor pastimes could blur the memory of the dark-haired, violet-eyed girl he'd shared such an adventure with. If only there weren't Brockhaven, he'd marry her in a trice and count himself the most fortunate of fellows.

He finished his drink and put aside the decanter and glass. He could afford nothing less than a clear head at this point. Reaching for his foil, he sat back and flexed the long, thin blade against the palm of his hand. He wasn't even sure what he meant to do with Brockhaven. Now, if the man had dared to touch her, the choice would have been made: the baron's life would be forfeit. But Gerald was right: killing a man to get his wife would ensure scandal. And a divorce would be disastrous. An annulment would be best, of course, but then it would be difficult to get a pompous fool like Brockhaven to admit to the world that he'd never bedded his young wife.

He was still mulling over the possibilities when he heard the baron below trying to rouse his household. He leaned back in the wing chair and waited, savoring the thought of the impending meeting. The next few minutes would determine his future, and he was ready.

After persistent knocking failed to bring any servants, Brockhaven had to let himself into the house. Oddly, there was no sign of anyone in the hall nor in the kitchen. Hmmmm—it must be earlier than he'd thought, he decided as he weaved his way upstairs. His thoughts too turned to Ellen Marling and a sense of injury came over him. It seemed that his encounters with her were never to live up to his expectations. Even now, instead of welcoming him as her savior after Trent had discarded her, the chit flung insults at him! He stopped at a mirror in the upstairs hall and tried to make out his reflection in the dimly illuminated mirror. How dare she make such remarks about his dress!

He turned sideways to study his rose-point tapestry coat with its exaggerated swallow tails and then held it open to admire the robin's-egg blue satin lining. No, he was as fine as fivepence, he consoled himself.

He moved on to his bedchamber, satisfied with his good taste. It suddenly occurred to him that there was no sign of the ever-present valet hovering about to help him undress. And as he walked into the room, he could see out of the corner of his eye that the door to Ellen's makeshift cell was open. He *knew* he'd locked it before he'd left. If one of those incompetents in his household had taken pity on the girl, he'd turn him off in a trice. He pushed his door wider and was totally unprepared for the scene of devastation and disorder that greeted him. Bedclothes were torn off the bed, drawers had been ransacked, and wardrobe doors hung open with empty hangers dangling off them.

"Ellen," he called out in alarm. "Ellen!"

Black-clad legs swung around the side of the wing chair as the Marquess of Trent righted himself with his steel-bladed foil bent into a bow between his hands. Towering over the stunned Brockhaven, he asked softly, "Tell me, Sir Basil, have you ever seen a hog butchered?"

"Milord!" Brockhaven goggled as he backed toward the door.

"Your servant, Baron," Trent acknowledged with a mocking bow. "Well, have you?"

"What?"

"Seen a hog butchered?" Trent released the point of

his blade and brought it to rest against the baron's quivering fat stomach. "Dear me, do you call this hideous thing a waistcoat, Basil? I find it offensive in the extreme." With a slight flick of his wrist, he deftly removed one of the buttons of the garment in question, causing it to fly off. "Ah, definitely offensive." Another button sailed off and pinged against a windowpane. "Do let me help you out of it," he murmured as he flipped off the last one.

"W-what t-the d-devil d'ye think you are d-doing?" Brockhaven whimpered while beads of perspiration popped out on his forehead.

Trent raised his blade to the base of the baron's earlobe. The point pricked and drew blood. Brockhaven squirmed as he felt a warm rivulet trickle down his neck and disappear into his neckcloth. He wet his lips nervously and stared helplessly at the marquess.

"But I return to our earlier conversation, dear Basil. I have only seen it once," Trent went on, "and I have never forgotten the scene. You see, they . . ." He paused briefly to dig the blade against Brockhaven's ear. "They slit its throat from ear to ear, and then they hang it upside down until all the blood drains out. Have you ever been hung by your heels, Brockhaven?"

"Wh-what do you w-want?" the baron's voice croaked and cracked.

"You trespassed, Basil. I cannot allow that to go unchallenged."

"You had my wife!"

"Not your wife, Brockhaven—the lady you forced to wed you," Trent pointed out reasonably. "Not the same thing at all. She doesn't want to be your wife—she never did. And I do not wish to see her do anything she does not wish to."

"But she married me!"

The blade moved lightly along the fold of Brockhaven's chin, drawing blood in its wake. The baron closed his eyes and swayed in terror, too afraid to move and too afraid to stay.

"You definitely have too many chins, Sir Basil. I wonder, perhaps you would look better without one of them," Trent mused aloud.

"For God's sake, Trent!"

"I may be forced to take your life, Brockhaven."

"No." It was a bare croak. "F-for the love of G-God!"

"For the love of the woman you call your wife, Basil. I want Ellen Marling. Tell me how I am to get her with you alive and I will listen." The blade reached Brockhaven's other ear, leaving an ugly scratch across his throat. "Well?"

"I-I-I'll d-divorce her! I will, I-I swear! I'll put up the b-bill myself!"

Trent appeared to consider and then shook his head. "No," he decided finally, "I don't think so. Too much of a scandal, you know, and I am afraid I cannot allow her to be publicly embarrassed."

"B-but I'll be a b-bigger embarrassment dead," the baron expostulated. "You cannot murder a man for his wife in England, sir."

"Can't I?" Trent asked softly. "I would not be so sure, my dear baron. But you could be right. I might consider letting you keep your miserable existence if you seek an annulment."

"An annulment!" Brockhaven said the word with such indignation that Trent felt compelled to increase the pressure on the blade tip until the baron capitulated. "All right," Brockhaven muttered finally with a mouth almost too dry for speech.

Trent dropped the rapier tip to rest against his own thigh and stepped back. His eyes were mercilessly cold as he nodded curtly to Brockhaven to sit. The baron dropped heavily into the nearest chair and grasped the wine decanter, uncorking it and drinking straight from the bottle to wet his mouth. He wiped his full lips with the back of his hand and eyed the rapier to ensure that it was well out of range. "I don't see what you want with her, my lord. She must've shown you more than she showed me. She ain't exactly in your style," he sneered nastily.

"We are not here to discuss her," Trent interrupted coldly. "I believe the subject was an annulment."

"Annulment—divorce—what difference?"

"Because when I marry her, Brockhaven, I do not wish her to live under any more scandal than necessary. With a divorce, people might intimate that things are not exactly as they should be."

Brockhaven forgot himself and lurched forward with a start. "Marry her!" He nearly choked on the words. "You are a bigger fool then than I have heard, sir! Marry your mistress?"

The blade arched swiftly up and pricked the baron's stomach. "I will say this one time and one time only," Trent bit off each word precisely. "Ellen Marling has never been my mistress and never will be. I intend to make her my marchioness—with your blood on my hands, if need be. Let me remind you"—he dug the point uncomfortably into the fat man's corset—"I can disembowel you easily with one quick turn of my wrist, and I should enjoy doing it. Now, the choice is yours: an annulment and your total silence on the matter, or a period to your existence."

"I said I'd give you what you want." Brockhaven shrank back against his chair in alarm. "I will!" The blade was lifted and he fell limp with relief. "I should have taken the younger one, anyway," he muttered.

"No, I don't think it wise." Trent shook his head. "For it was for the younger one that she was brought to sacrifice herself. You will find someone totally unknown to Ellen Marling to spare her the pain of thinking herself somehow responsible for another female's suffering." Trent reached across Sir Basil and picked up the decanter. Moving to fill the glass he'd used earlier, he poured himself a drink and pulled up a chair facing the baron. Taking a sip, he leaned forward and fixed the baron with those cold eyes. "Remember, I have a damnable temper when I am lied to. Breathe a word of this to anyone and I will be compelled to finish what I came here to do this morning. Say even one disparaging word about her to anyone and you are a dead man. Attempt to see her again and your miserable life is forfeit. And should the occasion arise that you ever meet in society, you will meet her direct, be pleasant, and move on. Do you quite understand me, sir?"

Brockhaven shuddered and looked away before nodding. "Aye, I understand, but you cannot keep the *ton* from talking, my lord. Do not be blaming me for what is said— you cannot escape the scandal even if my lips are sealed. People will want to know why I am seeking an annulment."

Trent appeared absorbed in buttoning the stud at his wrist and adjusting his sleeve. "I believe consumption to be your best explanation, Sir Basil. 'Twill be said merely that you wished for a healthy heir."

"And then how's it to look when you turn 'round and marry her?"

"I expect to be out of the country then for her protection. I daresay when we return, 'twill be found she was misdiagnosed and has made a rather remarkable recovery. No doubt being removed from the presence of your altogether hideous waistcoats will have a reviving effect on her spirits—after a decent time, of course." Trent slid his foot forward to slip on one of his shoes. "Get the other one for me, will you? And be a useful host, Basil, and hand me my coat. I really must be off if I am to get her on a packet by nightfall." He reached to take the shoe from the baron's hand and eased it onto his other foot, and then stood to shrug into his perfectly cut coat. "You really ought to try Stultz, my dear fellow—he is an excellent tailor." He eased the shirt cuffs to the edge of the coat sleeves and then turned back to Brockhaven with the faintest smile. "I regret that I am afoot and have need of one of your nags, but I shall send it back later today." He smoothed back the unruly black locks and set his hat at an angle. "Until next we meet, Brockhaven."

"I assure you there is no need, my lord. 'Twill all be as you ask."

"Ah, but I intend to leave nothing to chance. You will apply immediately and I will see that you get the Prince Regent's backing for it. Good day, Basil."

Trent let himself out of Brockhaven's house and made his way to the carriage house behind it. Whistling softly, he led out a horse, saddled it, and mounted. Riding around to the front, he stopped to look up at the window where she'd jumped into his arms, and he saw Brockhaven watching, white-faced. He lifted his hat in mock salute, and then, still in full evening dress, he edged the horse out into the early-morning bustle of the London streets, fully satisfied with himself.

15

DRAWING BACK THE heavy matelassé hangings, Ellen stared out at the wispy snowflakes falling from the overcast sky to the slushy, dirty Parisian street below. The weather, she sighed as she dropped the hanging, was very much like her own spirits: poor and unlikely to improve.

It had been almost seven weeks since they'd fled London, and her situation was still unresolved. Seven weeks since Trent had hastily brushed a brotherly kiss across her cheek and pushed her aboard the packet with Gerald at Dover. He had business to finish in London, he'd told her, but would follow as soon as he could. Business. She'd overheard Timms and Crawfurd marveling that Gerry'd dared to invade the Mantini's house to get Trent that night, so she knew very well what business Alex had meant. Well, she'd chided herself often enough, why shouldn't he entertain himself with his opera singer? Plain Ellen Marling had no real claim to him anyway. And yet, when he'd come for her at Brockhaven's . . . She let her thoughts wander back to that night as she often did these days. He'd been so kind, loving almost, but then he'd sent her off. She sighed heavily again and moved to warm her hands at the fire that blazed in the marble hearth.

Behind her, Gerald set aside the English paper he'd received in the last post and murmured sympathetically, "Weather got you blue-deviled again? Tell you what, Ellie. As soon as it clears enough, we'll bundle up and take a drive. Perhaps you would like to see if Madame Latille has an idea for the blue velvet Alex sent over—a new pelisse perhaps?"

"No." Without turning around, she muttered under her breath, "I have enough clothes for three females now—and I have nowhere to go to wear them."

"I like to see you in pretty things, Ellie," he reminded her quietly, "and so does Alex."

"Does he? Then why isn't he here?" A sob caught in her throat and she had to swallow hard to stifle it. "Gerry, it's been seven weeks. Count them—seven weeks!"

"He told you—he had business left in London. Ellie . . ." He rose and came up behind her, taking her by the shoulders and turning her to face him. "You know that. It isn't like he's forgotten you, my dear, when he writes to us every week, and at Christmas he—"

"He writes to you and asks about me."

"He sent you the amethysts for Christmas," he persisted.

"That I cannot keep! Gerry, I am beholden enough to the both of you that I cannot repay what you have expended on me if I live to be a hundred. I-I cannot take jewelry—like—like I am some sort of fancy piece! And do not be talking to me of his business, Gerry, when I know very well what it is."

"Ellie, Ellie, you do not know at all."

"Gerry, I am so miserable. You do not understand," she cried as she burst into tears.

He wrapped her in his arms and held her close. "I know you love Alex, if that's what you mean," he told her softly as she gave full vent to her frustration and wept into his shoulder. "You do, don't you?"

"No! Oh, yes, but . . ."

"Then everything's going to be all right, Ellie, I swear. Alex should be here soon and everything will be fine. Here . . ." He fumbled in his coat pocket for his handkerchief and handed it to her. "Blow your nose, my dear, and pull yourself together. You are getting one of Stultz's finest coats all wet. Come on," he coaxed gently, "all you need is some sunshine and Alex to lift your spirits."

"No." She shook her head as she took the kerchief. "What I need you will not hear of, Gerry. I need to get on with my life and quit hanging on the Deveraux sleeves for everything."

"Best let Alex take care of you."

"I cannot let him take care of me. 'Tis not his responsibility—can you not understand?" she cried out in frustration. Then, seeing his sympathetic expression, she relented. "I am sorry, Gerry. I am out-of-reason cross and I know it. I rip up at you for what is not your fault." She turned away and blew her nose, sniffed, and tried to compose herself.

"Tell you what," he offered. "Since we cannot go out, we can play cards and have ourselves a touch of that hot punch the cook makes."

"Only if you promise not to let me win again." She managed a contrite little smile and nodded. "I know you think you are finding a polite way to give me an allowance, do not think I do not, but no one could be as decidedly unlucky at cards as you have been these past weeks."

"Untrue. Whether you admit it or not, my dear, you are a veritable Captain Sharp. However, I promise to do my best to win back some of my money if that will satisfy you. You shuffle and I'll get the punch."

She sat down and quickly mixed the cards several times. Setting them aside on the table, she picked up the paper he'd been reading and cast a desultory glance over the front page to find that the Whigs were still crying foul over the Prince Regent's abandonment of them since his authority had been proclaimed five years before. Opening the paper, she scanned the various announcements of betrothals and the few winter events before a small article caught her eye. It was a brief note that Signora Sophia Mantini had completed her London engagements and would start a Continental tour in Paris beginning with a private party given at the British embassy for Lady Augusta Sandbridge and her niece. Her heart beat faster as she reread the short piece several times while trying to credit it. Aunt Gussie in Paris! And Amy! She had her answer to everything. If she could but get their direction, she could throw herself on her aunt's mercy and then perhaps everything would be all right. Augusta Sandbridge was a *grande dame* of the *ton* and could smooth things over and maybe even avert a scandal. She chewed her thumbnail nervously and tried to think how she could ever explain to her Aunt Gussie about her flight from

Brockhaven—or Lord Trent's part in it—or her living with Gerald Deveraux. The story sounded sordid in the extreme, but perhaps if she could actually face her aunt, she could somehow make her understand. There was no doubt that she would be scandalized, but would her aunt turn her away?

"Are you quite all right, Ellie?" Gerald asked as he set down the pitcher of steaming punch and lit the candle-warmer underneath.

"Gerry, 'tis the answer! Aunt Gussie's in Paris! Don't you see . . ." She rose in agitated excitement and began to pace in front of him. "I can go to her and everything will be all right."

"Who's Aunt Gussie? Ellie, what the devil are you talking about?"

"Here." She picked up the paper and handed it to him, pointing out the small article at the bottom of the page. "Lady Sandbridge is my aunt, and she has always had a particularity for me, Gerry. If I can but find her, I can explain it all to her. She's the one Alex was taking me to in the very beginning. I won't have to be a trial to you or Alex any longer, Gerry."

He studied the announcement for a moment and then shook his head. "I'd wait for Trent if I were you, Ellie. He should be here any day."

Reflecting that since the Mantini would be in Paris, Trent would probably come at last, Ellen shook her head. She had no wish to watch him come and go to his assignations with his mistress. "No, I am decided, Gerry. If you will not take me to my aunt's, I shall get her direction from the embassy and find her myself." When he made no answer, she raised her hands to plead. "Gerry, you are my dearest friend and have borne much for me, but please—oh, *please* help me find Aunt Gussie. Trent will not care, I swear, for it was what he meant to do in the first place. Gerry, please!"

"But Alex—"

"He will have my direction, Gerry. If he has anything to say on the matter, he can find me there. But she is my aunt and it would look ever so much better if I am discovered living with her."

There was more animation in the violet eyes, more

purpose in the set of her chin than he'd seen since they'd rescued her from Brockhaven that night in London. And she was right: no matter what Trent intended to do about pursuing his suit, it would probably be easier for everybody if she lived with her female relation until things were settled. He drew in a deep breath and nodded to the entreaty in her face. "All right. I suppose I can call on our ambassador and find her for you. When do you want me to do it?"

She moved to lift the heavy hanging again and looked out. "Well, do you think the streets still passable?"

"Today? Ellie, it's snowing!"

"I know, but . . ."

More than half in love with her himself, he was never proof against that look she gave him. "All right," he sighed, "I'll go."

"I'm going with you."

"In this weather? You'll catch an inflammation of the lungs, girl."

"Nonsense," she dismissed firmly, "I am never ill."

"If we are to pull this off, my dear, you cannot be seen in my company and you cannot be remarked by the embassy staff."

"I know. I mean to wait in the carriage." She could see his hesitation and she pressed her advantage. "We can go to my aunt's together, Gerry, so that if she will not believe me, I can come back with you."

"You wouldn't rather that I spoke to her first? What if she will not let you stay?"

"Then I will accept it and return with you."

"All right. You'd best warm yourself with a cup of the punch, Ellie, for it's deuced cold outside. And pour me one, too, while you are about it. I'll alert Timms and let his complaints fall on my ears."

16

FORTUNATELY, THE INTERVIEW with Augusta Sandbridge went better than either Gerald or Ellen had expected. After the initial surprise of seeing her niece, that lady welcomed her with open arms and then, over glasses of burgundy brought out to celebrate, listened intently to the story of Ellen's odyssey from Brockhaven's window to Paris. Gerald, finding Ellen far too modest for her own good, had to interrupt from time to time to tell of how she had saved his brother's life. Only one thing puzzled him: either Lady Sandbridge was a tough old Tartar or she knew far more than she let on, for she was not in the least shocked by the story.

"Well, my love," Augusta told Ellen when she'd finished, "you did quite the right thing in coming to me. The scandal has already broken to some extent, but—" She looked up and caught Ellen's stricken expression and hastened to add, "No, no, not that sort of scandal, my dear. Quite the opposite, in fact, for more than one has laid blame at Sir Basil's door." She stopped for a moment and looked at Gerald. "That is—well, have you heard anything about what has happened?"

"Alas, we have not," he admitted. "Alex has written often enough, but he's said little on that head."

"Well, then I shall leave most of it to his telling. Suffice it to say that Brockhaven has applied for an annulment and has offered for my sister-in-law, Lady Leffingwell. Naturally, when the news was out, the entire *ton* could speak of little else, but the reason given for Sir Basil's action was Ellen's ill health. With two wives already buried and no heir, it is believed that he has put her aside for a healthier female."

"You mean he offered for Aunt Vinnie?" Ellen asked incredulously when she finally found her voice. "But she's too old."

"She is not as old as you might think." Augusta smiled. "And although you will scarce credit it, she has developed quite a *tendre* for Brockhaven. *I* think they quite deserve each other," she added smugly.

"He's getting an annulment and not a divorce?"

"Yes, well, I believe Lord Trent can be most persuasive at times, my love."

"And I shall be free," Ellen mused slowly as her aunt's news sank in. "Gerry, did you hear? I shall be free, I shall be free!"

"Aye, I heard." He grinned as he reached to squeeze her hand. "Ellie, I am quite happy for you."

"Well, it is not quite over yet," Lady Sandbridge cut in, "for there are those among Brockhaven's friends who will have it that the fault was Ellen's and that Sir Basil is merely being gallant. There have been whisperings about her whereabouts, and some have even insinuated that he found her not to be all she was supposed to be."

"What?"

"Oh, 'twill die down in time as some new *on-dit* takes its place, my dear, so I would not refine too much on the gossip. And since Amy is to be out this Season, I brought her here ostensibly for a little town bronze, but in reality to escape any association with the unpleasantness."

"And Papa?" Ellen had to know.

"I leave that to Lord Trent to tell. Surely he will be coming to Paris to apprise you both of what has happened." Turning to Gerald again, she nodded her approval. "But I cannot but confirm that you have done the right thing. We will give out that Ellen has been recovering at Greenfield from an unknown malady once suspected of being consumption, and is now joining me and her sister for a holiday abroad. 'Twill be said she came to escape the scandal, but what's that to the point, anyway? At least it will be shown that we mean to stand with her and hold her blameless."

"Aunt Gussie, I am sorry you had to do this for Amy. I would not have had this touch any of you."

"Nonsense," Augusta dismissed briskly, "I have always liked Paris and am glad to be back now that that lunatic Bonaparte is done, dearest child. And Amy is finding herself the belle of the diplomatic corps, I assure you. Indeed, the only regret I have is that your Mr. Farrell was the only man we could impress on such a short notice to accompany us."

"John? Here? Oh, dear, what a lowering thought!"

"Yes, and I cannot tell you enough how very right you were to decline his offer, my dear, for I have never met such a prosy bore in my life. He and Amy are forever at daggers drawn, as he will not desist in telling her how to go on, which to him means to be quite insipid."

"And you simply cannot depress his pretensions," Ellen said, "for I have tried for years. There was no way that I could make him see that I truly did not want to be Mrs. Farrell." She looked up at Gerald and explained, "I know it is quite unbecoming of me to say so, Gerry, but it was true."

"Well, my dear, I believe he has not given up hope in that quarter yet," Augusta informed her with a sigh. "I vow that I had not gotten halfway to Dover before I was heartily sick of his telling me how your father refused his suit when he knew full well that you were quite willing."

"Surely he never said that."

"Over and over again."

"Aunt Gussie, I told him outright that we should not suit!"

"Reverend Farrell has the most selective hearing I have ever witnessed, my dear. I am afraid that nothing short of seeing you wed again to another man will ever convince him that his case is hopeless, and I am not even sure then. From what I have seen of the man, he will simply wait until you are a widow."

"Nonsense, Ellie." Gerald rose to take his leave. "If the fellow gets too persistent, just apply to me. I have not the least compunction about sending him on his way—and neither will Alex."

"Oh, your pardon, Aunt Gussie." Amy Marling stood in the doorway for a moment and then saw Ellen. "Ellie!

Oh, whyever did you not call me down, Aunt Gussie? I heard voices but thought 'twas the servants. Oh, Ellie!"

Gerald watched as a girl he could only describe truly as a vision of loveliness flew across the room to envelope Ellen in an enthusiastic embrace. She was laughing and crying and altogether absorbed in taking stock of her sister.

"You've grown prodigiously prettier, Ellie, I swear. But let me just look at you. I knew you would not live with Brockhaven—I knew it! And Papa was mad as fire until—"

"Amy! Your manners, miss," Lady Sandbridge interrupted sharply.

"But . . . Oh!" She looked up suddenly and saw Gerald Deveraux, and her beautiful face flushed in confusion. "Oh, dear, how I do go on, uh—"

"Amy, may I present Gerald Deveraux? Gerry—my sister, Amy Marling."

"I should have known her anywhere." Gerald smiled as he bent gallantly over Amy's small hand. "She is as pretty as you said she was."

The girl blushed furiously but did not draw away from the pressure of his fingers on hers. Instead, she stared almost dumbly at the twinkling blue eyes, the finely chiseled face, and the unruly black hair. "Oh, but you are funning, sir," she managed finally, and felt incredibly stupid for saying so.

"I assure you I am not."

"But you look very much like—"

"Amy!" Augusta cut in again with a warning look to her younger niece. "Captain Deveraux is brother to the Marquess of Trent."

"Oh, I was about to say—"

"I know what you were about to say and I would ask you not to."

Amy shot a questioning glance at Augusta and then nodded. "Oh. 'Twas not important, Captain Deveraux. I merely meant that you reminded me of someone," she recovered. "Someone I quite like, in fact."

"Amy, would you take Ellen upstairs to freshen for tea while I see the captain out?" Lady Sandbridge asked in a firm manner that brooked no refusal.

"Surely." The girl held out her hand to Gerald and murmured, "I do so hope you mean to call on us again, Captain. I am sure that Ellie and I would both be pleased to see you."

"Miss Amy, I quite expect to run tame in this house if your aunt will but let me."

"Good. Then we shall expect to see you." Her wide blue eyes met his candidly and she smiled in such a way that Gerald could not mistake her sincerity. "And pray do not let Reverend Farrell discourage you, sir, for he has such a way about him."

"I do not discourage easily, miss."

He watched the Marling sisters leave and then turned back to Lady Sandbridge. "I collect, ma'am, that you knew more of this than you admitted at first."

"Just so. Your brother sought us out in London shortly after you took Ellen out of the country. He apprised us of the annulment and prepared us for the scandal. Indeed, 'twas his idea that I should bring Amy here and that Ellen should join us to lessen the effect some of the stories will have on her. I believe him to be most protective of her."

"He is."

"In fact, I am certain he means to make her an offer."

"Then why the secrecy, ma'am?"

"Because, Captain, I believe a man should do his own courting, for one thing, and I would not push her into anything she does not want to do, for another."

"You may rest easy on that head, Lady Sandbridge. I know for a fact that she is not indifferent to him; she has admitted as much to me."

"Then we shall just have to wait for him, shan't we?" She smiled serenely up at him. "I mean to support my niece."

"I believe we understand each other." He smiled back.

"Gerry!" Ellen flew back down the stairs and caught both his hands while her eyes brightened with tears. "Gerry, I . . . Oh, my dear, *dear* friend, I cannot let you go without telling you again how very grateful I am for all you have done for me and for your friendship. I shall miss you so!"

"Ellie, Ellie, I meant it. I mean to run tame in this

house if your aunt will let me. I'd not leave you until all is settled, my dear—word of a Deveraux," he murmured softly.

"And—and—" She sniffed to hold back the flood of tears. "You will tell Alex how m-much I-I shall miss him, won't you?"

"I swear it, Ellie. Come, 'tis not over yet."

"And t-tell him I shall see him repaid for everything—I will."

"All right, I'll tell him anything you wish."

"No. That's it, Gerry. Oh . . ." She raised on her tiptoes and hastily gave him a quick kiss on the cheek. "Good-bye, Gerry." With that, she turned and fled.

"You aren't in love with her yourself, are you?" Lady Sandbridge asked after Ellen had gone.

"No." He reached for his cloak and fastened it around his shoulders before adding enigmatically, "I am excessively fond of Ellie, ma'am, but I believe I have interests in another quarter."

Upstairs, Ellen threw herself across her bed to listen forlornly to the ticking of the ormolu clock on the mantel. She ought to be happy to be restored to at least part of her family, she told herself, but instead she felt infinitely saddened. She'd had such an adventure with Trent and his brother, an adventure that no one would believe. Others could speak of their shocking reputations and of their coldness, but she knew better. No, she'd done the right thing, she tried to convince herself: she'd saved them from the consequences of her scandal. Trent was now free to pursue his other interests.

"Ellie, are you quite all right?" Amy asked from the doorway.

"Oh, of course I am all right." Ellen sat up and wiped her face before managing a tremulous smile. "I-I am so glad to be with you and Aunt Gussie."

"You don't look very happy," her sister pointed out doubtfully.

"No, really, I . . ." Ellen could not finish before she buried her face in her hands. "Oh, Amy, I am the most miserable of creatures!" she burst out.

Later, when she cornered her aunt alone, Amy told of Ellen's strange behavior. "Do you think all she has been through has affected her mind? I mean, Ellie's never suffered from an excess of sensibilities in her life."

"No, she's head over heels for Trent, unless I'm very much mistaken in the matter, and she don't want him to know it."

"And you would not let me even tell her about his visit to Papa."

"It's his business to tell her, missy, and do not be forgetting it," Augusta told her sternly.

"But what did Papa say?"

"Humph! What could he say? As much as it distresses me to say it, your father is a coward, and certainly no match for the likes of the Marquess of Trent. Wouldn't have made any difference, anyway. His father was just such a one, Amy, and he stole Lady Caroline quite literally from her family and her betrothed, made off with her straight out of the house in front of everyone."

"I wonder they survived the scandal."

"Survived it? They thrived on it, child! He was such a scapegrace that it was almost taken for granted by everyone but her family, of course. By the time he brought her back, she was in the family way with Lord Trent, and what could they say then, anyway?"

17

AFTER ONLY TWO days in the house, Ellen could quite see what her aunt meant about John Farrell and Amy. They kept the place at sixes and sevens with his attempts to depress the girl's natural liveliness despite Augusta Sandbridge's best efforts to keep the peace. On this particular morning, they'd quarreled over his insistence that they should all take an extended tour of the city, and Amy had demurred. It was not so much that they did not wish to see everything, Amy had pointed out with wounding candor, but rather that she'd no wish to sit hours in a closed carriage listening to him expound on what he'd never seen before either. "For in spite of what you must believe, John," she'd finished almost acidly, "we can read the guidebooks also." The end result was that he had taken himself off to explore Paris by himself, and Amy and Augusta had gone shopping. Thankful for the peace, Ellen had pleaded a headache to remain at home with Jane Austen's *Emma.*

She was quite absorbed in enjoying Miss Austen's social observations and missed the sound of the knocker until she heard his voice in the hall. Panic seized her momentarily and she cast about wildly for the means to escape, not because she did not wish to see him desperately, but because she knew she could not maintain her composure. To her horror, she could hear the butler directing him to her.

He walked in and gently shut the door behind him. Her heart skipped a beat and then began to flutter wildly as the blood pounded in her temples. When she could bring herself to look up, he was standing before her.

Without speaking, he reached into his coat and drew out a document wrapped in oil paper.

"I've brought you a gift that you can accept this time, Ellie," he told her quietly as he laid it in her trembling hands. "It's already in the papers, I am afraid. I couldn't quash the story because it had to be a matter of public record." He watched her open it up and read it silently, her lips moving soundlessly as her eyes traveled down the page. "I am sorry, my dear. I tried."

"Sorry?" She looked up finally. "How can you be sorry, my lord, when you have given me my freedom?"

"At a price, you know. There is much talk, and not all of it is sympathetic to you."

"I don't care what they say, Alex. I am free of him, and Aunt Gussie will support me against Papa—and—and I owe it all to you. I can never thank you sufficiently for all you have done for me. I know I have been a said trial to you, my lord, and I shall always be grateful. I-I will never forget your kindnesses."

"Ellie, we are not done yet." He moved to stand so close that his leg brushed against her bent knee. She looked up and sucked in her breath at the intensity mirrored in those blue eyes. "Do you remember what I said to you that first day we were on our way to York?"

"I remember that we said quite a few things to each other then," she reminded him nervously.

"Ellie, listen to me, hear me out, will you? I said we'd be in the basket over this, and we are. But the thing is I do not mind at all, Ellie." He reached to grip her cold fingers. "Wed me and Brockhaven will not dare to tell the story no matter how great the outcry. Do you understand me, my dear? I am asking you to accept the protection of my name. I offer you what I've never offered to anyone. I know I am not the man you would have—God knows I am not proud of what I have been—but I can give you greater protection from the scandal than any man I know."

"Please, Alex . . ." She twisted her hand away and wrenched her body out of the chair to turn away from him. "There is no need, my lord. I assure you there is no need. I-I cannot accept your generous offer, but believe me that I am grateful for it."

"Ellie, turn around and look at me," he ordered even as he grasped her shoulders. "Listen to me! You have to wed me, my dear, you have to! Whether you will it or not, we are scandal bound to marry."

"No." She shook her head as he turned her around to face him. Her throat ached from the effort of maintaining her composure, and her voice was hollow. "Alex, I am free, and that is all that matters, my friend. There is no need for either of us to do anything we do not wish to do."

Mistaking her meaning, he dropped his hands. "I see." Exhaling slowly to hide his bitter disappointment, he stepped back and managed to ask quietly, "You decline, then?" She nodded mutely. "Well, then there is not much else I can say, is there? It appears I have mistaken the matter, and I would not distress you for the world, Ellie, by pressing a suit I can see is distasteful to you." He turned to walk away.

"Alex," she wrenched out miserably, "please—"

"It is all right, Ellie, I understand, I think. Good-bye, my dear."

Numbly, she watched him go, his footsteps echoing on the floor. For a brief moment, she wanted to run after him, to tell him she'd take whatever he could offer, but in the end, she could not. No, he did not understand at all, he could not even guess the pain she felt knowing she probably would never see him again. As she heard the front door slam shut, she flung herself on a nearby settee and gave in to an overwhelming need to cry. No, she could not hold him, she sobbed, and she had to accept that she would get over him easier now than if she had to see him spend his evenings with one mistress after another. He would come to regret his nobility in offering for her and she could not bear that. Why should he be the one to suffer for having the misfortune to catch her beneath Brockhaven's window? But, oh, it was so very hard to let him walk out of her life. Great, painful, convulsive sobs racked her body until she had no breath, and then subsided into a pitiful sniffling. She had no idea how long she lay there in her misery, hours perhaps, for it was not until she heard her aunt and her sister come in that she even tried to compose herself.

"Ellie, only fancy!" Amy waltzed into the room in high spirits and then stopped suddenly at the sight of Ellen's tear-ravaged face. "Ellie, what is it? What is the matter, love?" her voice dropped in concern, and she knelt by the settee.

"Well, my dear," Augusta murmured as she came through the doorway, "you were wise to stay home. I vow I am exhausted. Oh, dear!" she drew up short. "Oh, my dear," she clucked sympathetically, "it cannot be that bad. Amy, fetch some brandy, child, and a bowl of lavender water." Moving to sit at Ellen's feet on the settee, she patted her consolingly.

"Oh, Aunt Gussie," Ellen wailed miserably, "Trent was here!"

"But whatever did he do to overset you so, love?"

"He—he came because he thinks himself o-obliged to marry me. He thinks he has to p-protect me from the sc-scandal!" She turned her head into the soft leather and sobbed anew.

"He cannot have said that," Augusta was positive.

"Yes, he did, and I-I refused him!"

"You cannot have heard him aright, child."

"I did! He—he said we were scandal bound to marry, if you want the whole."

"Surely he spoke of his regard for you, or said something else, Ellen."

"No," she sniffed, "he did not, I swear. Aunt Gussie, it was a bl-bloodless offer!"

"The noddy," Lady Sandbridge muttered succinctly under her breath. "And so you have refused his suit?"

Ellen straightened up and nodded as she dabbed at her face with a thoroughly soaked kerchief. "I had to, Aunt. I could not force him into a distasteful marriage, could I?"

"No, no, of course you could not, dearest," Augusta soothed while mentally consigning the marquess to perdition. "Here . . ." She looked up to where Amy was coming in with the requested brandy and lavender water. "Let me pour you a sip of brandy, love, and after you have drunk it, we'll wash your face to make you feel better."

"Aunt Gussie, what happened?" Amy demanded as she handed over the tray.

"Lord Trent bungled his offer," was the terse reply.

"But he has such address! I mean, that is—never say she *refused* him!"

"Of course she refused him, child!" Augusta snapped with unwonted temper. "How could she not when he said he was obliged to offer?"

"But surely—"

"Amy," her aunt cut her short, "we will talk no more of it just now. She will partake of the brandy and then we will help her to her bed. You will read the rest of her book to her this afternoon, and then, when she feels better, she will bathe and dress and come with us to the embassy reception tonight. If she is to recover from her disappointment, she must put it behind her." She patted Ellen again. "You must not think me unfeeling, child, but I know what is best."

Augusta waited until her program for Ellen's afternoon was well underway before sending a tersely worded letter to the marquess. After all the effort and care he'd put into arranging things for Ellen, she knew quite well that he was in love with the girl. She certainly meant to speak her mind to him and give him some advice, whether he wanted to hear it or not. How so very like a man, she reflected in disgust, never at a loss for some inane compliment for a bit of fluff but unable to offer for a respectable female.

It did not take him long to respond to her summons, and when he arrived, Augusta's heart almost went out to him. Had it not been for her niece's own unnecessary suffering, she could have cried for his. Instead, she greeted him crisply and pulled him into the small parlor to complain, "My dear Trent, in all of her twenty three years, I cannot say I have ever known Ellen to suffer from an excess of sensibilities, but she is prostrate in her bed now. What on earth did you say to the girl?" she demanded.

He ran his fingers distractedly through the thick, unruly waves of black hair and shook his head ruefully. "I did not say much at all, madam, for she would not let me say my piece. I offered for her, of course, and my suit distressed her so that I had to leave."

"Yes, I heard how you offered, my lord," Augusta

noted dryly, "and I own that I had expected you to have more address in the matter. She believes now that you merely felt obliged to save her from the scandal."

"Obliged?" he repeated in dawning horror. "No! 'Twas not my meaning."

"But did you not say you were obliged?" she persisted.

"I don't remember—perhaps. But she should have known—"

"My niece is an intelligent girl, Trent, but she ain't clairvoyant. To put it bluntly, sir, she described it as a bloodless offer. I could scarce believe my ears after all the trouble you've been to to get the chit," she told him flatly with the tone of a barrister resting his case.

"I've got to speak to her, Lady Augusta. Surely I can make her understand—" He stopped and shook his head. "No, she would not believe me now, would she? She'd think you read me a peal and brought me to heel, I suppose. But she has to know I obtained her annulment for her with the express intent that we should marry."

"But did you tell her that?"

"No, I wanted her free to accept me before I said anything. You are certain she cares for me?"

"She is besotted! But do not be looking to me to do your courting for you, my lord. It was outside of enough that I had to endure bringing Lavinia and Sir Basil together, after all. But I will tell you this much: nothing short of drastic action will remedy the situation."

"I see. You do not think perhaps I should try for another interview with her?"

"No, for you will have her turning into a watering pot again. However, I mean to take her to the affair at the embassy tonight whether she wishes to go or not. And," she added conspiratorially, "I am sure you will be able to obtain a card, won't you?"

"Lady Sandbridge, you may depend on it. And I hope I do not shock you too much with what I mean to do."

18

As she looked around the crowded room, Ellen noted the hushed whisperings and the furtive nods in her direction, and devoutly wished she had not come. While no one gave her the cut direct, there was a certain reserved curiosity about her. Well, she braced herself, she was made of stern stuff, and she would muddle through whatever came her way. At her side, her sister made polite small talk with a couple of well-favored young gentlemen.

"Look, Ellie!" Amy turned around suddenly and drew her attention to an extraordinarily beautiful, vivacious woman entering the room amid a crowd of admiring men. "I vow 'tis the Mantini herself!"

Ellen craned her neck for a better look at Trent's mistress, and her determined smile froze on her face as she took in the raven hair, dark eyes, perfect skin, and exquisite figure of the other woman. And it was apparent that Sophia Mantini meant to display her charms, for her red silk dress was cut so low that it nearly exposed full, creamy breasts, and so tight that it was obvious that she wore not even a pair of pantalettes beneath the clinging skirt.

"Hallo, Ellie."

Ellen spun around and nearly stumbled into him. "Trent! Oh, you startled me!"

"I thought you might be here, my dear, and I would come offer my support." He smiled easily. When she just stared, he nodded at the card that hung from her wrist. "If there is dancing, I believe I should like to put my name there unless you already have a full card."

"No, there is no one on it, my lord. You would be the only one brave enough to stand up with Brockhaven's castaway."

"I feared as much, Ellie, but I daresay I can remedy the situation."

"No, pray do not trouble yourself, Alex," she put in hastily. "If you are determined, I shall stand up with you, but I don't think I could face the prospect of trying to converse politely with anyone else."

"Not even Gerry?"

"Well, maybe the two of you, but pray do not try to force anyone else to stand up with me."

"Poor Ellie," he sighed, "still determined to be selfish with her scandal."

He signed her card in four places—two more than was polite or acceptable—and then moved on to pay his respects to the ambassador and several members of the mission. Try as she would, she could not help following him with her eyes as he crossed the room, his tall, well-proportioned frame dominating those around him. He would have been remarked in any crowd, she was certain, for she could think of no more attractive man in the world. And he was dressed even finer than she had ever seen him, so elegantly correct in a perfectly tailored dark-blue jacket, burgundy velvet waistcoat, and buff trousers. Even his neckcloth was understated, tied in an Oriental rather than one of the more intricate styles. Other men might have to resort to ridiculously high starched neck points and fancy cravats, but Trent could set the fashion merely by being himself. It was rumored that Stultz, tailor to the Beau himself, had said he ought to pay Trent for wearing his clothes.

As Ellen watched, Sophia Mantini disengaged herself from her little court and caught at his arm, hanging there to whisper something in his ear. Whatever it was, he appeared less than amused, shook her off with bare civility, and turned back to Lord Halsingham.

John Farrell, having escaped by mutual consent from Lady Sandbridge, made his way ponderously toward Ellen, and she could not help comparing him to the marquess. While John was exceedingly handsome in a well-chiseled way and his body nearly of a height with

Trent, he lacked both the physical and social grace of his lordship. Everything about him was stolid, from his manner to his walk, and he fairly exuded pomposity even before he opened his mouth. And once again, he was making it quite plain to everyone that he expected to wed Miss Ellen Marling as soon as her papa could be brought about.

"I thought perhaps that I might have the honor of a dance with you, Miss Ellen," he began.

Resigned, she opened her card and started to write him in, but he read over her shoulder and shook his head repressively. "I should not allow you to dance with the Marquess of Trent, my dear, for if I may presume—"

"No, John, you may not presume," Ellen snapped.

"Nevertheless, my dear, in your circumstance, it would not do to be seen in his company. After all, it is important if you are to reestablish yourself that you be circumspect in the extreme."

"The last person to tell me that was Brockhaven," she muttered with asperity, "and I do not propose to reestablish what was never established in the first place."

"A vicar's wife has a position in society."

"But I do not aspire to the position."

"You are overset merely," he continued placidly, "for this is your first time out since your illness."

"Ah, there you are, Ellie. Still got room on your card for me?"

"Miss Marling regrets—"

"Miss Marling is delighted, Gerry. There's naught but you and Trent and John—and I am certain that John does not waltz."

"I feel that touching the female form breeds familiarity," Farrell retorted stiffly, "and I have made myself plain on that head."

"So you have, John," Ellen agreed smoothly, "Therefore, I shall save the waltzes for Captain Deveraux and his brother." Then, knowing that she had wounded his sensibility, she laid a hand on his arm and gave him a weary smile. "John, would you be so kind as to procure a glass of something for me?"

"Poor Ellie," Gerald teased lightly, "is that your worthy suitor?"

"He thinks so," she answered pointedly, "and he is nearly as obtuse as Brockhaven much of the time."

"Should've taken Trent, my dear. Much more fascinating, I should think."

"Gerry, please, if you are my friend, you'll not remind me. I have the headache, my face hurts from smiling when I know people are talking about me and speculating just why Brockhaven discarded me for a middle-aged prattle, and my spirits are about as low as they can get."

"Ellie, I am sorry. I just don't understand it, that's all. Alex has taken it quite badly, my dear—says his hopes are all cut up. I thought he'd be too foxed to bring tonight."

"He seems to have recovered rather well."

"Captain Trent, we meet again, do we not?" a soft, throaty voice spoke from behind Ellen's shoulder. "And I daresay this is Miss Marling, the one that was Lady Brockhaven?"

Without turning around, Ellen knew it was Sophia Mantini, and was instantly on the defensive. "I am Ellen Marling," she answered almost warily as she moved closer to Gerald Deveraux.

"And you are not at all as I would have thought," the Mantini murmured less than pleasantly, "and certainly not in Alex's style. Tell me, Miss Marling"—her mouth twisted bitterly—"what is it about you that would make a man leave me in the middle of the night to come to you?"

Ellen could hear Amy gasp indignantly behind her. "I have not the slightest idea, Madame Mantini," she replied coolly, "as to what you mean."

"Do not come the innocent with me, Miss Marling," the Mantini retorted, "for I know why Brockhaven was persuaded to give you up."

"Sophie!"

"It is quite all right, Alex. I was but making the acquaintance of Miss Marling," Sophia purred as Trent caught up to her.

"Sophie, I ought to wring your wretched neck," he hissed low for her ears alone.

"Ah, but you will not, I think, for I am tonight's entertainment," the Mantini reminded him with a triumphant smile at the white-faced Ellen. "And do not be thinking you can stop the story, my dear Trent, for it is quite around already. Good evening, Miss Marling."

"Devil a bit, Alex," Gerald muttered. "What now?"

"We proceed as planned, but we do so earlier. Ellie, I am sorry if you had your heart set on waltzing away your evening, my dear."

"No." She shook her head. "But I have to find Aunt Gussie. I hope this does not overset her. I shall plead the headache and get my cloak and see if John can take us home."

"Er, I believe he is occupied getting a fruit punch out of his clothing, my dear, and do not be worrying about Augusta Sandbridge. She's more than able to deal with Sophia's mischief. Are you ready, Gerry?"

"Happy to get the door for you, Alex." Gerald grinned.

"Then, dearest Ellie, I see no reason to wait. Gerry, stand ready to hold any who would stop me." Trent slipped his arm easily around Ellen's waist and lifted her up before she could fathom his intent.

"Alex!" she squealed in alarm. "What in the world—?"

"Hold still, Ellie, and hang on. Here's where I put it to the touch and hope you do not bring the house down." He adjusted her in his arms and headed for the double doors at the end of the ballroom. "And do not be kicking, either, for I should hate to look like the veriest fool."

"Alex! Put me down! People are looking at us," she hissed.

"I certainly hope so, my dear, for you find me quite determined to share your scandal to the fullest of my ability. But it's all right, love," he added conversationally as he carried her past a stunned audience, "for 'twill be said the blame is mine—we Deveraux are a hotheaded lot—and I've waited quite long enough for you."

"Listen, Alex, I can walk," she choked in embarrassment under the bemused stares of the ambassador and his entire staff. "If you will but put me down—"

"I know you can, love, but this way I can depend on your coming with me," he soothed as he shifted her before he reached the doors.

"Alex!" She clutched at his shoulder for fear of being

dropped. "Listen, you cannot just do this. I mean, are you abducting me?" she demanded incredulously.

"Well, I should prefer that you think of it as a romantical elopement, of course, but I suppose you could call it an abduction."

Gerald threw open the doors and swept Ellen an elegant bow. "Good luck, both of you. And Ellie, I am quite determined to be your brother, one way or another, my dear."

Several of the guests still in the ballroom broke into applause as they cleared the door. Ellen clutched at him tighter when the cold winter wind hit them. "Alex, this is ridiculous! We shall be a laughingstock! Alex, you have taken leave of your senses! I think you are foxed!"

"Not at all, my dear. I am in full possession of all my faculties."

"Everyone will be talking. Alex, please set me down."

"In a minute. We've not too much farther to go. You know, Ellie, you are not as light as I thought you were."

"Thet Miss Ellie?" Timms asked as he opened the coach door. "Ah, miss, 'tis good ter 'ave yer back."

"Timms," Ellen tried desperately, "tell him he cannot do this!"

"Eh? Why not?" the driver responded cheerfully as he climbed up on the box and waited for Trent to thrust her inside the carriage. "Seems right ter me, miss!"

"Alex, we will not have a shred of reputation left," she tried to reason as Trent heaved his tall frame through the door and settled onto the seat.

"I hope not," he agreed while pulling her onto his lap and cradling her against his shoulder. "In fact, I am quite depending on it. You see, Ellie, you think I think I am obliged to marry you because Brockhaven let you go."

"You said we were obliged to marry—'twas you who said it."

"Well, maybe we weren't then, but I mean to make damned sure that before this night is over, I *am* obliged to marry you. Your aunt said I bungled it, that I didn't make it plain that I wanted you, Ellie."

"Alex, this is insane. Think of the scandal."

"Aye." He nodded imperturbably. "I thought of it. Here—you haven't a cloak and neither have I." He pulled a heavy lap robe around them and held her closer. "I haven't forgotten the last time we got chilled together."

"There's no reasoning with you," she decided with a sigh as she shivered against him.

"Shhhhh, just let me get you warm, love."

For a time, he contented himself with holding her and dropping an occasional kiss on her hair and down to where the blanket lay against her nearly bare shoulder. His breath on her skin sent tantalizing shivers down her spine. His arms were warm and strong around her. And then his fingers began working the hooks at the back of her dress.

"Alex, no! Please, I can't!"

"Shhhhh, it'll be all right, I promise."

"No!" She twisted in his arms and tried to face him. "Not like this!"

"How?"

"I . . . Please, my lord . . ." Her mouth went dry and her heart pounded harder as his fingers slid beneath the taffeta and began to knead the flesh of her shoulders.

"I've been wanting to do this for a long time, Ellie," he whispered in the darkness.

The carriage rolled to a halt and Timms jumped down from the box to open the door. Alex quickly rehooked the dress beneath the blanket and slid her off his lap. Climbing out, he turned back to lift her out.

"I am not an invalid!"

"If you do not cease wiggling, Ellen, I'll put you over my shoulders like a feed sack," he threatened as he carried her into the house and started up the tall staircase. "Don't look down. It'll scare you."

"For the last time, Alex, put me down!"

"For the last time, I will not."

He kicked open the door to his bedchamber and walked to dump her unceremoniously on the bed. She fell back into the feather mattress and lay staring up at him like he'd lost his mind. He turned to latch the door. Slowly, deliberately, he undid his cravat and discarded it on the back of a chair before removing his coat and waistcoat and draping them over the cravat.

"What do you think you are doing?" she demanded nervously.

"Undressing."

"Alex, this is ridiculous. I mean, you cannot mean to—"

"I mean to."

She rolled off the bed and scrambled for the door. "But—"

"I am afraid it's locked, Ellie."

"Alex, be reasonable! Now I know you have taken leave of your senses. You cannot wish to marry me!"

"And that is a lie."

She licked her dry lips nervously. "I will not be your mistress."

He stopped unbuttoning his shirt to consider quite deliberately for a moment. "Did I ever ask you to be my mistress? No," he decided finally, "I did not." He drew his shirttail out of his trousers and removed the shirt. "In fact," he added, "I am quite positive that I asked you to marry me."

"Because you felt obliged to! You thought I could not take the scandal of Brockhaven's getting the annulment."

"You know, Ellie, you have been so deuced possessive about your scandal that I have had to come up with one we can share."

"Alex, there is no need! Do you think I do not know that I am not the sort of female you would choose on your own? I am not such a fool that I do not know you could have a Toast, a Diamond of the First Water, a—"

"I don't want one of them." He turned around and gave her a wry smile. "I know it sounds perverse of me, Ellie, but I have the strangest notions about what I want."

"But you could have someone quite beautiful, like the Mantini, or—"

"I think I have one. Look at me, love," he commanded. She raised her eyes to his bare chest and looked away. "You've seen it before," he reminded her, "for it is the same chest you spread onion poultices on, remember? Now, let me tell you some things, Ellie. I am afraid I will not be your conventional sort of husband, my dear. You see, I shall expect to live with you, not just politely share my house. Get used to the sight of my skin, because I expect you will see a lot of it over the years. I know I shall expect to see a lot of yours. And I am not one for undressing in closets, either—nor do I plan to sleep alone. I do not plan to get up from your bed to seek mine."

"Alex—"

"No, let me finish. I know it is common for our class to live separate lives except for the necessary begetting of heirs. That is why so many of us keep mistresses, if you want my opinion of it. Not me. I don't ever want to seek any company but yours. I want to wake up with my wife, Ellie. I think it will be a comfort to me to have you with me because I never expect to be bored with you. You see, you little wretch, I know I love you. Now, shall I continue removing my clothes or do you wish to marry me first? By now, Gerald will have arrived with an English divine from the embassy to take care of the matter. But if you require further proof of how I feel about you, I am prepared to continue until we are both as bare as we were born and I'll show you."

"Oh, Alex!" Her voice had taken on that husky quality of one deeply moved as she smiled up at him mistily. "I quite believe you, and if you are that determined to share my scandal, then you are quite welcome to share my life, too. I do love you, you know."

"I know." He reached down to pull her up against him and bent to kiss her mouth, gently at first and then with deepening passion. She twined her arms around his neck and pressed closer until at last he released her and stepped back shakily. "We will have such good times together, Ellie, I swear. I shall take you to Italy—maybe Spain, too—and we'll not go back to England until the tale dies down. And everyone will blame it on my wild Deveraux blood instead of you by then. I gave it out tonight that I've had a long-standing attachment for you—and I have."

"Alex, would you mind very much if we did not go to Italy?" she whispered against his shoulder. "I know where I should like to go."

"Greece?"

"No. Little Islip."

"Then Little Islip it shall be, my love, but I warn you—no pork jelly."

Prologue: May, 1085

An expectant air hung over the small, high-walled garden set within the lower bailey at Nantes. Herleva, nurse to Count Gilbert's three daughters, fought a losing battle to keep her young charges busy, while the sounds and smells of festival preparations competed for their attention. Somewhere in the town below the castle, carpenters hammered on stands and hung gaily-dyed bunting, while cooks tended pits and spits of roasting meat and bakers kept ovens going day and night baking enough bread and pastries for noble and peasant alike. From time to time, the clatter of newly arriving lords and their retinues carried upward from narrow cobblestone streets. Most would seek lodging within the town, but a few of the more distinguished of the nobility would enjoy Gilbert's own hospitality.

Herleva watched as the eldest girl, twelve-year-old Eleanor, struggled reluctantly with her needlework. The girl held up the altar cloth she had been working on, surveyed it with disgust, and slowly began to pick out the stitches she had just completed. No, the girl would never be noted for her skill with the needle, or for any other housewifely accomplishments. Well, it would be a rare lord that would care, anyway, because the girl was already much remarked for her beauty. Unlike others her age, Eleanor of Nantes lacked that awkwardness so often associated with the approach of womanhood. With long dark hair that hung in a thick curtain to her tiny waist, clear fair skin blushed with health, and a pair of fine brown eyes fringed with thick black lashes, she presented as pretty a sight as flesh and blood could make. At twelve, she was small and delicately made, but her young breasts already outlined the smooth samite of her silver-threaded purple gown. It was rumored that Count Gilbert intended to negotiate for her marriage soon, and the servants of Nantes hoped that their demoiselle would go somewhere where she would be more valued.

A mild oath escaped the girl's lips as she threw her work down in frustration. Abruptly, she stood up and began to pace impatiently back and forth along the narrow flagstone walk.

"Demoiselle!" Herleva's voice rose in reproof.

"I don't care," Eleanor muttered mutinously. "It is easy to chide when you sew a fine hand. Mine is naught but a batch of knots that I should be ashamed to offer for Christ's altar." She kicked the crumpled cloth with a dainty leather-clad toe.

"Child, would you have it said that I taught you nothing?" Herleva asked quietly.

"Nay, but I cannot be what you would have me." The girl looked longingly at the high rock wall that enclosed them. "I would rather be a peasant out there tasting, seeing, feeling the festival. Instead, I sit unraveling poor stitches—and so it goes on and on." She hugged her arms to her. "Why is it that none but Roger can understand?"

The old nurse sighed in sympathy. "You cannot follow Roger around much longer, Demoiselle. It will soon be time to prepare to be a lord's lady." She stooped to retrieve the discarded cloth. "Here—it cannot be so very bad. Let us work on it together." Closer inspection caused her to shake her head.

"See, even you who love me must own it hopeless."

"Let me see," piped ten-year-old Margaret, "though I know mine's better."

Herleva whisked the cloth behind her. "As for you, little Margaret, you need to know there's more to being a lady than stitching," she admonished the younger girl.

"At least *I* do not spend my time in the courtyard with a bastard stableboy," the child retorted. "Maman says ladies do not follow stableboys."

"He's not a stableboy! For shame, Maggie. He's your own brother."

"Half-brother," Margaret sniffed disdainfully, "and bastard at that."

"Through no fault of his own," Eleanor defended.

"Roger's a bastard," seven-year-old Adelicia chimed in. "Everyone knows he's a bastard."

"See, even Lissy knows what he is. Maman says he is only fit to feed the horses."

"Maman is just jealous because she never had a son," Eleanor shot back.

"Mmmmm, I'll tell Maman," Adelicia threatened.

"You'll do no such thing," Herleva intervened, "unless you want to spend the festival in the nursery while the rest of us see the company. The duke himself comes to Nantes."

"The Old Conqueror?" Even Eleanor was diverted by the news. "I thought him on the French border. Will he bring England's crown to wear?"

"As to that, I cannot say. All I know is that I heard he comes to ask for the count's levy against King Philip."

"Well, he wastes his time," Eleanor pointed out with an insight beyond her years. "If he would have Nantes' levy, he'll have to demand it. My father is too careful of his own skin to fight another man's war. He'll claim he cannot fight because he is a vassal to both Duke William and King Philip."

"Nonetheless, he comes here—mayhap today or tomorrow."

But Eleanor's attention suddenly became intent on sounds coming from beyond the castle wall, sounds of a fight brewing in the field by the drainage pond. She could barely make out taunts of "Bastard! Bastard! Your mother's a Saxon whore!" Instinctively, she gathered up her skirts and moved purposely toward the gate.

"Demoiselle! Eleanor!" Herleva implored. "He can take care of himself!"

Eleanor broke into a run, passing sentries who hesitated to lay a hand on the heiress. As she cleared the gate, she could see a crowd gathered at the edge of the foul-smelling ditch. It appeared that Roger was cornered at water's edge by a group of boys brandishing swords. He was parrying off thrusts with a stout pole held in front of his chest. She hurled herself headlong into the startled group, panting for breath and pushing her way to the forefront. That these boys were sons of the greatest noble houses in Normandy, Maine, and Brittany bothered her not at all. To her they were nothing but a group of bullies intent on harming her brother.

"Foul! Foul!" she cried. "Does it take all of you to beat one boy? For shame! Where is your honor? Where is your chivalry?"

Roger's chief tormentor, a tall, black-haired boy, growled back, "Hold her. She can watch me drown the bastard."

The others were hesitant. By the richness of her gown, it was evident she belonged to a great family. She took advantage of this hesitation to rail against them. "Fools! Dare you put a hand on Nantes? I shall have you whipped if you do!"

"Lea, get out of here!" Roger called to her. " 'Tis no place for a maid."

"Nay, brother, I'd not see you harmed in an unfair contest." Turning back to the group, she continued, "Art cowards all! He can take any one of you. Why must it be all against one?"

"Nay, he cannot take Belesme," someone called out.

"Then let Belesme fight him alone."

The black-haired boy sneered, "I'd not sully my honor meeting the Saxon bastard."

"Fie! Shame! You call it honorable to fight eight or ten to one? You are not fit to bear the sword you hold."

They were so intent on one another, girl and squires, that they did not notice the approach of several riders. It wasn't until the leader, a thick-set, graying warrior rode straight into their midst and dismounted that he got their attention. Expressions of shock, disbelief, and horror spread across the boys' faces. From behind Eleanor, the old man called out, "What goes here?"

The crowd fell strangely silent and uncomfortable. Eleanor whirled to face the newcomer while the others looked at their feet. The old man's black eyes raked the group until they focused on her. "Well," he asked finally in a rough and raspy voice, "is there not a man among you save for the maid? She stands brave while you cower." In spite of the challenge, none dared to answer. "Well, Demoiselle, I leave it to you to answer. What goes here?"

"These—these squires thought to amuse themselves by harming my brother for no reason other than that he is bastard-born." She pointed accusingly at the tall boy identified as Belesme. "He threatened to drown him."

"Robert"—the old man scowled at the black-haired youth—"is this true?"

Robert's answer was evasive. "Sire, he would use the quintains with us and he has not even fostered. 'Tis plain he's baseborn and not fit to meet with us."

"And why should he not use the quintains?" Eleanor questioned hotly. "They are his. He set them up and this is his practice field." She faced the tall boy defiantly. "What right have you to come to Nantes and to taunt Nantes' son?"

"If he's so noble, why hasn't he fostered?" Belesme countered.

"Silence!" There was unmistakable authority in the old man's voice. "I would only know if the quarrel is over bastardy. Is there any here who can say it isn't?" He motioned Roger forward and stared hard at him. "Well?"

It was obvious that Roger had no wish to be a tale-bearer, but Eleanor refused to allow his tormentors to go unpunished. "Sir, my lord," she cut back into the old man's attention. "they were all taunting him—calling him a bastard and calling Dame Glynis a Saxon whore. They fault him for what he cannot help."

"I know much about bastardy, Demoiselle," was the terse reply. "Gilbert's by-blow, eh? You have not the look of him."

"I favor my mother, my lord." Roger met the black-eyed gaze squarely. "My mother is daughter to a Saxon thane and no baseborn whore."

The old man rubbed his chin thoughtfully. "A pity Gilbert's only son had to come from the wrong side of the blanket. I wonder . . ." He let his train of thought trail off unsaid. "Never fostered, eh?"

"My mother would not hear of it," Eleanor inserted herself back into the conversation. "She hates him."

"I can well believe that of Mary de Clare," he commented dryly. "How are you called, Demoiselle?"

"I am Eleanor, heiress of Nantes," she answered proudly, "and this is my brother Roger, called FitzGilbert."

"I see. And how old are you, Roger?"

"He is nearly sixteen, my lord," Eleanor responded.

"Demoiselle, he does not appear addlepated," the old man told her. "Surely he can answer simple questions by himself."

Eleanor reddened and bit her lip to stifle a retort. Roger had to smile at her discomfiture as he answered for her this time. "Your pardon, my lord, but Lea is strong-minded and always ready to speak on my behalf whether I need the service or not."

"I see. Well, Roger FitzGilbert, you have not trained in any household, yet your sister says you can fight. Can you indeed acquit yourself with any skill in combat?"

"Aye, my lord, I can fight with lance, ax, or sword," he answered simply.

Those around them laughed derisively. The one called Robert of Belesme snorted, "That marks him for a liar, sire, for a broadsword is nigh as big as he is."

"I think we'll see, Robert," the old man glowered warningly. "If this fellow can account for himself against you, I'll foster him myself. When all's said, I think we bastards should stand together."

Roger was dumbfounded by this sudden change in his fortune. When he could finally find his voice, he managed, "But, my lord, you do not know me, nor do I know you."

This brought another derisive snort from Robert of Belesme. "The fool knows not Normandy and England, sire."

A boy little older than Roger edged his horse forward from where he had been watching with the others who accompanied the old man. "Aye." He leaned forward to address Roger. "FitzGilbert, you stand before your duke." His face broke into a friendly smile even as Roger's reddened, adding not unkindly, "My father will give you justice even though you recognized him not."

Both Roger and Eleanor sank to their knees beneath Duke William. The newcomer turned his attention to the kneeling Eleanor. "Art a fine champion for your brother, Demoiselle. I would that any of my sisters were half so spirited in my defense."

William gave the crowd one last withering look before allowing them to rise. With his own hand, he lifted Eleanor to her feet and studied her intently. Apparently, he liked what he saw as his face softened into a smile.

"Henry," he addressed the rider above them, "see the Lady Eleanor back inside while I deal with those who would taunt a bastard." His weather-roughened hand still enveloped hers in a firm grip. "Are you betrothed as yet, Demoiselle?"

Eleanor colored under his gaze. "Nay, my—Sire."

"Art a fierce little maid, Eleanor of Nantes, and worthy to be a warrior's bride. Mayhap I should speak to Gilbert about a suitable husband for you." He released her hand with a sigh. "I've five daughters of my own, and not one has your spirit. I pray you are allowed to keep it." Motioning her over to his son's horse, he bent and cupped his hand. "Up with you, child," he rasped as she hesitated before stepping into the palm. With a quick boost, he put her in front of the prince. Henry slid back on the saddle to make room for her slender body and slipped an arm easily about her waist to steady her.

"Sometimes, my father finds particularly pleasant tasks for me, Demoiselle," he murmured from behind her.

"Wait. What of my brother?"

Duke William answered her. "Your cousin Walter will lend his mail so that young FitzGilbert has his chance to meet Robert in a fair match. After that, I intend to birch Belesme myself."

Prince Henry twisted behind her to loose his sword. Raising it hilt-first, he proffered it to Roger. "Give a good account of yourself, FitzGilbert, and when you join my father's household, you shall ride in my train. Until then, I lend you Avenger. Use it well, boy, because you have a chance to do what I have oft longed to try."

"But never dared," Belesme taunted.

The prince ignored the gibe. "Remember, FitzGilbert, you shall ride with me."

"Henry," William the Conqueror warned his son, "I would have him learn warring rather than wenching."

The remark drew laughter from the rest of the boys. It was well-known among them that the seventeen-year-old prince had an eye for beauty and a lusty appetite for the favors of some of the married ladies at his father's court. Henry laughed good-naturedly with them while tightening his arm around Eleanor. "Pay them no heed, Demoiselle, for today I am slave to you."

Roger frowned, his blue eyes narrowing at Henry's words. He moved protectively toward his half-sister, but stopped when he saw nothing but open friendliness and teasing in the prince's expression. Instead, Roger tweaked the toe of Eleanor's shoe for attention. "Lea, if I am to meet Belesme, I would wear your favor."

She flushed with pleasure at the request, given as gravely as though they were knight and lady. Nodding, she removed the enamel brooch she wore pinned to her shoulder. Leaning as far as she dared while Henry held her waist, she kissed him solemnly. "May my token bring you good fortune today, brother."

Prince Henry nudged his horse away. As they began the climb up the rocky road, Eleanor strained to watch as Walter de Clare began divesting himself of his mail and his gambeson.

"Do not fear for him, little one," the prince reassured her. "While I doubt very much that your brother can best Belesme—I doubt anyone can—you may be assured that my father will not let the boy come to harm."

It was then that the full import of the day's event came home to Eleanor, and she fell silent. For Roger, gaining a place in William the Conqueror's household was a great honor. For Eleanor, it meant losing the person dearest to her heart. She tried hard to focus on the thought that it was at least an opportunity for him to make his way in a world that denied him an inheritance. Besides, had he been a legitimate son of a noble house, he would have fostered at seven or eight. At least she'd had him a lot longer than most sisters had their brothers with them.

"Why so silent, Demoiselle? You were full of words back there."

"I—I shall miss my brother," she managed.

"My sisters could scarce wait to see me gone," Henry told her conversationally, "and I thought much the same of them. My sister Adela has the temper of a viper."

Eleanor spoke before she thought. "It cannot be the same for you, Your Grace. Your father does not hate you for being a girl, and I am sure that your mother did not hate you either. My parents have never forgiven me for what I cannot help. I suppose that is why Roger and I have always meant so much to each other: we are both despised for what we were born. Only he, Dame Glynis, and my old nurse care about me. And I love Roger above all things." Her shoulders began to shake slightly.

"Demoiselle, you weep too soon. Your brother will be back often enough to visit, I promise you." Henry's words only seemed to increase her anguish, causing him to try another subject. "Even if your lot is unhappy for the moment, little one, it will not be too long before you will be betrothed to a lord that loves you." He shifted his arm to cradle her against him. "Nay, sweet child, none could look upon you and not love you."

"You are kind," she sniffed, "for you do not know me. My lord will most probably beat me because I cannot sew and I have not the least ability in household accounts."

Her innocence brought forth a fierce desire to protect and comfort her. "Believe me," Henry told her, "when I say that such accomplishments are commendable, but they have little to do with a lord's love for his lady. A man can pay to have his sewing done, and he can get a steward and a seneschal to run his household. On the other hand, it is a rare marriage contract that yields a beautiful wife."

"Your Grace—"

"Demoiselle, you may call me Henry. Come, I am not much older than your brother. Can we not be friends?"

She half-twisted her body to look at him. The friendliness in his face was unmistakable as she studied him. Unlike his father, he was not dark. His open countenance was framed with light-brown hair cut straight across the forehead in Norman fashion, and his eyes, while brown, were not nearly so dark as the Old Conqueror's. But it was his easy smile and gentle manner that made her think that this surely must be the best of Normandy's sons.

"I am but seventeen and yet to be knighted," he

continued conversationally. "While there is some small difference in our ages, I hope your brother and I may become friends. Perhaps we will both be able to visit you, and mayhap my father will order you to court when this quarrel with France is done."

She leaned her head back against his chest much as she would have done with Roger. As the prince's arm tightened protectively around her, she was suddenly struck by the picture of impropriety they must present. She tried to sit upright before any could see her, but found herself held so tightly against him that she could feel his heartbeat.

"Your Grace . . . Henry," she protested, " 'tis unseemly that you hold me thus, though the fault is mine."

He relaxed his arm reluctantly. "Nay, Eleanor, the fault is mine."

"The black-haired one—the one called Robert—I didn't like him at all," she changed the subject to safer ground. "Is he always like that?"

"Always. The young Count of Belesme is excessively proud, excessively cruel, excessively vain. No one likes him and everyone is afraid of him. He's Mabille's spawn."

"Mabille?"

"They say she's a witch." Henry crossed himself with the hand that held the reins even as he added, "I do not put much store in such tales, but she is said to have poisoned Robert's father. There are other things said of Robert and his mother that I dare not tell you."

"What things?"

"I say too much. What I have heard is unfit for your ears. Suffice it to say that my father is the only thing Robert of Belesme fears. When he is gone, I fear the devil will be loosed."

"And you, my lord, are you afraid of him?"

He shrugged behind her. "I? I am not much the soldier, Demoiselle. I fight if I must, but I'd rather not. I have not the quarrelsome nature of Curthose and Rufus. Besides, as the youngest son, I have little enough to fight for." There was a faint trace of bitterness in his voice that faded as he added, "Alas, Demoiselle, we are arrived, and by the look of things you have been missed."

About the Author

Anita Mills lives in Kansas City, Missouri, with her husband, four children, sister, and seven cats in a restored turn of the century house. A former English and history teacher, she has turned a lifelong passion for both into a writing career.